THE AUTHOR

Clifford Henry Benn Kitchin was born in Harrogate, Yorkshire, in 1895. He was educated at Clifton College, Bristol, from where he won a classical scholarship to Exeter College, Oxford. From 1916–8 he served with the British Army in France, and after the war turned to the Law, joining Lincoln's Inn and being called to the Bar in 1924. Later, like the hero of his crime novels, Malcolm Warren, he became a stockbroker, but a huge inherited fortune allowed him to leave his profession and to concentrate on his great love, writing.

His first two novels, *Streamers Waving* and *Mr Balcony*, were published by Leonard and Virginia Woolf at The Hogarth Press in 1924 and 1925, and he won wide popularity with his first detective novel, *Death of My Aunt* (1929, also published as a Hogarth paperback). Over the years, more crime fiction appeared: *Crime at Christmas* (1934), *Death of His Uncle* (1939) and *The Cornish Fox* (1949), interspersed with more serious novels, the most famous of which is *The Auction Sale* (1949).

The unique atmosphere of Kitchin's detective fiction owes a lot to his own eccentricity. Scholarly, humorous, given to sudden caprices, he was an expert botanist, poet, linguist, fine chess player and talented musician, with the unnerving habit of composing improvisations to illustrate his friends' characters. An avid collector of priceless objects, whether Georgian silver or Meissen teapots, he was also well known as a gambler on London greyhound tracks and in Riviera casinos. In the end, however, despite his daunting, rapier wit, his death in 1967 drew tributes to, above all, his sensitivity and generosity of spirit.

CRIME AT CHRISTMAS

C. H. B. Kitchin

THE HOGARTH PRESS
LONDON

Published in 1988 by
The Hogarth Press
30 Bedford Square
London WC1B 3SG

First published in Great Britain by The Hogarth Press 1934
Copyright Francis King

A CIP catalogue record for this book is available from the British Library.

ISBN 0 7012 0673 X

Printed in Finland by
Werner Söderström Oy

CONTENTS

CONTENTS—*continued*

TO

KENNETH RITCHIE

I. PRIDE

AT twenty minutes to four on Christmas Eve, I made my way through a circle of roisterers who danced and sang and pelted one another under the big dome of the Stock Exchange, to the public telephone-room, where I asked for the number of my most important client. This client was so important that he was worth all my other clients put together.

" Is that Hampstead o-nine-one ? This is Mr. Warren speaking. Will you tell Mr. Quisberg that I am on the telephone ? "

During the pause which followed, I put my jobbing-book in a convenient position, and gave a turn to my Eversharp.

" Well ? "

It was the well-known voice, as usual abrupt, nervous and excited.

" There has been hardly any change since I last spoke to you. The price is, of course, tending to widen, as people don't want to increase commitments before the holidays."

" Could you buy *d*em at forty shillings ? "

His pronunciation of " th " was not quite " d," but nearer " d " than " z."

9

"No, I could sell them at forty and a penny halfpenny."

"If I pay over forty shillings, you charge me sixpence commission ? "

"Yes."

"Instead of *d*e fourpence halfpenny *d*at I have always paid ? "

"That's because you've never bought them at over forty shillings before."

"But you prefer I should buy *d*em over forty shillings ? "

"Of course we do," I said pertly. It was, I think, my pertness which enabled me to keep his business, for he was always running after different brokers and playing them off one against the other.

"Driffield told me he could get *d*em at *d*irty-nine and nine."

"When ? "

"Just before lunch."

"So could I, then. Can Driffield do that now ? "

"No."

Some little grunts told me that he was thinking. I held my pencil poised.

"I want to buy ten *d*ousand. What will you have to pay ? "

"I can't possibly say offhand. It will probably be very difficult if not impossible to deal in such a number. I think I can promise you one thousand at forty and tenpence halfpenny."

"One *d*ousand! I want ten. Buy me as many as you can *d*en, up to forty and tenpence halfpenny. No, forty-one and *d*ree. No, forty-two shillings, if

you must give it. I want *d*e shares. Run along now
and deal, and ring me up."

I repeated the order in my professional voice.

" Buy up to ten thousand Harrington Cobalts up
to forty-two shillings. Thank you so much."

He gave a grunt and rang off.

My firm's two dealers whom I consulted hurriedly
as to our best tactics, were all excitement. What a
windfall, what a Christmas present! As I walked
down Old Broad Street to the office I felt exhila-
rated. My firm was a small one, but we had already
gained prestige as big dealers in Harringtons. I
foresaw the day when the leading jobbers would
tremble at my approach and say nervously to one
another: " Look out, here come Heavens and
Slicer. What are they up to now ? "

Largely by good luck we were able to complete the
transaction by about ten minutes past four, and I
rang up Mr. Quisberg again.

" Good, good, very good," he said. " Now I want
eight hundred for Dr. Green."

" Dr. Green ? " I asked, elated at the thought of a
new client.

" Dr. Martin Green. I will be responsible for him.
Get him eight hundred as cheap as you can, and
send *d*e contract note to me. No, you needn't ring
up again. I'm very busy. You'll meet Dr. Green at
dinner to-night and can tell him what you've done.
I shan't be *d*ere, I'm afraid. I have to be at *d*e
Carlton at seven-thirty to meet G——. *D*is is, of
course, confidential."

My answering " Oh " was full of admiration.

G—— is a name of such magnitude in financial circles that I dare not even write it in full.

" And buy yourself as many as you can," he said with a sudden kindness in his voice which made some amends for his many exasperating qualities.

I bought three hundred at forty-two and nine, and my partner, Jack Slicer, did the same.

" Now we're for it," he said, as we were having our tea. " What does old Q. know, do you suppose ? "

" What the shares are going to be taken over at, I imagine," I said guardedly.

It was no secret that the Universal Canadian Mining Corporation, of which G—— was president, was eager to buy the Harrington Cobalt Company, though there were very contradictory views of the purchase price.

" In spite of that denial in the papers ? "

" Oh, that means nothing."

" Well," he said, " we should have had a pretty lean account without you. As it is, it must be a record."

I glowed with pride—an ominous pride that went before a fall.

As soon as I had signed the contracts and the remaining letters and given the usual seasonal greetings to everyone in sight, I locked up my desk and went to my flat near Berkeley Square. I was to spend Christmas with my client and his wife—his wife, especially—and had little time in which to wash, change from my City serge into something cleaner, and pack. The Quisbergs, except when they were giving a formal party, dined at half past seven, and I had promised to arrive about a quarter to. It was actually about twenty minutes to seven when I left my flat in a taxi, and began the well-known drive along Mount Street, northward up Park Street, Gloucester Place, Wellington Street, Finchley Road, Fitzjohn's Avenue to the summit of the heath by the pond and flagstaff at the top of Heath Street, then down the West Heath Road to Lyon Avenue, in which the second house on the right, Beresford Lodge, was my destination.

I had met Mrs. Quisberg about eleven months before, when dining with some of my grandest acquaintances. One's social judgments of people— if one must make them—are largely based upon the medium of one's introduction. But I think as soon as I saw Mrs. Quisberg, I realized that she did not belong to the world in which we were both, for the moment, moving. There were about her an effusive-ness and an eagerness to please which I could not associate with my other fellow-guests. We were partners at bridge. She played badly but with enthusiasm, and when I was lucky enough to make a redoubled little slam, she could hardly contain her joy.

" I do hope you will come and see me sometime," she said, as we were beginning to say good-bye. " I'm sure you're a rising junior at the Bar, aren't you ? "

" No, I'm on the Stock Exchange."

" The Stock Exchange! My husband will love that. You must come and meet him. And you will

have music in common, too. I heard you talking so
learnedly about Wagner to Lady Geraldine Richings
during dinner. I'm afraid I don't know one note
from another—quite a barbarian—but we can
always play bridge, can't we ? "

She spoke with a slight Irish accent which gave
point to her flattest remarks. She was good-looking
in a mature way, and might have passed for forty-two
or three. Her dress was elaborate, but gave an
impression of slovenliness, as if she could not trouble
to be really tidy even in the houses of the great. I
caught a glimpse of a slightly soiled shoulder-strap
which had won my sympathy by slipping from its
niche of brocade. As she drove away in a splendid
Rolls-Royce, I felt that she was one with whom one
could take liberties and be forgiven. I resolved to
accept the invitation when it came.

It was not long in coming and I paid my first of a
long series of visits to Beresford Lodge on a dull
Sunday in February. By the early summer I found
myself going there more often than to any other
house in London, and barely a week passed without a
meeting between myself and one of the Quisberg
family. There was nothing romantic, I hasten to say,
in my friendship with Mrs. Quisberg. She liked me,
and even showed me a sentimental fondness, but so
she did to everyone she liked. She was, as they say, a
devoted wife and an indulgent mother.

Mr. Quisberg was her third husband. There were
five children, all by his two predecessors. The eldest
son, Clarence James, was about twenty-four and did
not live at home. I think he was Mrs. Quisberg's one

disappointment. He had never taken kindly to her remarriages and had wayward and artistic tastes which perplexed the rest of the family. On leaving Cambridge he refused to go into any business, and began to paint. After many quarrels and reconciliations, he was given a small income by his stepfather, and established himself in a cottage in the old part of Hampstead. He had become greatly entangled with a coterie in Bloomsbury, and I had actually met him at a party in that district—where I myself had a somewhat doubtful footing—a few months before I met his mother. When, afterwards, he learnt that I was a friend of his parents, and a Stock Exchange friend at that, he took a dislike to me. It is my fate, in Bloomsbury, to be thought a Philistine, while in other circles I am regarded as a dilettante with too keen an æsthetic sense to be a responsible person.

The second child, a daughter named Amabel Thurston, was, like the remaining children, issue of Mrs. Quisberg's second marriage. She was just twenty, very pretty in a peroxide fashion, and formidably self-assured. She was engaged to, and very much in love with, a stalwart ex-tea-planter named Leonard Dixon, for whom I could not entertain any affection. I have often noticed that wherever I go, I seem destined to have as one of my associates a man who gives me a sense of awkwardness and physical inferiority. In the old days, my tormentor had been my cousin, Bob Carvel,* and when the catastrophe in which we were both involved put me on a different footing with him, his place was taken

* See *Death of My Aunt*.

by an ex-naval half-commission man in my office.
Hardly had I laid my successful plans for ridding
myself of this thorn in the flesh, when I realized that
as long as I went to the Quisbergs' I was bound to see
too much of the man Dixon, as I called him oppro-
briously. Mrs. Quisberg had no very delicate
perceptions and was too much inclined both to think
the best of people and to accept them at their own
valuations. She confessed to me, however, that her
husband did not much care for the proposed
marriage, and would have been glad to know a little
more about his future stepson-in-law. Apparently
both his parents were dead, and the only relative of
whom he spoke was an aunt who lived near Gosport.
I was not surprised at Mr. Quisberg's dissatisfaction;
for the young man, in addition to those qualities
which made him specially antipathetic to me, had
traces of vulgarity in his nature such as my cousin
Bob and the ex-naval man had never possessed. I
should have said that Amabel's passion for him was
largely physical, had not their tastes seemed to
coincide in everything.

I liked the third child, Sheila Thurston. She was
nearly eighteen, less blonde and pretty than her
sister perhaps, but, to my mind, of far pleasanter
disposition. She had only lately left school, and
was still wrapped up in the friends she had made
there.

Next came two boys, Richard, aged fifteen, who
was spending Christmas with his cousins in Switzerland, and Cyril, aged twelve, who was at home
recovering from appendicitis. He had been operated

on only a fortnight before and still had to keep to his room.

I remember hoping, as my taxi clambered painfully up the steep curve of Heath Street, that I should not find too boisterous a party. I felt rather tired with a long innings at the office, and singularly ill-provided with the puckish spirit which the season required. However, it was a pleasanter way of spending Christmas than staying at home, or going to an hotel. My mother and stepfather and unmarried sister had gone for three months to the South of France where my stepfather had been offered the chaplaincy of one of those English churches which flourish so amazingly among the baccarat players. I knew the Quisbergs well enough to be misanthropic if I found my vitality pitched in too low a key.

After the run down West Heath Road and an abrupt left turn into Lyon Avenue, my taxi passed through the iron gates of Beresford Lodge. It could not, however, set me down at the front door; for the circular drive was blocked by the Quisbergs' Rolls-Royce which stood with the engine running and chauffeur in readiness. Harley, Mr. Quisberg's spectacled and freckled little secretary, was waiting by the chauffeur, and looking with such concentration at his watch that he hardly noticed my approach. I got out of my cab with my suitcase, paid the driver and told him to back into Lyon Avenue. As I went towards the house, I saw my host and another man pacing up and down the small front lawn in the light of the electric gate-lamps. They were talking so earnestly that I thought it better not to interrupt, and was about to ring the bell when Quisberg turned round and saw me.

" Hello! " he shouted, " I'm just off." Then, after an irresolute pause which was characteristic of him, he ran up to me and shook hands.

" *D*is," he said, pointing to his companion, " is Dr. Green. Well, I shall hear your news to-morrow, I hope. Good night! "

At that he got into the car, followed by Harley, who carried an attaché case, but the car had barely begun to move when he rapped on the window and jumped out, calling, " Martin, ano*d*er *d*ing——" The doctor, who had not yet shaken hands with me, took Quisberg's arm and led him, rather quickly, I thought, out of earshot, to the end of the lawn. At that moment my hostess came to the door with the footman.

" So there you are at last, Malcolm," she said. " Come in and leave those men. I don't know what they're up to, but something terrific seems to be in the wind. I expect you're rather tired. Will you have a cocktail before you dress, or when you come down ? Or shall I send it up to you ? Oh, you must have one. Amabel's had three already. I'm afraid I've had to give you the nastiest little room—the bogy-hole beside the drawing-room. You see, we're crowded out. I hoped we should have got rid of nurse by now, but Dr. McKenzie thinks she ought to stay another week, though Cyril's getting on simply splendidly. You haven't seen her yet, have you ? She's so

pretty, mind you don't make me jealous. Then
Clarence is here, which is something of a surprise.
He's in a tiny attic right at the top, a box-room
really. Lucky we've plenty of beds. And there's
Mrs. Harley——"

" Harley's wife ? "

She roared with laughter.

" No, you goose! His mother. A nice little body.
Must have been beautiful once. And there's Dr.
Green, and Leonard, of course. Here you are."

We had reached the first landing, and she opened a
door on the left of the drawing-room and went before
me into a room which looked smaller than it was
owing to the height of the ceiling.

" Well, I'll leave you now. Let Edwins unpack
for you. Here he comes with your bag. Half past
seven, remember! " And she bustled out.

She had done everything she could to make me
comfortable. An ormolu chest had been turned into
a dressing-table, and there was a compactum wardrobe against the opposite wall. I had indeed all I
needed, a complete, if composite, bedroom suite.
It irked me a little, however, to know that Dixon
had been given a proper bedroom, while I had a
makeshift one. No doubt, I thought naughtily, he
and Amabel like their rooms adjoining! At all
events, I was on the first floor and could thus easily
slip away from the party when I wanted, provided
always my room was not used as a dressing-room for
charades.

My knowledge of the house was naturally restricted
to its lower floors. The building was, as might be

expected, most elaborate in construction and design.
On the ground floor, after passing through a lobby,
one reached an enormous hall, more ornately
panelled than anything I have ever seen. The
dining-room was on the right, or north-east side, and
gave access to a moorish conservatory, known
popularly as " the Aviary," though happily no birds
were kept there. The hall extended so far to the
north-west that the room opening out of it in that
direction was absurdly narrow from door to windows,
though it stretched nearly the whole breadth of the
house. It was known as the " Terrace Room," and
had four french windows all leading on to a broad
covered terrace from which one went by a poor
imitation of a Louis Quinze staircase into the
garden—the real garden; for the strip of lawn on
which Quisberg and the doctor had been walking,
was as nothing compared with the vast area behind
the house. On the left, or south-west side of the hall,
was a passage which led to a big cloak-room and
lavatory on the garden side, and a green baize door
on the road side, through which only the staff had
the privilege of going. On the same side as the green
baize door, but before one reached it, was the door
of my host's study—a narrow room facing the road.
There was also a door from this room leading
directly into the hall, but it was kept locked, and was
concealed on the inside by a bookcase. The main
servants' quarters were in an airy basement which
ran the whole width of the house on the road side.
The staircase giving access to it was to be found
somewhere beyond the green baize door, which

meant that to go from dining-room to kitchen one
had to cross the width of the house twice. All food,
however, was conveyed straight to the dining-room
by a service lift. The ground, as in many Hampstead
gardens, sloped steeply—in this instance away from
the road. Thus it was that the terrace was fully
twelve feet high and the path below it was below the
level of the basement floor. The basement rooms,
however, had no windows on the garden side.

The first floor was occupied almost entirely by the
drawing-room—a room for which I can find no
adequate superlative. Its area was that of the
dining-room, a good piece of the hall and the
terrace-room, the dining-room part making a
monstrous L with the rest. Its windows on the
north-east side faced to the glass roof of " the
Aviary," and those on the north-west faced the garden, though there was a broad balcony with a
spiky railing which formed the roof of the terrace
below. My own room was really a little slice of the
drawing-room, cut off no doubt to satisfy the caprice
of some former owner, and had access to the same
balcony as the drawing-room. I wished that, as in
hotels, there had been an iron railing separating
mine from the communal territory, so that I might
enjoy the afternoon sun on it, if there was to be
any. On the same landing there were three rooms
looking over the road, one of them Sheila's bedroom,
another the bedroom of Mrs. Quisberg's maid, and
the third the bedroom of Harley, Mr. Quisberg's
secretary. All I knew of the south-west side of the
landing was that the wall contained another green

baize door, hidden as a rule by a huge lacquer screen.

The bathroom—that is to say, the bathroom which I used—was half-way up the next flight of stairs.

Mrs. Quisberg's enormous bedroom, into which I had been once when she had a cold, was on the second floor, on the north-east side, so that she should get the morning sun. On the same floor there must have been at least five other rooms, Mr. Quisberg's, Amabel's and a spare room, all probably over the garden front of the drawing-room, and two more spare rooms on the road side, not to mention bathrooms and domestic offices.

The third floor was devoted to the night and day nurseries, servants' rooms, box-rooms and the " attic " allotted to Clarence.

The less I say about the furnishing and " appointments " of the house, the better, perhaps. Both Bloomsbury and Belgravia would (for different reasons) have described them as appalling. A few pieces of furniture were beautiful. All of them were expensive, but the general effect was deplorable. Somehow everything about the house was a little wrong. Despite the size of the rooms, they seemed too full. The electric light fittings, specially made in Paris, I was told, did not harmonize with the carving on the walls and doors. The colour schemes were at once nondescript and crude. In the drawing-room, for example, some exquisite Samarkand rugs were killed by the brocade curtains, which, as Amabel jauntily let out, cost one and fourpence an inch. The dining-room was the least unsuccessful room in the house; for there Mrs. Quisberg's taste, which really ran to a nineteenth-century splendour, could gratify itself unabashed. It was when she tried to copy the neo-Georgian interiors of her Mayfair friends that she failed most dismally.

While I changed for dinner, my thoughts were chiefly occupied with Harrington Cobalts. At one moment I wished that I had plunged really heavily, at the next I feared I had been foolish in buying as many as I did. When the gong sounded, I was beginning to wonder what my bank would have to say if things went wrong.

II. A FALL

THERE were eight of us at dinner. Mrs. Quisberg sat at the head of the table, with me, Sheila and Leonard Dixon on her right, and Dr. Green, Mrs. Harley and Clarence on her left. Amabel sat at the other end, between Clarence and Dixon. In the first conversational " set " I was paired off with Sheila, but as she was not talkative and devoted herself greedily to her food, I had leisure to observe the two members of the party whom I had not met before—Dr. Green, who was opposite me, and Mrs. Harley.

The doctor was a big florid man, blue-eyed, rather bald, with a red-brown complexion and a bristly fair moustache. He might have been any age between forty-five and sixty. He laughed and talked loudly and incessantly, emphasizing his remarks by waving his big hands in the air, drumming on the table and winking. He was clearly not English, though he spoke with unremitting fluency, and gave the impression, whenever he misused one of our idioms, that he had done so on purpose. He was so full of vitality that he made even my hostess seem languid. Mrs. Harley was small and sallow, with large brown eyes which she had probably rolled to effect in better days. She spoke huskily, and was full of nervous mannerisms. She seemed most grateful to be where she was, and perhaps a little overawed. Once or twice I caught her looking at Mrs. Quisberg half sadly and half resentfully. " She is wondering," I said to myself, " why some women should live in boarding-houses, while others live in crystal palaces."

All serious table talk was reduced to incoherence by a sudden shout from Amabel: " You pig, Sheila; hand over those almonds. Take them, Len."

" Don't you be bullied," I said to my neighbour. " We want them here."

This drew Amabel's attention to me.

" Oh, so you like our almonds, Mr. Warren," she answered in a drawling voice which she affected, when she remembered, for my special benefit. " Tell me, did you condescend to notice the close of Harrington Cobalts, Mr. Stockbroker ? "

" They closed quite firmly," I said guardedly.

" Now, Amabel," her mother put in, " don't talk about things you don't understand one little bit."

" But I do thoroughly understand them," was the reply. " Don't we all know that if they touch—that's the *mot juste*, isn't it—fifty-five bob, we shall buy Paragon House ? "

" You know nothing of the sort," said Mrs. Quisberg, looking round nervously to see that none of the servants was in the room.

" What and where is Paragon House ? " I asked.

" Paragon House is that hideous derelict building

in Strathsporran Road we can see in winter at the end of the garden. In summer, of course, the plane trees hide it."

" Is it empty ? " asked the doctor.

" Yes, empty and for sale. It's near enough the Finchley Road to make people want to pull it down and build a block of flats, and we're naturally not very eager for that. It's a great pity, as it's the only building which overlooks us in any way."

" How much do they want for it ? " I asked.

" Twelve thousand."

" Good gracious! "

" Prices round here are terrific. Sir Samuel Baruch paid twenty-seven thousand for Darlington Lodge—that's the corner house next to this, you know."

" But," persisted Amabel, " you can't compare Lyon Avenue with Strathsporran Road. It's practically a slum and ends up in shops and the kind of bungalow female Labour members would live in. Personally, I think the whole idea's damned silly. All right, Mumsie. Dad had far better double my allowance. Don't you think so, Len ? "

" Besides," said Clarence, while Dixon was hesitating over a facetious reply, " the female Labour members will probably tax you out of it, if you do get it."

" I believe you'd like them to, Clarence. Do you know, Len, he's written three articles on *art* for the *Daily Herald* ? "

" Well, I'm blowed! What sort of art ? The altogether, eh ? "

Meanwhile, having delivered his spirit of venom, Clarence turned disdainfully back to Mrs. Harley.

"I am afraid you must consider us a most ill-mannered family."

"On the contrary," said Dr. Green, who seemed to hear everything everybody said, "nothing is more agreeable than to hear young people saying exactly what they think, even if they don't think what they should. I was staying with a family once where there were eight daughters—all very pretty, high-spirited young ladies. One day the third daughter, whose name was Waterloo—they were all christened after the famous British victories——"

He went on to tell a rambling story, which was only entertaining through his manner of telling it. Noticing that Mrs. Quisberg was not listening to him, I asked her what her husband would do with Paragon House if he did buy it.

"It's most unlikely," she said. "But I suppose, if it went very cheap and we did get it, we should just pull it down. You see the ground slopes very steeply the other side of it, and we should get the view of the Harrow Ridge that you get near the top of the Heath. I dare say Axel would use some of the ground to build another hot-house. He's always wanted to experiment with some kind of tropical melon that needs heaps of space and attention. And we might make a bathing-pool. But it isn't worth talking about, it's so improbable. And it might be rather silly. After all, I don't suppose we shall live here for ever."

I remember noticing that Mrs. Harley, though she

was one of the doctor's audience, seemed to have caught my hostess' last remark, for she half looked up and seemed about to say something and then turned her eyes to her plate again and fiddled with a walnut. She must, I thought, be suffering badly from an inferiority complex.

" I suppose you expect Mr. Quisberg back about eleven," I asked, changing the subject.

" No, not to-night at all. He and Mr. Harley are sleeping at the Carlton. Mr. G—— seems to be a most peculiar man—full of fads like so many of these multi-millionaires. He always goes to bed at half past ten, and gets up at half past six, and poor Axel will have to do the same. When the big men have finished their talk, I believe the small fry—the secretaries, accountants and such-like, you know— have to agree to some figures, and then they all have another meeting to-morrow morning at half past seven, before Mr. G—— flies to Brussels in his own aeroplane at about ten. Poor Axel, he does hate hotels, but it was obviously better for him to sleep on the spot. I do hope he'll get a good rest there. I thought he seemed so strung up to-night. Now I suppose I ought to make a move. Don't be too long. We have coffee in the drawing-room in about ten minutes. Amabel——"

The women left the room, and Dr. Green at once moved into Mrs. Quisberg's chair, as if he was not going to allow anyone else to dominate the table. He poured himself out large glasses of sherry and liqueur brandy, and sent the bottles round the table.

"Fill up, fill up," he said. "It's Christmas Day to-morrow."

"Not for me, thanks," said Clarence, who seemed in no way surprised that, though he was our hostess' son, he was ousted from the position of host.

"I'm practically T.T.," said Dixon. Oddly enough it was true. He had been most abstemious during dinner.

"Don't they teach you to drink in the tropics, Dixon?" asked the doctor.

"Some fellows do. I've always found myself fitter without it."

The doctor looked at him with an irritating smile, and I looked at him too. He certainly was incredibly fit, and I compared his healthy brown complexion enviously with my own, which betrayed lack of fresh air and too many late hours. How did he do it? How did he manage to make me feel so like a rat beside a stallion? Even his dinner jacket put mine to shame.

We were an ill-assorted group, and I hoped the doctor would not keep us too long at the table. As if realizing, however, that conversation was not going to be gay, he began to tell smoking-room stories, including a grossly medical one of a patient who had to be operated upon for the strangest of self-inflicted injuries. Clarence looked bored, and Dixon (a puritan, like so many people, when confronted with the unfamiliar), shocked. I felt I had to make some response.

"I can only say, Doctor," I said, "that I'm glad you're my client and not my medical attendant, if that's the kind of thing you specialize in."

" Who knows ? " he replied. " You may need me before so very long. Always at your service. Always at everybody's service."

" You are a doctor of medicine, then ? "

" I am a doctor of science at the University of Vienna. And there is no degree more distinguished in this world."

" The School of Freud, you mean ? "

" Pah! Freud! Psychoanalysis is pure common sense. Nothing more or less. There's nothing new in it. Freud's great work has been to knock another nail in the coffin of prudery. That's all he's done. And now, I suppose, as you all seem so eager to be reunited with the fair sex that you can't even drink Axel's good brandy, we had better leave the table."

He drained his goblet, which held about a port glass full of brandy, in one gulp, and led the way upstairs.

" Bridge, my dear lady ? " he said to Mrs. Quisberg. " I play bridge very well. And so, I am convinced, does my friend Malcolm here."

I noticed that he called us all by our Christian names, except Dixon. Mrs. Quisberg led the way to the table.

" Clarence, you'll have to make the fourth," she said. " Mrs. Harley positively won't play."

" Can't play, you mean," she said timidly. " But I shall love looking on, if you'll just excuse me while I fetch my needlework."

She gave an apologetic little smile, and hurried out of the room, as if afraid of being called back.

" What's the matter with her ? " asked the doctor.

" She suffers terribly from nerves. Insomnia, you know. And when she does get to sleep, she walks in it. I feel so sorry for her. She's really come to London to see a nerve specialist. Harley, Axel's secretary, you know, didn't like letting her stay in an hotel alone, and as Axel couldn't spare him to go to her just now, owing to this Mr. G——, we thought she'd better come to us. And I'm glad she has. I hope we have the chance of feeding her up, poor thing. She looks so dreadfully worn. Now, Clarence, put down that book, dear."

Clarence got up to join us, and Amabel pulled Dixon from a sofa by the fire.

" Come on," she said, giving us a scornful glance, " let's leave them to their frowsy game, and have some ping-pong in the terrace-room."

I watched them go out of the door with satisfaction, and so, I thought, did Clarence.

" I didn't know you played bridge," I said to him.

" I don't, as a rule. I prefer intelligent conversation, but if——"

He shrugged his shoulders and sat down.

The game began. Mrs. Quisberg played vilely, but Clarence much better than I had expected. He wishes to show, I thought, that the man of intelligence can beat the Philistine on his own ground. There was, indeed, something about him which annoyed me. I was convinced, without good cause, that I knew much more about the game than he did, but everything he did seemed to be lucky and to bring him an unmerited prestige. When, for example, he trumped my ace of diamonds in the

first round of the suit, his gesture almost implied
contempt for " city " brains, and whenever he made
a declaration, he appeared to correct mine which had
preceded his. At length I became more angry with
myself than with him, for being so sensitive to his
superior airs, of which, perhaps, he was quite
unconscious, and I began feebly to try to imitate the
doctor in his flippant attitude to the game. The
doctor was quite clearly far better than any of us, but
would not for one moment treat the game seriously.
He kept up a flow of ridiculous conversation,
whistled, sang, shuffled the cards spectacularly with
his big hairy hands, patted his tricks, drummed on
the table, and seemed continually on the verge of
cheating, though he never actually did so.

" Come, Malcolm," he would say, " play the
queen now if you have her. Come along, little lady.
Hoop-la! There she goes. And now there's the
knave, this naughty little knave we have to get hold
of. Who has the knave of hearts ? If it's in Letty's
hand, I give you two tricks more. Yes, only two
tricks. Your king of clubs ? What care I for your
king of clubs ? I trump him—so. Letty has the
knave of hearts. I knew she had. She had to have
it, by all the rules of the game. And by all the rules
of the game the other tricks are mine—for I have
nothing but trumps left! Isn't it wonderful ? Oh, I
have such an unlucky partner—so unlucky, he must
be in love, to have given me such a be-autiful hand.
Does she not love you at all, partner ? Well, I hope she
won't till the rubber's over. After that, may she love
you as much as you like, and God bless you both."

Clarence, at whom these thrusts were directed, grew very red and seemed about to throw his cards on the table.

" Come, Doctor," said his mother, " it's too bad to tease him like this. He may really be in love, for all we know. After all, we usually were at his age, weren't we ? "

" Oh, Madam, how you flatter me. But you know nothing of my early life, and don't you pretend you do. No tales of me to these young innocents. Not a word, I beg you. Now! I bid three spades, and if nobody says anything I shall be very much surprised. You, Malcolm ? Ah, I thought so. Lying low! You, partner ? "

" Five clubs."

" Ah, capital. And, Madam ?

" Sweet Gretchen's pretty ankle
Would make my . . .

" Sh! Five hearts, you say ? What do I care for five hearts ? Six no trumps. Oh, it's an easy game, bridge. You, Malcolm ? No bid again ? Oh, aren't you a shy boy! Partner ? Thank you for your implicit confidence in me. And, Madam ? Madam doubles. Madam would—and I redouble Madam—just for the sake of introducing a little gallantry into a game which is, in its essence, completely unchivalrous."

And so on. By half past ten, the doctor had won four rubbers. Mrs. Harley, who had crept into a chair near the table and been watching us like a little cat, folded up her embroidery and was clearly about to say good night, when Amabel burst into the room followed by Dixon and the Drews, a young married couple who lived in the neighbourhood.

" Oh, Lord, I'm thirsty; aren't you, Doris ? " said Amabel when the new arrivals had been briefly introduced. " We've had eleven sets, Mums. I caught Doris as Edwins was showing her upstairs, so you must thank me for not having your precious game interrupted. Oh no, you can't begin another rubber. You really can't. It's Christmas Eve, not the eighth Sunday after Trinity. What about some musical chairs ? Come on, everybody. Yes, Mrs. Harley, of course you must."

" But Mrs. Harley wants to go to bed, dear."

" Oh no, she doesn't. Do you, Mrs. Harley ? Now, Sheila, be an angel and leave your Ethel M. Dell and perform upon the pianoforte—didn't I say it well ? "

I was indignant that our game had to give way to such a rough and dangerous pastime, but Amabel was so insistent and so ably supported by her friends, that there was no help for it. Clarence and I cleared away the card-table, while the others prepared the room. Sheila, who had some talent at improvisation, drifted to the piano.

" Mind you," said Amabel menacingly, " this is only a beginning. There's no knowing what we shan't be doing in an hour or two. So you'd all better get the party spirit right away! One, two, three, go! "

The pianist struck a loud chord, and we pranced foolishly round the polished floor, my own concern

being to be " out " as soon as possible. It was
wonderful how much horseplay four people with the
" party spirit " could introduce into the preposterous
game. I found myself jostled and harried in all
directions, while mocking shouts assailed my efforts
to be unruffled. I was just vowing that never again
would I visit Beresford Lodge during a festive season,
when I caught my foot in the leg of a chair that someone had pushed out of line, slithered over the floor,
and fell with a crash beside a big Chinese cabinet.

I seemed to lie for a long time, wondering what had
happened. Then, as people began to crowd round
me, I felt a violent pain in my right arm and
another, only a little less severe, in the fingers of my
left hand. The doctor took me gently by the
shoulders and pulled me to a sitting position. I
looked up stupidly. Then the whole room swam
round me and I was violently sick.

" Lord! How beastly! "

It was Dixon who spoke first. I think even Amabel
felt that he rather than I had committed a breach of
good manners, for she darted to the table of refresh-
ments and brought me some brandy. Meanwhile,
Mrs. Quisberg was wringing her hands and murmuring endearments.

" Oh, the poor boy. Is he very much hurt, Doctor ?
Oh, I hope it's not concussion of the brain. All
right, Malcolm, dear. We'll look after you. We'll
soon have you comfortable. Doctor, do you think
you can do everything, or shall I ring up Dr.
McKenzie ? Perhaps Nurse is still up."

" I'll go and see," said Clarence.

" She's in the grey room," his mother shouted, as he went precipitately through the door.

" The nurse can do nothing that I can't do," said Dr. Green, who still supported me. " Nor your Dr. McKenzie either. Leave him to me."

" I'm so sorry," I gasped, feeling oddly revived at the sound of the doctor's voice. " I shall be better in a few minutes. Just leave me, will you ? "

" There's only one place for you, and that's bed," said the doctor. " Where's his room, Letty ? "

" Next door to this—the bogy-hole. Oh, but let him have Axel's room, or mine, now. And do you want Nurse ? "

" I hate all nurses," I said. " They make me feel ill. If Dr. Green will help me to my room——"

He raised me to my feet, and to my great relief I found that I could walk without any difficulty. Evidently I still had legs, if not arms. Mrs. Quisberg opened the door and went before us down the long corridor to my room. A big fire was burning, and a mound under the bedclothes denoted a hot-water bottle.

" It does seem pitifully small," she said, looking round at the congested furniture, and shuddering.

I reassured her and the doctor bustled her away. He then took off my coat, waistcoat and shirt and examined my arms. Apart from a little bruising of the fingers of my left hand, my left arm was unhurt. My right arm, however, was very painful and had begun to swell from the elbow downwards, while I could not move the fingers of my right hand at all.

" Broke your fall, you see. That's the trouble,"

he muttered. "When you fall in future, always remember to let yourself go. You'll do far less damage. Well, my boy, if I had a professional reputation (which, I'm glad to say, I haven't), I'd stake it on your having broken no bones. An ordinary doctor wouldn't know. He'd either hope for the best, if he was a country one, and do nothing, or if he was a Londoner, he'd hustle you off to a radiologist who'd charge you five guineas for a snap-shot. Of course you can go to one if you like."

"I don't in the least want to," I said.

"Well, I'm an extraordinary doctor, and I'm positive there's no need. Just a little soothing massage first—so—so—and so——"

As he spoke, his chubby fingers wandered lightly but skilfully over the painful area, and brought an amazing relief. Suddenly he chuckled.

"You said you hoped you wouldn't be a patient of mine; don't you remember? Oh, these prophetic words spoken so lightly—these little kinks in the film of the future which get mixed up in the present! Don't you like it? Isn't it comforting? And what a thin skin! There now. No, lie quite still. I shan't hurt you. Ssss!"

He made the noise of a man grooming a horse.

"Now, have a little rest, while I fetch some balm and a bandage from my room. Shut your eyes and think of all the money you've made to-day, and don't move."

He went out, and in obedience to his orders, I began to wonder what was happening at the Carlton. Was "the deal through," or was G—— trying to drive too hard a bargain? As the owner of three hundred Harrington Cobalts (for which I should have difficulty in paying) I felt Mr. Quisberg ought to let me know as soon as he came in. But, of course, we were not to expect him till Christmas morning. Christmas! Stockings, holly, crackers, carols, too much plum-pudding, and the vague depression which even in childhood had seemed to surround the whole business—and the summer still so very far away.

I was embarking on one of those gently doleful reveries to which I am often liable, when the doctor came back, with his appliances.

" First," he said, " I'm going to give you something to make you sleep. No protests, please. An ordinary doctor wouldn't have thought of this. Your arm will become very painful in the night, and you won't get much rest if you don't do as I tell you. An ordinary doctor wouldn't mind that, of course. He wouldn't be interested in you. He'd be interested only in your case, and pain is the last thing which concerns him. I, on the other hand, think of everything, including your general well-being. Now drink this."

I drank.

" It will have effect in about half an hour. Now for the embrocation and the bandage, and a little look at your legs, to see if there's any more trouble, and I'll put you to bed. Your left hand will be well to-morrow, and your right arm—provided always that I am privileged to continue treating it—in three days, or less. But don't try to use it just yet."

As he spoke, he started on his programme. The

bandage, though very tight, gave me a feeling of confidence, and I was delighted to think that my injuries were to be cured so soon. Was it faith-healing, I wondered? At all events, I put myself completely in his hands, while a slight drowsiness helped to blunt my critical sense.

"May I come in?"

It was Mrs. Quisberg again.

"By all means," shouted the doctor, "if you wish to see him naked!"

She came in, undeterred, barely giving him time to throw something over me. But I was no longer uppermost in her thoughts.

"Doctor," she said. "I wonder, could you spare me a little of the draught you're giving Malcolm? It's Mrs. Harley, who's having a fit of nerves or something. She says she's afraid she won't get any rest to-night. Being in a strange house seems to have upset her, or perhaps it was that noisy game and Malcolm's fall. At any rate, she's all trembly, and when I saw you come down with the drink——"

"Oh, these women!" he answered. "All right. Leave me five minutes and I'll get you some."

She smiled and looked down at me.

"Isn't he a boor? Well, dear, I do hope you'll be comfortable. Is there nothing more I can do? A little brandy, do you think, Doctor, in case he feels faint?"

"Certainly not," he said. "He'll be asleep five minutes after I get his pyjamas on, and as I can't do that—without offending the laws of propriety—as long as you are within sight, dear lady, perhaps you'll say good night to Malcolm and wait for me outside."

" All right, but don't keep me too long. I've got *my* patient to consider. Good night, Malcolm, dear, and sleep well."

As she went out, the doctor made a face.

" There now," he said, when he had tucked me up in bed, " go off to sleep at once, and don't dare to move till I come to see you in the morning. Shall I hang up a Christmas stocking ? No ? Perhaps you're right. It might tempt our hostess to come back and fill it. Hush-a-bye baby! Sweet dreams! "

He turned off the light and went out. As the door shut, I remember hearing him say, " Now what about this poor lady ? " and the voice of Mrs. Quisberg in voluble reply. Then I fell asleep.

III. DISCOVERY

Christmas Day—Dawn

I SLEPT very soundly till an hour or so before dawn,
and then dozed, becoming with each spell of wakefulness a little more conscious of discomfort in my
right arm. By about half past seven I was in possession of my senses, and somewhat restless. The doctor
had left the window-curtains pulled together the
night before, thus violating one of my habits, and I
got out of bed to let the daylight in. It was a very
misty morning and apart from a few gaunt trees near
the window I could see nothing of the garden. Then
suddenly I noticed, on the extreme right of my piece
of balcony, a most peculiar shape resting obliquely
against the railings. The top end was hidden from
my view by a pillar which jutted out from the wall,
but the end which rested on the stone floor looked
like a bundle of underclothes. Very slowly I came to
realize that it was a body.

I have sometimes wondered what my feelings would
be on finding a body, and how much revulsion and
horror the discovery would bring. In this instance I
felt nothing but bewilderment and the wish to make
further investigations. I tried the handle of the
french window, but it was too stiff for me to open
with my left hand. Then I paused irresolutely.

Clearly I needed Dr. Green, and it was inadvisable that anyone else should share my knowledge till he had the situation in hand. I pulled down the blind again, got into bed and rang the bell. It was answered by Edwins, the footman.

" Will you go to Dr. Green, please," I said, " and tell him that I should like to see him at once. It's most urgent. No, don't bother about the blind. Go straight to the doctor, will you ? "

He went out in some surprise, and in a few minutes I heard the doctor's self-important footsteps echoing in the passage.

" Well," he said rather impatiently, " what's the trouble ? Can't you give me time to dress in peace ? "

He was wearing shirt, trousers and a dressing-gown.

" I haven't asked you to come and see *me*," I said, as he approached the bed. " There's a body on the balcony, and I can't open the window to get at it."

He looked at me in amazement.

" Have you been having nightmares, young man ? "

" It's quite true. I went to the window to pull up the blind, and saw—— "

As I spoke, he went to the window himself, pulled up the blind, gave a guttural cry, opened the window and walked through it. After a moment's indecision I got out of bed and threw a dressing-gown round my shoulders. As the doctor re-entered the room, carrying the human bundle, I said, " Ought you to have disturbed the position—— "

" Good Lord," he answered, " you're living in a detective story. I can't make my examination while the patient's feet are tangled in the balcony railings, can I ? I've got to be sure, first, that it is a corpse I'm handling. I am sure, as a matter of fact, though an ordinary doctor wouldn't be. Keep away now. It isn't a pretty sight, and I can't do with you in hysterics. Get back to bed and look the other way."

He put the body on the floor beside the fireplace, and without waiting to see the face I did as I was told.

" It's Mrs. Harley," he said. " Broken neck. Dead."

" Oh, dear. I suppose she must have walked——"

" In her sleep. Yes! I'll telephone for their imbecile family doctor first, and then we'll go to her room, if you will accompany me. You're on guard now. You won't scream if I lock you in for a minute or two ? I'll cover it with this."

He pulled down my bedclothes, ripped off the sheet, and put it over the body. Then he took the key, went out and locked the door.

It was perhaps fortunate that it was early in the morning; for at such an hour my emotions are rarely acute. While shaving, I can forget even that I am in love. My chief feeling, I think, was one of annoyance. There we were, all gathered together for a Christmas party, and plunged suddenly into gloom and the menace of official inquiry. " This time, at least," I thought, with the memory of my aunt's violent death in my mind, " it devolves on others to bear the burden of the arrangements. I can still be a petted invalid, inquisitive, importunate. And, of course, an accident is very different from murder. Unless perhaps it is suicide ? "

Poor Mrs. Harley—and her poor son, too. What a sad home-coming it would be for him after the night of high finance!

The key turned and the doctor came in again.

" I routed McKenzie out and he'll be here in half an hour. Meanwhile, shall we go upstairs ? "

He helped me to put on my dressing-gown properly, opened the door, and locked it when we had left the room.

" Do you know which her room was ? " I asked.

He looked at me sharply.

" Of course I do. I had to take her a sedative last night. She was jumping about like an electric flea, poor woman. I thought I made it strong enough to give her eight hours' good sleep."

" Mine wore off before seven," I said.

" Perhaps the prescription was not quite up to strength."

" Can you walk in your sleep after taking a sleeping-draught ? "

" It depends on the draught. After a mild one such as that which I administered, it is quite possible—though unusual."

" In any case, I thought sleep-walkers never came to any harm."

" That is an old wives' tale."

" How long has she been dead ? "

He looked apprehensively at the landing above and below.

" Sh! not so loud. After exposure to the cold, like that, I cannot say. Not more than eight hours, and not less than two. No doubt the good Dr. McKenzie will be more precise in his verdict. Here we are."

Mrs. Harley's room was immediately over mine, though it was larger and had two french windows, one corresponding to mine, and one to the right, over the drawing-room. This second window was wide open, and gave access to a very broad sill with low metal bars on the far side, which might have held a big window-box in position.

" Did she sleep with her window open ? " I asked.

" I suppose she must have done. I presume she slept, and we know she went to bed."

He pointed to the tumbled bedclothes, partially thrown aside, and the dented pillow. I looked round the room. On the mantelpiece was a photograph of the dead woman's son, in a leather frame. Her poor little evening dress and under-linen lay on a chair, while a quilted dressing-gown hung from one of the bed-posts. The sadness of the scene began to affect me, and so that the doctor should not see my distress I walked over to the window and looked out.

The garden was some fifty feet below me. If one jumped from the window, I thought, one might just clear the balcony outside my room. If one fell, one would be caught by it, impaled possibly on one of the

spikes. Had Mrs. Harley been impaled ? I shuddered, partly at so painful an idea, and partly with
cold, and was returning to the bed, when I was
struck by the contrast between the fresh air outside
and the air of the room.

" Well ? " said the doctor, as I sniffed.

" Do you smell anything ? " I asked.

" No. Do you ? "

" Yes—something a little odd. My sense of smell
is very acute."

" All your senses are very acute."

I was beginning to glow at the compliment when
he went on, " That's partly what makes you such a
nervy fellow. There's nothing to be said for hyper-
æsthesia, let me tell you."

" At all events," I replied, somewhat testily, " it
seems to give me an advantage over you now. The
smell is like—like, chloroform or ether—some
medical smell."

The doctor grinned wickedly. " Allow me to
congratulate you, Mr. Warren, upon a most
important discovery! Perhaps, however, I am more
familiar with ladies' bedrooms and their habits than
you are. What you smell—I confess I can't smell it,
but no doubt you're right—is Antaronyl, or a similar
preparation." He then gave me a gross explanation
of the uses to which Antaronyl could be put, and
concluded, " I've no doubt we shall find a bottle
among the poor lady's effects, but I suppose we had
better not derange them. Meanwhile, it is extremely
cold and I am more than a little hungry. If you will
go to my room, I will see to your arm and help you

to dress. Then I will complete my own toilet. By that time Dr. McKenzie should be here, or breakfast should be upon the table. Hurry up now, before the whole house is astir."

He pushed me out of the room across the passage, and into his room which was immediately opposite and faced the road.

"Now," he said, "you stay here in patience till I come back. I'll lock Mrs. Harley's room and fetch your clothes. There's a bathroom through this door. If you like to use it, you can, but you'll find it hard to soap yourself with one hand."

It was very true, and while the doctor was performing his errands about the house, I was only able to give myself a most ineffectual wash. I was drying myself in cold discomfort when I heard him come back.

"Sorry," he said through the door. "I'd valet you if I had time. As it is, I've got to dress myself and rub your arm before this doctor of theirs comes on the scene. Now! Sit down there, and let me see the damage."

He removed the bandage, and I was delighted to find that his patting and probing caused very little pain, while after a few minutes' massage, I felt almost as if I could bend my wrist again.

"I'll put back the bandage," he said, "anyhow for to-day. And you must wear a sling for a bit. I don't mind your moving the fingers, but be careful not to . . ."

There was a knock at the door and Edwins, the footman, came in.

" If you please, sir, Dr. McKenzie's waiting below. I showed him into the dining-room because the fire's going well there."

" Right! I will go to him at once. No, you stay and help Mr. Warren to dress. Mr. Warren had an accident while dancing in the drawing-room last night. I want you to fix him up with a sling. Do you know how to do it ? "

" Yes, sir. Had to wear one myself once."

" Most excellent."

He gave me a nod and went out. For a while Edwins helped me without speaking. Then, finding my silence unbearable, he said suddenly, " Not a very merry start for Christmas, is it, sir ? "

" Good heavens," I answered. " I'd quite forgotten that it was Christmas Day."

" Had the poor lady's accident anything to do with yours, sir, if I may ask ? "

" No, absolutely nothing. I'm afraid I don't feel at liberty to speak about it for the present."

" Sorry, sir. I don't wish to be inquisitive, but the door of your room being locked, and Dr. Green telephoning for Dr. McKenzie almost as soon as I'd asked him to come to see you——"

" What did Dr. Green tell you ? " I asked in as masterful a tone as I was able to assume.

" He said that Mrs. Harley had met with a serious accident, and that he must get hold of the family physician as soon as he could."

"Yes," I said vaguely, "that is all perfectly correct. And now about breakfast? I suppose nobody else is up yet?"

"Nor likely to be, sir, I think. The mistress has her breakfast in bed, and Miss Sheila's always a late riser. Both Miss Amabel and Mr. Dixon have got the cards on their doors."

"The cards?"

"You know, sir, like they have in hotels: 'Don't disturb me till noon '—' *Ne derangy par* ' it used to be at Deauville. I was in service there for a season, and there were cards almost permanent on all the bedroom doors."

"Miss Amabel and Mr. Dixon," I murmured.

"The master and Mr. Harley are breakfasting in town, sir."

"Oh, of course they are." I had quite forgotten the deal in Harrington Cobalts. "So that accounts for everybody."

"Oh, there's Mr. Clarence. I don't quite know what he's doing."

The man spoke as if Mr. Clarence were of very small consequence. "But if you would like breakfast, sir, it should be ready now, if you care to go down. I can then fix you up with a sling from the master's silk scarves in the hall cupboard."

He paused in the act of trying to brush my hair.

"Oh, I'll brush it myself somehow afterwards. Let me have breakfast first. I hope the doctors aren't still in the dining-room."

My fears on that score were soon relieved, for I

heard the sound of their voices coming from my bedroom, as we passed it on our way downstairs. In the hall Edwins equipped me with a creditable sling, and then conducted me to a chair by the dining-room fire, where I sat while he went to fetch my breakfast.

IV. BREAKFAST (FIRST SERIES)

Christmas Day—9 a.m.

AFTER eating my breakfast—a magnificent breakfast
of scrambled eggs with mushrooms and stuffed
tomatoes—I sat once more by the fire in meditation.
Christmas Day. Harrington Cobalts. My wrist.
The death of Mrs. Harley. These four strands of
thought twisted round one another lazily in my
mind, and kept it fully occupied. Christmas Day.
The present I had brought for my hostess, still in my
bedroom by the body of Mrs. Harley. Christmas
Day. Another year over. (At least I have done
something in the City.) Harrington Cobalts. Was
the big deal through? Would Mr. Quisberg shortly
return in triumph? "My boy, we have made a
fortune! You have made a fortune too!" Mr.
Quisberg and Harley. "Harley, your poor mother.
. . ." Surely it could not be a very festive Christmas Day? We should sit reading in isolated chairs,
I with a book in my left hand. How long should I be
maimed? At least I could excuse myself from
another outburst of musical chairs. But there could
be none. No dancing, no music. Sheila would read,
Amabel and her Dixon would suppress their titters,
Mrs. Quisberg would go about the house wringing
her hands, and ordering poor Harley an extra large

helping of plum-pudding which he couldn't eat.
And Clarence ? What on earth was he doing in the
house—neither gay himself, nor adding to the gaiety
of others ?

Then the door opened and the two doctors confronted me.

" This is Mr. Warren, Doctor," said Dr. Green.
" Malcolm, Dr. McKenzie would like a short conversation with you. I suggest the terrace room or the
drawing-room; for I am inordinately hungry."

He touched the bell and sat down at the table.
Dr. McKenzie, lean, tall, grey and pale, nodded at
me with his chin and held the door open.

" The terrace room ? " I asked.

" By all means."

A fire had been lit in one of the two grates, and we
sat down facing it in two chairs.

Dr. McKenzie coughed and began.

" I dare say you realize, Mr. Warren, that there
will be certain formalities in connection with Mrs.
Harley's death. I have telephoned to the police,
and they are good enough to say that they would
appreciate my evidence and dispense for the time
being with the services of the police-surgeon. I have,
as a matter of fact, acted in that capacity on occasion. Naturally, if I should find anything untoward
in the case, I shall at once put it into other hands.
But I do not anticipate anything of the kind. Now
will you be so good as to tell me in detail all your
actions from the time when you first awoke this
morning ? "

I told my story.

" You did not, I take it, see the face of the corpse ?"

" No, Dr. Green told me it was not a pretty sight."

" As a matter of fact, one of the spikes of the balcony railings had entered the cheek. Not that there will be any difficulty as to identification, evidence of which will be provided by Mrs. Harley's son."

I shuddered for him.

" I am told," Dr. McKenzie went on, " that the lady was in a condition of neurotic instability. As to that, of course, you can have no knowledge, but it will assist me to form my ideas, if you will give me your impressions."

" I saw her at dinner," I said, " and after dinner, while she watched us playing bridge. I thought her not quite normal. She twitched her fingers, and bit her lips, and seemed terribly timid. Mind you, I had been told by Mrs. Quisberg that she was to see a nerve specialist. . . ."

" Quite so. I shall, of course, have a talk with Mrs. Quisberg. In fact, I think it falls to me to break the sad news to her. Now as to the bedroom of the deceased. Did anything strike you about it ? Did you notice the bed ? "

" The bed looked to me just as if someone had spent the night in it, and got up in the usual way."

" A very restless night ? "

" No, I don't think so."

" Did anything else suggest itself to you while you were in the bedroom ? "

" No."

He looked at me interrogatively for a few seconds.

" Dr. Green told me," he said, " that you detected a faint odour, which you described as chloroform or ether. Is that so ? "

I blushed for my forgetfulness.

" Oh, yes. Dr. Green suggested that it must be Ant—Ant——"

" Antaronyl. Very possibly. Dr. Green apparently smelt nothing. Nor did I, and I have a keen sense of smell."

He sniffed as if to indicate that I must have been romancing, and got up from his chair.

" Let me see. To-day is Friday. The inquest should be on Monday. You will have to attend, and—er—testify. It will not be in any way an ordeal for you. I trust your arm is giving you no trouble ? "

He looked with suspicious curiosity at my sling.

" Oh, it's going on splendidly, thank you."

" Dr. Green is apparently an able manipulator ? "

The words were uttered as a question, but I preferred to accept them as a statement.

" Most able."

" Well, I will join him in the dining-room, if I may. I have had only the most slender meal so far. By the way, the—er—body of Mrs. Harley is in your room, I think. No doubt the ambulance, for which I have telephoned, will soon be here to remove it, but if, in the meanwhile, you need any of your effects, perhaps you will come and collect them with me now. I prefer that the door should remain locked for the present, and Dr. Green has very properly given me the key."

We went into the hall and upstairs together, and Dr. McKenzie unlocked the door of my room. The body was lying on my bed, covered with a sheet. I collected my possessions as quickly as I could with my left hand, and the doctor stacked them together in a little heap on the landing.

" I should ask one of the servants to find you temporary quarters," he said, nodded a distant farewell, and went downstairs.

Not a very pleasant man, I thought. Still, he hadn't had breakfast. For a while, I paused indecisively. Then I went into the drawing-room and rang the bell. A housemaid answered it, and I had to ask her to find Edwins for me. He came up ten minutes later, and on hearing my needs, suggested that I should make a temporary home in the bathroom on the half-landing, where there was a dressing-table, in addition to the usual appliances.

" I take it, sir," he said, while putting out my things, " that the poor lady's dead! "

" Really! " I exclaimed. " What on earth makes you think that ? "

" Oh, these things get about, sir. We're not all fools."

The remark was not all it should have been, but it was probably very true as far as he was concerned. He was a tall slender man, rather like Clarence James in appearance, though not so young. His alert bearing might have seemed rather formidable in a house with guilty secrets. To be sure, I suspected nothing of the kind at Beresford Lodge, but I felt that Edwins' views on the household might not

be unamusing, and resolved to give him a chance of
gossiping.

" I don't remember meeting Mrs. Harley here
before," I said, after a short pause.

" No, sir, this is her first visit—and her last."

I ignored the dramatic ending to his sentence.

" How long have you been here, Edwins ? "

" Five years, sir."

" Oh, have you ? That's longer than Mr. Harley,
isn't it ? "

" Mr. Harley took up residence three years ago,
sir, in April."

" Dr. Green's a new visitor, as far as I'm concerned."

" Yes, sir. He hasn't been here for fully a year,
and then only for one night. I believe he travels a
good deal on the continent. But he's a very old
friend of Mr. Quisberg's. Writes to him regular
once a week if not more."

" How do you know ? "

" Oh, I know his writing. He's given me letters to
post for him."

" He is certainly a very able doctor—at least, if I
can judge from my wrist."

" A very able gentleman in every way, I should
say, sir. And strong—my word! It isn't a thing I
ought to repeat, sir, and I shouldn't do, to any
gentleman except yourself, but one evening, two
years ago about, Miss Amabel was giving a kind of
party—quite in the modern style, sir, if you understand me—and one of the guests had brought a
prize-fighter to the house. At least, that's what I

took him to be. Well, this prize-fighter got absolutely drunk—stinkin' drunk, sir, if you will excuse the phrase—and cut up very nasty down in the terrace room, where they were playing some game or other. He gave poor old Mr. George—that's the butler, sir —a punch on the shoulder, and, I am told, forgot himself with one of the lady guests. Dr. Green was there and told him to stop, but he whipped his coat off and turned on the doctor like a whirlwind. Well, what do you suppose happened, sir? The doctor gave him one blow, fair and square on the jaw, and completely laid him out. One of the gentlemen and me carried him to a car, and he was got home somehow or other. My word, but there was a row afterwards! No more parties for Miss Amabel here!"

"But now," I said, rather naughtily, "there's Mr. Dixon."

"Yes, sir. I shouldn't like to get the wrong side of Mr. Dixon either. But I don't think he'd be a match for the doctor. And now, if you'll excuse me, sir, I'd better go downstairs. Mr. George doesn't hold with taking in breakfasts, and it's quite possible Miss Sheila or Mr. Clarence will be down."

"Breakfast seems to be served in instalments here."

"Yes, sir. Quite on the cards it'll go on till eleven."

"Well, Edwins, I'm much obliged to you."

"Not at all, sir. Only too glad."

I sat down—on a white-enamelled cane chair. What should I do next? There were no papers to read, no *Telegraph* or *Mirror*, no comforting pinkness

of the *Financial Times*. I didn't want to see Dr.
McKenzie again, and I dreaded the series of festive
greetings that sooner or later I must endure. Christmas Day. Harrington Cobalts. My wrist. The
death of Mrs. Harley. Sooner or later, Mr. Quisberg
and Harley would return from London. It would be
just my luck to be the first to meet them. What
should I do ? Smirk nervously and wish them the
season's compliments ? Or blurt out wretchedly the
tragic news ? It was really better to meet no one,
till the air was clearer, till the first shocks had been
given and received. If I had had a sitting-room of
my own, or even a proper bedroom, I could have
resumed my sluggish reading of *La Chartreuse de
Parme*, but Stendhal in a bathroom seemed altogether too cold a prospect. Why not a little walk ?
On the Heath, or in the garden ?

I went down to the hall again, where George, the
butler, helped me on with my overcoat. I do not
think I have mentioned that there was a small
telephone room leading off the lobby. There were
lines to the terrace room, Mr. Quisberg's study and
Mrs. Quisberg's bedroom, but the telephone room,
though not guaranteed to be sound-proof (as
Amabel once said), was the most suitable place for a
private conversation. As I walked through the
lobby, the door of the telephone room opened and
Dr. Green came out. I thought he looked a little
displeased.

"So you've got rid of Dr. McKenzie," I said.

"For a time, yes. I find the man an insufferable
boor."

" Has the ambulance come ? "

" Not yet. I have been telephoning to the Carlton, in the hopes of catching Axel and warning him to break the news to Harley on the way back. But, it seems, they've just left the hotel. So we shall have another nasty scene when they arrive."

" I'm going out for a walk in the garden. Are you coming ? "

" No, I am not."

He turned his back on me abruptly and went into the hall.

Outside, at last, I took a path that bent round from the drive to the left, past the length of the aviary and thence by a steep little zigzag to the foot of the north-east end of the Louis Quinze staircase by which one went up to the terrace. At this point, having no mind to remain within hail of the house, I took another path which ran behind a shrubbery and along the far, or north-east, side of the two tennis courts. Beyond them was my first objective, the rock-garden and pond.

It was one of those mild indefinite days, which we now associate with Christmas in England, a day which had in its clouded sunlight nothing of autumn and nothing of winter, but seemed rather to suggest the spring—a feeble spring seen in a looking-glass. The night (at least, at dinner-time) had been clear and star-lit, though a mist had developed before dawn. These meteorological reflections of mine were prompted entirely by the feeling that I was perhaps wearing too thick an overcoat. I did not for one moment realize how important it might be to seek knowledge as to the exact time when the clearness of the night gave way to mist.

The rock-garden was most excellently made, and I spent about ten minutes admiring it. As always, I was fascinated by the labels indicating the plants— either above or below ground—Primula Denticulata, Japonica, Sikkimensis, and Florindæ, Gentiana Sino-ornata, Iris Pumila, Iris Kæmpferi, Veronica Rupestris, Helianthemum and many more. The Iris Kæmpferi were planted most correctly on the artificially boggy bank of an irregular pond, about eighteen feet long and eight feet wide. This, as I knew, was the home of a score of goldfish, and I was bending down to see if I could detect a glint of red and gold amongst the water-weed, when my eye caught sight of a pink and blue cardboard object floating on the water in a clump of Scirpus Zebrinus, or variegated reed. Shocked by such untidiness, I picked it up, and found it to be part of an empty firework. A pink label running round the conical top bore the following legend: " The Jubilee Flash. Novelty. Price 2s. 6d. Place blue end in muzzle of detonating pistol. Hold pistol almost vertically above the head and pull trigger. Bright silver flash and stars." No doubt, I thought, a relic of the fifth of November. But what careless gardeners to leave it lying there. Absentmindedly I put it in the pocket of my coat.

Behind the rock-garden, there was a shrubbery of low but choice shrubs, azaleas, heaths and so on, and further back, some uncommon specimens of

berberis, philadelphus and viburnum. Beyond this
shrubbery there was a patch of bare but well-
cultivated ground, which I supposed was used in
summer as a reserve garden for sweet peas and other
flowers suitable for cutting. At the back of it was an
old brick wall, about six feet high and covered with
ivy, which marked the limit of Mr. Quisberg's
property.

Behind the wall rose Paragon House, indignantly
referred to by Amabel at dinner on the previous
evening, as the only obstacle between the windows
of Beresford Lodge and the Harrow Ridge, which
lay miles beyond the valley of the Finchley Road to
the north-west. It was a big unpleasant building, I
thought, as I surveyed it between the bare plane
trees which in winter were quite unable to screen it
from view. The windows were all shut and very
dirty. The ivy wall prevented me from seeing into
the garden, but I had no doubt it was as derelict as
the house. It would indeed be a triumph, I thought,
if Mr. Quisberg could buy it and pull it down. As
long as it stood where it was, one had the sense
(except perhaps when the trees were in full leaf), of
being overlooked. In central London, where gardens
cannot be taken seriously, and windows are pro-
tected by net curtains, this would not have mattered.
But it was too bad to own three acres or so in costly
Hampstead, and suffer from lack of privacy. However, with Harrington Cobalts all things were
possible. Surely Mr. Quisberg should have returned
by now ?

It was now about half past ten, and I left the

rock-garden to walk along a broad herbaceous border, which ran parallel to the terrace but on the far side of the huge central lawn. But hardly had I emerged from the shelter of the shrubberies when I saw Sheila on the terrace, beckoning me to come in. She saw that I saw her, and there was no escape.

V. BREAKFAST (SECOND SERIES)

Christmas Day—10.30 a.m.

SHEILA came running down the Louis Quinze stairs
of the terrace to meet me.

" Good morning, Malcolm. Mother's fussing
frightfully about you. She's been told, of course.
We all know everything now. She sent me to make
sure that you've really had a proper breakfast, to
ask how you are, and say how sorry she is about
your room. Come along, I'm having breakfast
myself. You can talk to me while I eat. Amabel
and Leonard aren't down yet."

She led the way into the dining-room through a
french window opening on to the terrace, and sat down.

" Have some more coffee ? No ? Well, pass me
the marmalade. I say, isn't it awful about Mrs.
Harley ? The ambulance has just been. I saw the
stretcher carried down the steps. Father isn't back
yet. I dare say he's taken a drive round the Heath.
Do tell me everything you know. Mother said Dr.
McKenzie said the body was on the balcony outside
your room ? Was it ? "

She turned an excited gaze upon me. If she was
so lighthearted over the catastrophe, how would
Amabel behave ? Perhaps the season was destined
to be festive after all.

" I don't think I ought to tell you anything about it."

" Oh, rubbish! "

She made a face, her mouth half full of toast and marmalade.

" Well, I haven't much to tell you. I got up to pull up the blind, and saw the body against the railings."

" What did it look like ? "

" I didn't stop to notice. I sent Edwins at once for Dr. Green. Then he took charge, and bundled me out of the room."

" Oh, was that all ? Then what did you do ? "

" Had breakfast and walked in the garden. What time is Church ? "

" Church ? Oh, I don't think we shall go to-day. Mother might have, perhaps, but——"

The door opened and Dixon came in.

" Hullo, Sheila. Mornin', Warren. Seen anything of the others, anybody ? "

" Amabel's dressing," Sheila replied. " She ought to be down any minute. What time did you two go to bed, anyhow ? "

" That's nothing to do with you," he answered, settling himself at the table. " How's the wrist, Warren ? "

" Better, thank you."

" I suppose," Sheila asked him, " you've heard the bad news ? "

" Bad news ? No. What bad news ? "

" Mrs. Harley was found outside Malcolm's bedroom window with a broken neck."

He whistled.

" Lord love a duck! It isn't April Fools' Day or anything, is it ? "

" No, it's perfectly true."

" Well, I'm damned. Who found the body ? "

" Malcolm."

" What a jolly affair! What are we going to do about it, anyhow ? Shall we have to put off to-night's beano, do you think ? "

" What beano ? " I asked.

" Didn't you know ? There was going to be a supper-party, a fancy-dress and fireworks stunt."

" Fireworks ? "

" Yes, why not ? There's a whole stack of them in the shed next to where Amabel keeps her car. Old Q. wouldn't have 'em in the house in case of fire. Any objection to fireworks, Warren ? "

" Who's objecting to fireworks ? " said a voice behind me. It was Amabel, looking very radiant and blonde. " 'Morning, Len. Good morning, Mr. Malcolm Warren. How's our wrist to-day ? No, don't move. I say, it is pretty rough luck about Mrs. Harley, isn't it ? "

She went to the side-table, helped herself to a couple of poached eggs, and sat down beside Dixon.

" Has anybody seen our beloved brother Clarence this morning ? " she went on. " Flora—yes, Mr. Malcolm Warren, we really have a housemaid called Flora—that's my pat, you beast—Flora said he had a teeny-weeny little roll and a teeny-weeny little cup of tea in his bedroom, and went out about half past eight."

" Perhaps he went to early service," suggested Dixon facetiously.

" Not Clarence. He's frightfully agnostic and all that. He's probably gone for one of Nature's rambles round the Heath. Talking of Clarence, I found a find last night." She opened her bag and drew out a folded sheet of paper.

" What is it, and where did you find it ? "

" I regret to say I stole it ! It was in a book—one of Clarence's books, obviously—*The Place of Lytton in Literature*, or something of the kind—on the table in the terrace room. I wanted a bit of paper to put under the post of the ping-pong net, and pulled it out. Then I saw Clarence's writing. What on earth do you make of it, Malcolm ? *Is* it poetry ? "

" That isn't always a very easy question to answer," I said. " Have any of us any business to read it ? Oughtn't you to give it back to him ? Why didn't you give it back to him ? "

" Don't catechize me like that. I just didn't. I meant, as a matter of fact, to bring it out during the evening, but your sad accident, Mr. Malcolm Warren, clouded our high spirits."

Again she used the special drawl reserved for me.

" Give it to me," said Dixon. " I'll soon tell you if it's poetry or not. I bet I know more limericks than anyone in the house."

He made as if to snatch the paper from her.

" No you don't. Here, Malcolm, catch it, quickly."

She threw it across the table. Rather reluctantly I picked it up. Dixon stretched out a hand, but she smacked his arm away.

" No you don't, you bully. Remember, he's maimed and can't protect himself. Now, Malcolm, read it through like a good boy, and tell us what it's all about. If you don't, I shall loose Len upon you."

Fearing that this indeed might happen, I took the document to the window-seat, and read it while the others wrangled at the breakfast-table. The words were written in pencil, with more than one erasure.

" To—

" Ah ! Moon of my delight, that knowst no wane!
  Thy frozen fire hath quite consuméd me,
  Till I am grown too weak to worship thee
Or urge the suit I once had hoped to gain.

" Have mercy! Make an end of thy disdain
  And smile once more. Let not thy victory
  Be tarnished by the victim's agony.
Have mercy, grant assuagement of my pain.

" To thee possessing all, what can I give
  For tribute, save myself who am rejected ?
Thou art my strength. From thee my thoughts derive
Their substance, while my ravish'd soul discovers
  Solace in thee alone, all else neglected—
Thy mirror, and most faithful of thy lovers."

I was surprised at verse in so conventional a manner proceeding from anyone so advanced as Clarence. Was it a joke, an experiment, a parody, or a real utterance of the heart? In case it was the latter, I felt bound to safeguard the absent author's interests, and was about to ask Amabel quite seriously if she minded my keeping the poem and giving it back to Clarence myself, when the breakfast party was further swollen by the entry of Mrs. Quisberg and Dr. Green.

"Oh, there you are, Malcolm," she said. "I told Sheila to bring me news of you. I do hope the poor arm is better. Is it really better, Doctor? Now Amabel, and you, Mr. Dixon, you ought to have been out of the dining-room long ago, so that they can lay the Christmas dinner. Not that it can be a gay one, I'm afraid. I'm still so dazed by this terrible news that I keep forgetting it. Poor Malcolm, what a sad shock for you, and to be turned out of your bedroom and all. . . . I can't think what we shall do with poor little Harley. I almost feel as if we were responsible, sending him down to sleep in London, the one and only night his mother comes here. Why couldn't it have happened anywhere but here, if it had to be?"

She pulled out a handkerchief.

"Now, Mums," said Amabel. "Pull yourself together. You won't make things any better by giving way. Besides, you're making everyone feel uncomfortable."

Perhaps to relieve her feelings, Mrs. Quisberg turned almost savagely on her daughter.

"Uncomfortable! Why shouldn't we be uncomfortable? I suppose you'd be perfectly comfortable if it happened to me. You and your cocktails and your rowdy dancing! You're a hard-natured girl, that's what you are."

Amabel flushed angrily.

"At any rate I can keep my head. What are you going to do? Sit here all sobbing till they come in and find you?"

"What can I do?"

"Make some arrangement to catch Papa privately, so that he can tell Harley without any fuss."

"It won't be so easy to tell Papa even," said Sheila.

"Well," answered her sister, "I dare say Dr. Green will do that. If he won't, I will."

"That's the spirit," said Dixon, who had been shut out from the conversation too long for his taste.

Dr. Green turned to Amabel.

"It may interest you to know, most charming of young ladies, that I have already tried to speak to your father on the subject. Unfortunately he had left the Carlton just before I telephoned, and as he hasn't a portable wireless on his motor-car, I have not been able to get into communication with him since."

He uttered each word in a tone of rude hostility. Dixon stepped forward angrily, and there might have been a most unpleasant scene if Amabel herself had not interposed.

" I'm sorry," she drawled angrily, " I seem to have made myself so unpopular with the older generation this morning, especially as the situation is rather beyond their control. My feeling, for what it's worth, is simply this. You can't have Harley coming in here and finding us all chattering about him. What would you do, Mother, if he did ? Run up to him and shriek, ' Harley, your mother's dead! ' ? "

She finished her unfortunate sentence with a sudden shout, which made us all look at her in dismay. Then a cry was heard at the other end of the room, and we saw Mr. Quisberg and Harley standing in the open french window. Mr. Quisberg gasped, and leant against the wall for support, while Harley, a miserable little figure, walked towards us through the long room. Then, seeing our grave faces, he paused pitifully and said in a husky voice that made our silence seem the more terrible:

" What's this about my mother ? What were you saying ? "

Before Dr. Green or Amabel could prevent her, Mrs. Quisberg darted forward, her face streaming with tears, and caught the little secretary in her arms.

" Come with me, dear," she said. " Come with me. I'll help you to bear it. Come away." Her voice at that moment was exquisitely compassionate. Like a child, he laid his head against her shoulder and moaned, while he allowed her almost to carry him from the room, " Oh, my poor mother. My darling mother."

Then Quisberg, still by the terrace window, tottered and fell flat on the floor. While Dr. Green and Amabel rushed towards him, Sheila collapsed in sobs over the table, and my own eyes were filled with tears.

VI. THOUGHTS IN A BATHROOM

Christmas Day—11.30 a.m.

THERE was only one thing for me to do—to hide myself till both I and the household attained a calmer mood. On hearing Dixon saying something to me, I walked dazedly away from him, into the hall and up one and a half flights of stairs to the bathroom which was now all I had by way of private quarters. I sat down gloomily on the cane chair, and lit a cigarette. Christmas! Indeed, the festivity had gone out of life at Beresford Lodge. Amabel and Dixon might recover. I could not, and would not make the effort. What a terrible morning it had been. I reproached myself bitterly for my earlier callousness, the lack of imagination which had allowed me to remain absorbed in my own petty concerns—my bedroom, my breakfast, my wrist—instead of realizing at once that Harley and his trouble alone should occupy my thoughts. "Why," Amabel had asked, "should we put off the fancy dress supper-party and the fireworks?" And I had asked the same question in different terms. One is, at times, strangely slow to understand that one's destiny has, temporarily at least, taken a tragic twist, and that any attempts at frivolity will only attract a greater retribution. Henceforward, I

72

would be reconciled. It was to be no ordinary Christmas. It was to be a ghastly Christmas, every moment of it seeming an age, and requiring tact, presence of mind and unselfishness to carry it through. When Christmas was over, when the Stock Exchange reopened, when my London life resumed its comfortable, if unheroic, course, I might relax, perhaps, and begin again to study my own interests. But before that could happen, there was a dark tunnel to pass through—a tunnel stretching certainly till Monday's inquest, and, it might be, further beyond.

It was not an ordinary Christmas, nor an ordinary house-party. I think, on looking back, that it first occurred to me, during my meditation in the bath-room, what a very extraordinary house-party it was. True, Mrs. Harley's accident alone was quite serious enough to throw a distorting gloom over every-thing. If I had been at that moment sending my mother an account of my visit, this is probably what I should have written:

" I arrived here last night after a little pleasant excitement in the City. This house is very full. Apart from the Quisbergs, Amabel, Sheila, Cyril and his nurse—I think I told you Cyril was recover-ing from appendicitis—and Harley, the secretary, my fellow-guests are Leonard Dixon (Amabel's fiancé), Dr. Green, a strange and interesting foreigner, Mrs. Harley (the secretary's mother) and Clarence James, Mrs. Q.'s eldest son, by her first husband. Last night, unfortunately, I slipped while playing musical chairs, and sprained my wrist

rather badly. Dr. Green attended to it very com-
petently, and it feels better to-day. This morning
something much more terrible happened. Mrs.
Harley was found dead, with a broken neck, on the
balcony outside my bedroom. She walks in her
sleep, and must have fallen out of the window. I
shall have to give evidence at the inquest, I'm afraid,
for it was I who found the body. It is most sad, and
we are all rather overcome by the shock—especially
of course, poor Harley. Mrs. Q. is being very kind
to him, and to me, too, for that matter. . . ."

Something of the sort would have been a fair
précis of events, a little colourless in style perhaps,
but, after all, I should not wish to harass my mother.
Yet was it really adequate ? I had a feeling, even
then, that there were elements in the situation of
which I had no grasp. Foremost in my mind was
the strange bearing of Mr. Quisberg. To be sure, I
had always known him as a neurotic, jumpy little
man, kind and irascible by turns, excitable, erratic.
Much might be ascribed to the deal in Harrington
Cobalts—the biggest venture, I surmised, in which
he had ever been engaged. The whole circumstances of this deal were unusual, but then it was an
unusual deal. Perhaps in high financial circles,
midnight meetings in hotels and departures at dawn
in private aeroplanes were not very remarkable.
G—— was known to be domineering and capricious.
One could gather so much even from the newspaper
gossip about him. There was, therefore, probably
nothing abnormal in the fact that Quisberg and
Harley had to spend the night at G——'s beck and call

in London, even though it was Christmas Eve, even though Mrs. Harley was the Quisbergs' guest for the first time. After all, she was hardly their guest. They were being kind to her, as one is kind to a dependent. Harley could not have a holiday just then, and his employers had done the next best thing to giving him one. That Mrs. Harley should have chosen that one night for a fatal walk in her sleep was, of course, a lamentable coincidence—only on a par, however, with an attack of scarlet fever on the eve of a wedding, or the explosion of a kitchen range half an hour before one has to entertain a gourmet. A lamentable coincidence—but this did not quite explain Mr. Quisberg. There was something hard to understand, too, about his demeanour in the drive, at the moment of my arrival. His furtive, anxious manner had expressed something more than nervousness before a financial tussle. Why all that muttering with Dr. Green ? Had Dr. Green been in the secret ? From all I knew of Quisberg's business, Dr. Green played no part in it. There was evidently a hitch, an unforeseen complication, with which the doctor was acquainted. All this, however, sank into insignificance compared with Quisberg's reaction to the news of Mrs. Harley's death. He had fallen down and fainted, perhaps even had a stroke. Of course, the deal might have gone wrong. The sad news, received so abruptly at the moment of his homecoming, might have been only the last straw which broke down his self-control. How I wished I had seen him approaching the house, and observed whether his gait and appearance were quite normal then. Somehow I was inclined to think that they had been. He had evidently told the chauffeur to drive in by the garage entrance which was hidden from the road-side lawn by a thick shrubbery of evergreens. Otherwise, occupied though we were by the quarrel in the dining-room, we should have seen the car. I myself was standing opposite the window which looked on to the road. Why, then, had he gone to the garage ? Presumably so as to look at the green-houses which lay behind it. From there he must have walked along the path below the terrace, and mounted the north-east branch of the Louis Quinze staircase, the top of which was almost immediately outside the french window of the dining-room. He always moved quietly as a ghost, and little Harley no doubt tiptoed after him. We were all looking at Amabel and listening to her tirade. Small wonder that we had not observed the newcomers. Such, indeed, was the only way in which I could account for the manner of Quisberg's arrival—a visit to the greenhouses followed by a stroll through the garden. But this was not the procedure of a man in grievous mental stress. All therefore had been well until he reached the dining-room, and heard, so unceremoniously, the tragic news.

Here, so far as Quisberg was concerned, I came to the end of my tether. I think, however, that my mind continued to work unconsciously on the problem, and thus prepared the way for the illumination which later was to dawn upon me with such a dazzling suddenness.

And then the others. Of the whole party, Sheila and Mrs. Quisberg alone appeared quite normal. Poor Mrs. Quisberg! I had almost forgotten about Cyril with his appendix—or rather without his appendix—on the top floor. As for the nurse, I hadn't even seen her. " She's very pretty," Mrs. Quisberg had said. " You mustn't make me jealous." So far there had been no chance of any such behaviour on my part. An invalid and a trained nurse in the house. Was that not complication enough without these fresh calamities ? How good she was, how unselfish and how kind!

By way of contrast, my thoughts turned to Amabel —and Dixon. Surely they were both a little exaggerated ? I knew Amabel to be a slightly suburban type of " the modern girl." Had I not heard, that very morning, of her "party" with a drunken prizefighter ? But could she make no effort to be agreeable generally, no effort to help her mother and entertain her mother's guests ? She was no fool. Even if she were entirely selfish, she must see, at least, the ugliness of her conduct. Perhaps, as far as she was capable of that emotion, she was very much in love. The fact that Dixon was a vulgar and illmannered boor did not make that impossible. He had a fine physique, and no doubt Amabel, in her infatuation, took her cue from him. He puzzled me a little. To what niche in society did he belong ? I have called him " vulgar." I could not exactly call him " common." He had clearly been about the world, knew how to wear his evening clothes and so on. His face, with its " aristocratic " nose, was not a common face. Why then was he " letting himself go," instead of ingratiating himself with the family, into which he hoped to marry ? No doubt he thought himself less disagreeable than he was, and being, unlike Amabel, of very small intelligence, did not see how little he appealed to those who were not dazzled by his charms. At the same time, I had a feeling that his exuberance proceeded rather from desperation than conceit. Was he, perhaps, not sure how long he could maintain his hold ?

Then there was Dr. Green. Foreigners are always harder to " place " than one's compatriots, and I could not " place " the doctor anywhere at all. I agreed with Edwins in thinking him a very remarkable man. I liked him instinctively, but he fell into no category. When considering the other members of the party, I had tried to touch upon any aspect in their actions or behaviour which was abnormal. Dr. Green, being entirely abnormal, revealed no particular aspect on which to seize. He might, I felt, do anything and for any reason, nor would any knowledge of ordinary psychology be any guide to his. Apart from his kindness to me, he had shown only one human trait—his obvious resentment at Amabel's rudeness to her mother. And there he had made an error in exasperating the girl by his reply. I did not, somehow, associate him with errors. Perhaps he too was on edge, like the rest of us. But why should he be ? He was a doctor. Dr. McKenzie had shown no unprofessional distress, and he was a very humdrum little practitioner compared with Dr. Green.

Then Clarence—but Clarence, the last of the party to enter my thoughts, was not allowed to remain in them; for there was a knock at the door, and Edwins came in.

"Oh, there you are, sir. I've been looking everywhere for you. The mistress was most concerned, sir, at your having no proper room of your own, and Miss Sheila has been moved to the dressing-room next the master's bedroom. So now, sir, I must move you into Miss Sheila's. That's on the drawing-room floor. A nice room overlooking the road."

"Oh dear," I said, "I seem to be causing a lot of trouble. What has happened to Mrs. Harley's room?"

"It's still as it was, sir. I understand Mr. Harley will be going through his mother's things later, when he feels more up to it. Your room, I mean the room you had last night, is being turned back to a little sitting-room, which by rights it ought to be. I think the mistress felt you might not care to sleep in it again, as it must have painful memories."

"Oh, I don't think I should have minded. However, I dare say I shall enjoy Miss Sheila's room more."

He began once more to collect my possessions together.

"Is everything all right now?" I asked with deliberate vagueness.

"As far as I can tell, sir, yes. Mrs. Quisberg has been with Mr. Harley for some time, and a superintendent from the police called to see him about ten minutes ago. Mrs. Quisberg saw him for a moment and Mr. George says he heard the superintendent say he'd call again this afternoon. I understand that the master was taken unwell in the dining-room, but Dr. Green's been looking after him, and took him upstairs. I don't think it's anything serious. Master Cyril has been very naughty this morning, so Nurse says. Seemed to think he was neglected like. No wonder too, if he was, with all these goings-on."

" Well, it shows he's getting better, at any rate."

" Yes, sir. I don't think there's much wrong with him now."

" What time is luncheon ? Is it luncheon or dinner, by the way ? "

" Well, sir, it was to have been dinner, and still will be, according to the food. One o'clock was to be the time. I don't think the master will come down for it, nor Mr. Harley either, but I've laid for the mistress."

" One o'clock. That's in ten minutes. Perhaps you'll wash my left hand for me, will you ? Thank you very much. I mustn't keep you now."

" You'll find cocktails and sherry in the terrace room, sir," he said as he opened the door.

" Splendid. I feel I need one."

" And now," I thought, as I left my refuge and went downstairs once more, " the ordeal begins."

VII. THE SMILING NURSE

Christmas Day—12.50 p.m.

In search of the promised drink I went into the terrace room. Dixon was writing a letter at the far end, and Amabel was sitting with a white face near the fire—in the chair in which Dr. McKenzie had sat when he interviewed me. She looked up when I came in, and said, " Do help yourself. You must need one."

I did so, and took the chair opposite to her.

" I do hope your father's better."

" I think he is, thank you. Dr. Green said he was getting on very well."

" He won't come down to luncheon, I suppose ? "

" I'm afraid not."

She stretched out for an illustrated magazine and began to read it. I toyed with my drink for a moment, drank it, and rose to help myself again.

" Can I get you one ? " I asked.

She shook her head.

Apparently I was the only drinker in the room. " Better one than none," I thought, as I poured out my second glass. For want of anything better to do, I drank the contents quickly, and was wondering if I could with decency help myself yet again, when

Clarence came in, with very muddy boots. He looked tired, but strangely radiant.

" Hello," he said, joining me by the drink-table. " How's the wrist ? "

" Much better, thanks. Have you been for a walk ? "

" Since nine this morning. All over the byways of the Heath. It is a most exquisite morning. No, sherry, please. I often wonder why we bother to live in houses."

He looked round the room, but if his remark was meant to provoke discussion, it failed to do so.

" Where's Harley ? " he went on. " Could I be of any use there ? Oh yes, Edwins told me when he let me in just now."

(So Clarence had no latch-key.)

" Harley's in his room," said Amabel. " You can go up and see him if you want to. I don't suppose he wants to see any of us."

" Why ? " asked her stepbrother, but she didn't reply.

He sighed good-humouredly.

" And Cyril ? " he went on.

" Cyril hit Dr. McKenzie in the face with a wet sponge," said Sheila, who came in at that moment, followed by her mother and Dr. Green. Conversation began to flow more freely.

" I require," said the doctor, with something of his earlier manner, " a vast quantity of sherry. Letty, for this once only ? "

Mrs. Quisberg smiled and shook her head.

" So you drink cocktails, Malcolm! Have another."

" I'm already a little unsteady," I replied, allowing him to refill my glass.

" And who, pray, asked you to be steady ? " he said. " I abhor all steady young men. With your leave, my dear lady, I'll send a glass of this most excellent wine upstairs to our patient—and, why not? —a glass to Harley too. We must live, we must live while we can, nor should the sorrows of others, if we cannot alleviate them, be allowed to damp excessively our own good cheer. There, that's a sermon for you. Letty, you're missing something good."

It was wonderful to me how merrily he talked, with no sign of applause. I even felt that we were being ungrateful to him for his efforts, and was racking my brains for a witticism with which to urge him on, when Christmas dinner was announced.

Mrs. Quisberg took the head of the table, and Amabel sat at the other end, with her back to the french window. The vases and centrepiece contained holly and mistletoe, but there were no crackers. Dr. Green talked not unamusingly about the habits of birds. Clarence replied softly and sweetly to all my remarks—his mood seemed strangely enough to be one of kind acquiescence with all the world—and Shiela, Dixon and Amabel said little or nothing. Turtle soup, roast turkey, with innumerable garnishings, plum-pudding, dessert. What with my cocktails and mulled claret, I felt sleepy even before the end of the meal, and decided to slip away as soon as I could and lie down. It had occurred to me, however, that I ought to ask my hostess whether, in view of all the turmoil in the house, it were not better that I should leave the party. I should indeed have been glad to do so, except for the fact that I had given my housekeeper a holiday till the Sunday night, and should therefore have either to fend for myself or take refuge in an hotel.

When the meal was over, I waited about till I saw Mrs. Quisberg go alone into the drawing-room, and followed her in. Naturally she would not hear of my leaving Beresford Lodge.

" And what would you do, my poor Malcolm, with your wrist and no one to look after you ? Of course you must stay here. It's a comfort to have you, Malcolm. I feel somehow I can rely on you—even more than on some of my own family."

" I'm quite sure," I said boldly, " that Amabel didn't mean anything this morning. She was right, too, in a way."

" She was. But still, I can't help wishing——"

I approached and took her hand. (Really, the wine must have gone a little to my head !)

" What is it ? "

" Dear Malcolm, you are always sympathetic and so kind. I can't help wishing this engagement of hers were settled one way or the other. It seems to have upset her altogether. She never used to be . . . Of course, she's always been full of spirit, and I've never tried to curb her or spoil her fun. But she used to have a very sweet nature underneath, till lately——"

" Are they really engaged ? " I asked.

" So they say. But we haven't given our consent, and I won't, till Axel agrees."

" Does he not care for Leonard Dixon ? "

" He feels suspicious about him. I'm afraid Axel is suspicious of strangers. He's met so many bad lots in his life, you know. Amabel should be well off one day, and though you might say that's all the more reason for letting her marry a poor man, we have to be careful. She's very pretty, but if he only likes her in that way, and for what she may bring him, it can't lead to any happiness. Can it ? "

" No—if you really think that of Leonard Dixon. Has Mr. Quisberg actually refused his consent then ? "

" Oh, no. About three months ago he said he must consider it. I think he promised to say ' Yes ' or ' No ' before the end of the year."

" Then it must be a trying time for her," I said. " No wonder she's on tenterhooks. Suppose they ran away and married ? "

" Axel's quite firm about that. If they do, he says he won't give her a penny. He wouldn't either. You know how strong-minded he is over some things. He regards all my children as if he were their father—except Clarence, perhaps."

" Yes, there's Clarence."

" He and Clarence used to have the most frightful rows. It broke my heart to hear them. Clarence, of course, was very difficult, like his father, I'm afraid. Perhaps the present arrangement is the best, though it hurts me to think of Clarence living away from home. It was nice of him to come here for Christmas."

" I thought he seemed in very good form to-day."

" Did you ? I'm so glad. Well, Malcolm, it's a sad household for you to spend Christmas in—all the world thinking us so prosperous and happy too. But you've been most good and patient, with no one doing anything to entertain you. It's been a strain on you, I can see. You look so tired."

" I feel very sleepy," I said. " In fact I think I shall go and have a nap."

" The very thing. Come down just when you like and ring for tea to be taken up to you any time. I do hope you're settled in your bedroom. I wish I'd thought of moving Sheila out before."

" You've been in every way most kind and thoughtful for my comfort. Now look after yourself, and try not to worry about anything. *Au revoir*."

I gave her hand a little pat, went out and shut the door.

As I crossed the landing to go to my new bedroom I saw the nurse for the first time. She was standing at the far end of the passage by the lacquer screen in front of the green baize door, as if uncertain whether or not to go through it. She held what looked to be a letter in her hand, and was apparently absorbed in its contents ; for she was quite unaware of my presence. She was indeed extremely pretty, almost too pretty to be a nurse anywhere except on the stage. Despite the half-light in which she stood, I saw the deep brown hair beneath her cap, and the long dark lashes which could not quite veil the gleam of her vivacious eyes. Her nose was delicate and sensitively tipped, while on her lips, which were perhaps too full, played a most strange and interesting smile—the smile of a nun who yields to the allurements of the world, or, if there is such a smile (and I think there is), the smile of a woman who knows herself to be desired. As I held my ground and gazed, I could not help contrasting her insidious charm with Amabel's more boisterous sex-appeal—I am bound to say, not entirely to Amabel's disadvantage. How strange, I thought, to find such a creature in such a house at such a time.

I had now remained watching her for so long that I felt I could not continue on my way without speaking, in case she caught sight of me and thought that I was spying on her. Perhaps I was still emboldened by the unusual quantity of alcohol I had taken, for I advanced towards her and said, in as hearty a tone as I could assume, " Good afternoon, Nurse! I hear your patient's getting on splendidly. I should like to come up and see him some time, if I may."

She turned round with a little gasp, and then, recovering from the shock, gave me a smile. But it was not at all the smile she had worn before she saw me.

" Oh! " she said, " you must be Mr. Warren. Yes, the patient is doing very well. I'm afraid he won't need me much longer. He's a dear little boy —except when he's naughty. And he can be naughty, you know."

" I hear he threw a sponge at Dr. McKenzie this morning."

" He did. Wasn't it awful! "

" Well, you must tell me when I can pay my respects."

" He's asleep now, and Mrs. Quisberg has given me a holiday for the rest of the day. Why not come and see us to-morrow morning, after the doctor's been ? "

" Yes, I will," I said, realizing that I should probably do nothing of the sort. " And now I'm going to have a nap—after too much Christmas dinner."

She laughed, quietly but gaily, then with a little nod went behind the screen, and through the baize door, while I walked across the landing to my room. " She didn't mention my wrist," I thought. I was not hurt by this omission, but it seemed to show how far her wits had strayed from her professional tasks.

So she was holiday-making that afternoon. That might account for much. What kind of a man, I wondered, had filled her with such joy ?

A fire had been lit in my bedroom, and the bed looked most inviting. Had it not been for my injury, I should have undressed completely and put on my pyjamas, but I knew that though I could undress, I could not dress again without help, and did not wish to make too many calls on Edwins that day. Already I began to wonder how huge a tip I should have to give him when I left. I contented myself therefore with taking off my sling, my coat and waistcoat and my shoes, and lay down between the eiderdown and

the blankets. In two or three minutes I fell fast
asleep.

I awoke at half past five. The fire was still
flickering in the grate, and through the window I
could see the cedars lit up by the lamp down the
road. Christmas. Harrington Cobalts. My wrist.
The death of Mrs. Harley. What a pity it was that
I had to get up! At least the dreary day was ending.
I pressed the bell-switch by my pillow. In a few
moments there was a knock at the door and George,
the butler, came in with tea on a tray and turned
on the light.

" Thank God! " I exclaimed; " what a happy
thought! "

" The mistress suggested that I should take up tea,
sir, when your bell rang."

" You are all most kind."

" Is there anything I can do for you, sir ? Shall I
pull down the blind ? "

" No thank you. I like seeing the trees through the
window. There's only one thing. I wonder if you'd
mind helping me to put my shoes on. I can't tie up
the laces with my left hand."

I swung my feet from the bed, while the old man
knelt down heavily.

" Thank you so much. No, I can manage my coat
all right. I'll put it on when I've had tea. Is Mr.
Quisberg all right ? "

" Yes, sir; I understand that he is much better.
He will come down, I think, for supper."

" What time is that ? "

" Half past seven, sir. The gentlemen are not dressing."

My tea revived me, and I began to feel ashamed to think that, beyond my short stroll in the garden, I had spent the whole day indoors. Should I take a walk before dinner ? No, I really had not the energy. What with the heavy dinner, my potations, the reaction from my fall, the sleeping-draught which Dr. Green had given me, and the nervous strain of the morning, I was strangely languid and reluctant to do anything except lounge about by myself. Instead of stirring, therefore, I sat down in an easy chair close to the window and gazed idly on to the strip of garden and the road. How delightful, I thought, to live with trees in sight of every window. My flat in London was both sunny and airy, but day after day, the same walls confronted me through the net curtains. And even if one had trees in central London, they were grimy and unnatural, except at the time of their first greenery. The Quisbergs' house might have been a hundred miles away from all the hubbub of Piccadilly. Even the road was deserted—or nearly so ; for there was one figure standing near the gate, as if he were waiting for someone. A footman, perhaps, from a neighbouring house, waiting for one of the Quisbergs' maids. Then why didn't he go nearer the garage entrance and the back door ?

As this thought occurred to me, he pushed open the gate and walked furtively along the semi-circular drive. Then he looked up at my window, saw me, or at any rate the light in my room, turned round abruptly and walked away down the hill to the right. He was a big fellow, wearing a shabby cloth cap—clearly no footman. A tramp, I supposed, whose courage had suddenly failed him.

A few moments later the gate opened again. This time it was a policeman. He went straight to the front door, and I heard the bell ring. There was a pause, and then a knock on my door.

" If you please, sir, there's a constable would like to speak to you."

" Oh, Lord! Have I to go down, George ? "

" No, sir, I can bring him up here, if you prefer."

" It might be better, I think."

Whatever can this be, I wondered, as the butler left me. But it was only a formal summons to attend Monday's inquest on Mrs. Harley.

" All right," I said, " I will be there. Good night."

" Good night, sir."

I continued to sit by the window, in meditation. Christmas, Christmas in Hampstead! All round the Heath, in the Garden Suburb, in the little houses packed around the Finchley Road, there would be paper-chains in the windows, Chinese lanterns, balls of coloured glass and Christmas trees. I pictured a thousand small drawing-rooms, filled with smart " modern " furniture, the walls distempered a pale grey or a pale yellow, ornamented it might be with a ribbon-like frieze below the picture moulding, the mantelpiece covered with calendars and cards, the pictures—Medici prints probably, or minute etchings in black frames—each bearing a twig of holly. By every hearth two or three children would be playing with new toys, tearing the coloured ends of crackers into shreds, sucking whistles, blowing out balloons and bursting them. Father would have his feet up on the sofa. Like me, he had probably eaten too much in the middle of the day. Mother would be sitting in the easy chair, wearing a pink paper-cap, supervising the games, telling a story, and wondering how soon she ought to see about supper—for, of course, the maid had the afternoon and evening off. " Next year," said Father, knocking his pipe against the fender, " you won't see the road. The macrocarpa should grow another two feet." " No, Jimmy, don't do that, dear. Yes, we shall be quite private then." " Surely," she thought, " in another year we shall have blue curtains like the Smiths over the way! And Tommy will be eight, and go to school and come home every day with his little satchel. Now can it be that Eleanor forgot the cheese ? "

I became quite lost in the picture of suburban domesticity I was outlining for myself, and felt strangely drawn to those unknown lives by which I was surrounded—lives which seemed, falsely enough, so much simpler and easier than my own. Dear lives which make no mark upon the world. . . .

As this thought lingered in my mind, there were steps in the porch, which lay a little to the left of my window, and a man and a woman, Dixon and Amabel, walked round the longer arc of the drive which led past the shrubbery to the garage.

" Now, darling," I heard her saying, " throw it

all off and for God's sake forget about it. We're going to enjoy ourselves to-night, anyhow. Besides, there's nothing . . ."

Her voice tailed off in the distance. In a few minutes I heard the sound of a car starting up in the garage, and shortly afterwards a smart little two-seater, which I recognized as Amabel's car, passed the front gate and went up towards West Heath Road. Encouraged, perhaps, by the thought that the two most difficult members of the party were safely off the premises, I felt it was my duty to emerge from retirement again. Why could I not be more like Clarence—at least, the Clarence of that morning—and see what I could do for others ? A word of sympathy to Harley might not come amiss. There was Sheila to entertain. Clarence himself might like to talk to me, and Mr. Quisberg might be down at last, with news of Harrington Cobalts.

I went downstairs.

VIII. THE NEXT ALARM

Christmas Day—6.30 p.m.

I WENT first to the terrace room, but it was empty.
Much as I should have liked to settle down there
with a book, I had resolved to be sociable, and went
upstairs again to the drawing-room, where I found
Mrs. Quisberg, Sheila and Harley. Poor Harley
looked pale and shrunken, like a little animal that
has been ill-treated by its master. When he saw me,
he rose, as if to offer me his chair. " Oh, please
don't," I said, and gave him a look which I hope
conveyed some of the sympathy I felt. " I've been
eating and sleeping so much," I went on to the
company at large, " that I feel quite dazed. I don't
think you can ever have had a lazier guest. You must
make me do some work now. What can I do ?
Shall I teach Sheila to knit, or would you all like to
teach me to play ping-pong with my left hand ? "

Such an ordeal, fortunately, was not in store, and
we managed to talk very pleasantly for about half
an hour, when Mr. Quisberg came in, suddenly
and noiselessly, as was his wont. We shook hands.

" A very happy Christmas, Warren," he said.
" *De* greeting is belated but sincere. Now, as I
expect you are hoping for a Christmas box from me,
perhaps *de* company will let me give it you in my

study. But it is a very small Christmas box indeed, I fear."

He went to the door and opened it for me. I was surprised at finding him so calm, though he was very pale and had the air of one who has been through a painful experience.

As soon as he had shut the study door, he came straight to the subject—Harrington Cobalts. The meeting with G—— and his associates had duly taken place at the Carlton, and there was no doubt that G—— was eager to buy the company. He had actually made an offer at a higher price than any at which the shares had yet changed hands. "Higher than forty-two and nine ? " I asked timidly, remembering that I had bought myself some shares at that high figure.

"Higher even *d*an *d*at ridiculous price," he answered with a smile. However, my fortune was not yet made, it seemed; for the syndicate of which Quisberg was a member had rejected the offer, and were holding out for considerably more. Whether G—— would give more, depended, said my host, on the success or failure of certain continental negotiations. There was every reason to suppose that they would be successful, and for this reason I was advised to " hang on," even if there was a set-back when the Stock Exchange reopened. "*D*is advice," he said, " is your Christmas box. I have, of course, told you more than I should, *d*ough as you have *d*e privilege of being one of my official brokers, I have *d*e right to tell you my secrets. Hang on! You will get decidedly more *d*an your forty-two and ninepence! " He

smiled broadly, delighting, I believe, in the thought
that I, a stockbroker, had paid more for the shares
than he had.

" And now, my boy," he said, " we may as well
rejoin *de* ladies. I have been distressed, very distressed, you will believe me, at *de* deat(h) of *de*
mo*d*er of my poor little secretary. It has shaken me
severely—here." (He touched his heart.) " I have
been ill all *de* afternoon. But now I am better, and
hope to eat a happy Christmas supper wi*d* you all.
Let us now go."

We went. I was a little disappointed at my host's
financial news, though it promised well. He, at
least, seemed in no way disturbed at the delay in the
final settlement of the business. Indeed, I could not
remember ever having seen him less flustered or
apprehensive. Quite clearly his agitation of the
morning had nothing to do with Harrington
Cobalts. In the drawing-room we found Dr. Green.
He too seemed to have fully recovered from the
strain of the morning, and was in most excellent
vein, twinkling and joking and radiating in all
directions his satisfaction at being alive. I even felt
that such good humour was perhaps out of place
while Harley was with us. He did once move
towards the door, as if to escape from us, but Mrs.
Quisberg, who was watching him the whole time,
drew him back. " No, dear," I heard her saying,
" you mustn't be alone again. We're better company
for you than your thoughts. Come and sit down by
me."

At half past seven came supper. Amabel and

Dixon, we were told, had gone to dine with some friends and would not be back till late. I sat on Mrs. Quisberg's right and Harley on her left, while Sheila and Dr. Green were respectively on the right and left of Mr. Quisberg, who was at the other end of the table. Between Sheila and Harley there was a vacant place which Clarence should have had. Mr. Quisberg asked once, rather testily, where he was, and poor Mrs. Quisberg had to apologize vaguely in reply. " I haven't an idea," she said, in an aside to me, " what he can be doing. But with Clarence, one never knows! "

After coffee had been served, Mrs. Quisberg and her daughter went upstairs, leaving me with my host, Dr. Green and Harley. The two older men were still in excellent humour, and fell to bantering me on the score of my professional aptitudes. During the conversation Quisberg openly referred to the Harrington Cobalts which I had bought on his instructions for Dr. Green, and the doctor pretended to feel great nervousness over his commitments. " Look here, Malcolm," he said, " I rely on you. Here's Axel teaching me to gamble, and putting all my hard-earned savings into some wild-cat scheme or other. Why don't you stop him ? You should treat me as you treat your tenderest widow, and feed me exclusively with your excellent British government securities. I most strongly disapprove of these fly-by-night concerns. Harrington Cobalts indeed! Where's Harrington and what is Cobalt, anyway ? Answer me that! "

"Harrington," I said vaguely, "is somewhere in Canada, and cobalt is a metal—perhaps I should say, a mineral, which is used for—for the manufacture of paint, I believe, among other things."

The doctor snorted. "Now, Axel, you try," he said.

Quisberg, however, rose to the occasion, and delivered quite a sound serio-comic lecture on the mine, its situation and potentialities. No doubt, I thought, the doctor knows all there is to be known about cobalt, but it certainly seems as if, in this venture at least, he is merely following Quisberg's lead. I was destined, later, to reconsider this view, but although it was quite possible that the whole conversation that evening was a piece of buffoonery, I had a strong impression that, for once, Quisberg was really sure of himself, and on his own ground, while the doctor was little more than an interested spectator. As for Harley, he had been plied liberally with claret and a very good brandy, and sat listening to us with a dazed acquiescence. I was a little relieved, on his account, however, when we went upstairs; for the other two seemed to have forgotten all about him, and I feared that either of them might by a careless remark reopen the morning's wound.

In the drawing-room, of course, Mrs. Quisberg took charge at once, and suggested that we should all play "Word Making and Word Taking"—a game which Sheila had bought, intending to give it to Cyril. It promised to be a pleasant way of spending the evening, and with the exception of Quisberg we all seated ourselves round a big card-table in front of the fire, and did our best to concentrate. Quisberg declaring that he could not even spell words of one letter in English, sat in an armchair and read the paper. Harley and Sheila were both expert at the game, and Dr. Green showed great adroitness for a foreigner. He was always devising unusual words, many of them with a slight flavour of impropriety. Mrs. Quisberg just sat and smiled and failed to score a single point. Really, I thought, we are getting through the evening fairly well, all things considered. It was difficult to realize that only that morning I had found the body of Harley's mother outside my bedroom window. The nervous apprehension, which had troubled me almost ever since my arrival, became blunted. Surely, apart from the inquest on Monday, the worst was over. It was indeed delightful to enjoy a lessening of the tension, the feeling of backwash into calm waters.

" Now, Harley," said Sheila suddenly, " I'm surprised you missed that one."

(The whole family called him Harley, I noticed, as if it were his Christian name.)

I looked at him, and saw that, despite a poor little smile, he was on the verge of tears. Feeling that I could not possibly bear to see him break down, I was about to make some excuse for leaving the room when, luckily, Mrs. Quisberg, who had been watching him most of the time, gave an imitation of a yawn, got up, and said, " It's all very well for you young ones, but I'm much too tired to go on to-night with such a difficult game. I can see both Harley and Malcolm are tired too. Don't you think, dear, you should say good night now ? "

Her question was addressed to Harley, not to me.

" If you'll excuse me," he answered, " I think I will."

" Come along then," she said. " No, don't bother. The others will put the game away."

And for the second time that day she led him out of the room, with such a natural kindness that one could not be surprised.

" I must say," I said to Sheila, " I do admire your mother. She's wonderful."

We talked together and put the game away, while Dr. Green drew up a chair by Quisberg. Then the door opened, and I looked up expecting to see Mrs. Quisberg returning, but it was George, the butler, red in the face and somewhat flustered.

" Excuse me, sir," he said, and coughed importantly.

Quisberg looked round nervously.

" Yes ? "

" There's a—an individual come, sir, who wishes to see you on important business."

Quisberg rose, and walked towards the butler.

" One of *de* police ? "

" Oh no, sir. At least, he's in plain clothes."

" What name did he give ? "

" He gave no name, sir. He said his business was important and very private."

" Did you tell *dis* person *dat* I am not in *de* habit of

interviewing *d*ose wi*d* whom I am not acquainted—
least of all at such an hour ? ”

“ I did indicate as much, sir. But the—er—
person in question was so very urgent in his manner,
so to speak, sir, that I thought it best not to order
him off the premises. If you would just see him
for a moment, yourself, sir, no doubt you could
judge. . . .”

At this point, Dr. Green intervened.

“ It’s probably some touting rogue, Axel. I
shouldn’t go down if I were you.”

“ He said, sir,” resumed George (who was clearly
rather afraid of being called upon to eject the
visitor), “ that he had some information which you
ought to have.”

Quisberg rose and followed the butler to the
door.

“ Very well, I’ll go. No, Martin, I’m all
right.”

As he went out of the room, he looked perplexed,
rather than harassed. Sheila took up a book and
began to read, while the doctor paced up and down
by the fire. I made some remark to him, I remember,
but he only barked at me in reply. Then suddenly I
realized that Christmas Day was almost over,
without my having produced the present I had
bought for Mrs. Quisberg, and resolved to have it
ready for her when she came down again. I do not
know if this resolve was prompted by a wish to overhear any conversation that might be taking place
in the hall, but I certainly paused for a moment by
the stairs, on my way across the landing. I heard

nothing, however, and after reaching my bedroom, began to look for the parcel containing the rather horrible little green leather blotter, which was all that my feeble imagination had suggested as a gift for my hostess. It had evidently been put away somewhere by Edwins, and I had to search slowly with my left hand, through two or three drawers, before I came upon it. Then, as I was about to go back to the drawing-room, I suddenly heard voices below me—loud voices, seemingly raised in anger. Of course, I recollected, my room was immediately over Quisberg's study, where, no doubt, he was having his interview. A great desire came over me to hear what the two men were saying, and I longed for an excuse to loiter in the hall. I was afraid, and perhaps ashamed, to do this, but, finding that the sounds from below came most loudly when I stood near the fireplace, I knelt down by the hearth-rug and put my ear to the wall by the chimney, which was presumably carrying the noise. The voices were now clearer, and I could distinguish Quisberg's tones from the other man's, but even so I could not gather a single word of the conversation, till all at once I caught the following sentence, uttered by the stranger—" Why, in that light, I saw it as plain as I can see you! " This was followed by a low murmuring, and the sound of a bell ringing.

A feeling of guilt overcame me. "Do they realize," I wondered, " that I'm just above ? " Should I go back to the drawing-room with my parcel and present it as if nothing had happened ? But there were heavy steps on the stairs, steps on the landing and the sound of a door (probably the drawing-room door) opening, more steps and then the voice of Dr. Green, speaking quite close to my door:

" All right, George. If Madam asks where we are, say we are unfortunately involved in a business talk."

He spoke loudly ; for George was rather deaf. Then, after a pause, the door of the room below me opened and shut, and I heard the two voices again, reinforced by the doctor's. But this time they were calmer and, realizing that, short of another outburst, I should gather nothing more, I took up my parcel and crossed the landing to the drawing-room.

It was empty, except for Sheila, who was still reading.

" Dr. Green's been called downstairs to join Daddy," she said, barely looking up. " Where have you been ? "

Really, I thought, how tactless the child is!

" I've been looking for the Christmas present I wanted to give your mother," I answered. " I'm ashamed to say the wretched little thing I got for you must have been left behind. I can't find it anywhere among my things."

" Oh, Malcolm," she said with more animation, " that's too kind of you. Do tell me what it was! "

I had to think very quickly; for, to tell the truth, I had, in the rush before Christmas, completely forgotten to buy anything for Sheila at all.

" It's a—it's a kind of bead necklace—a very cheap one," I added hastily.

Her interest waned a little.

" Oh," she murmured, " I'm sure I shall love it. But you shouldn't have bothered about it. We've none of us, I'm afraid, got anything for you. We're a very poor family at giving Christmas presents. Mummy and Daddy, of course, give us presents, but the rest of us agreed not to bother, this year."

Evidently, I thought, in the houses of the rich, this aspect of Christmas is not so predominant as it is amongst the comparatively poor. And by way of contrast I pictured, with mixed feelings, the family Christmases of my childhood and adolescence, and recalled the blend of generosity and greed which that season used to arouse in us all.

" Do you think your mother has gone to bed ? " I asked.

" No. She'll come back to say good night. I expect she's trying to cheer Harley up. But don't you stay up any longer if you're tired. I'm quite happy with my book."

" I think I will go to bed, then," I said. " Good night! "

" Good night, Malcolm."

I was not altogether sorry to be dismissed.

I heard no voices from the study as I undressed by the fire in my room. Either the interview was over or they were talking very quietly. I did, however, hear from time to time doors opening and shutting, steps on the stairs and, after a long interval, the shutting of the front door. Was that the going of the unknown ? Like a trained spy, I switched off my light and raised a corner of the blind. A biggish man, with a cap on the back of his head, was walking down the drive. I watched him till he had opened the gate and turned to the left towards West Heath Road. All I saw was his back view, but the cap and the manner in which it was worn recalled to my mind the figure I had seen loitering by the gate before dinner.

So, I thought, switching on the light and resuming my undressing, it was no ordinary tramp that I had seen. If it had been, the discussion in the study would have been over much sooner. Were such mysterious visits part of the game of high finance ? Was it blackmail ? " Harrington Cobalts are worthless, Mr. Quisberg, and you know it ! Your returns are faked, your mining engineer's a crook, and I shall write to the papers unless you give me a hundred thousand shares ! " But what were the words which I had actually heard ? " Why, in that light, I saw it as plain as I can see you ! " Saw what ?

I got into bed with my book, but instead of reading I listened. From time to time I heard steps and the shutting of doors. Well, there were several people in the house who had still to go to bed—Mr. and Mrs. Quisberg, Sheila, Dr. Green—and several others who had not come in yet, as far as I knew—Amabel, Dixon, Clarence and the nurse. Do nurses use front or back doors, I wondered ? Really, my sense of hearing seemed, that day, to have been the most valuable of my senses. Perhaps it usually was, and for that reason I tended to remember people's words and voices rather than their gestures and faces— preferred music to painting or sculpture. Yet Dr. Green had said that all my senses were acute. No doubt they were, when I used them consciously, but when I was in one of the absent-minded, introspective moods that came upon me only too frequently, it was my sense of hearing that was paramount, noticing and registering impressions without any guidance from my will.

I was still analysing my faculties, with that gentle undercurrent of self-praise which usually flows beneath such reveries, when I heard steps approaching my door and Mrs. Quisberg's knock on the panel.

" I've just come," she said, " to say good night to you. I've had such a time with poor little Harley. He broke down completely when we left the drawing-room, and I had to take him to my room and talk to him for a long time before he recovered himself. He must have been a very devoted son. Or it may be that he wasn't. Why is it, Malcolm, that we can only realize how much people mean to us when we lose them ? It's a real tragedy."

She wiped away a tear, and began again.

" Well, Malcolm, it'll sound silly and artificial if I start apologizing to you again for this miserable Christmas. We shall have to get through it, some-how. There's Axel all upset again over goodness knows what. Martin Green's gone upstairs with him and is putting him to bed. Some business worry, he said, and told me not to make matters worse by

asking questions. He's coming to look at your wrist
when he's finished with Axel. Well, I'm going now.
You must be thoroughly sick of us all. No, I won't
stay. I'm really too worn out myself. I do hope you
will be comfortable and that things will seem
brighter in the morning. Good night, dear. You
have the switch and a bell by the bed, haven't you,
in case you want anything ? Good night, again, and
sleep well."

She left the room, barely giving me time to say
anything in reply. Poor angelic woman, I thought!
However, hers was a nature which would quickly
rebound. How, I wondered, was Dr. Green bearing
up amid these alarms ? I almost resolved to speak
my mind to him, and say: " Look here, Doctor,
what's up ? Why is Quisberg so jumpy ? Why is
Clarence so queer ? Who exactly is Dixon, and who
are you, prowling about among these mysteries like a
panther ?" But this would have been quite the wrong
way to tackle him. I could imagine his sardonic
laugh, his counter-thrusts, the way in which he
would soon turn the tables. " My dear fellow," he
would say, " we all know that your poor aunt died
in very dramatic circumstances. Don't brood on it.
Don't let it go to your head. You're among quite
ordinary people here. It's true, Harley's mother
was a somnambulist and a little deranged in the
head—women not infrequently are at a certain age
—and it's true that an annoying fellow visited
Quisberg to-night on business. It's true that Dixon's
a bounder, that Clarence James is a romantic young
man full of artistic rubbish, and that his half-sister,

Amabel, is a bright young thing whose behind
should be thoroughly chastised with my razor-strop
—and it's true I'm a character. But for the Lord's
sake leave it at that, and make some effort to adapt
yourself to us—(and you're a bit of an oddity too,
you know)—instead of indulging in these utterly
fantastic speculations! "

" But, Doctor,—" I would have said, and was still
prolonging an imaginary interview with him, when
he came in, and a real conversation, not at all on
preconcerted lines, began.

" And now for you," he said gruffly, leaning over
the bed and drawing my right arm towards him.
" You're better. You must wear the sling to-morrow.
You needn't wear it the day after. And begin to use
your fingers more. Use a pencil, or strum the piano.
Come on, turn over, I can't reach you there. I'm far
too tired to stand up while I rub you."

" Why are you tired ? " I asked.

" I'm tired of you—by which of course I mean
practically everybody in the house."

" I hear Mr. Quisberg's unwell again."

" Yes, another attack of the jimjams. Well, if you
will dabble in things that are too big for you, that's
usually the end."

" You mean this financial deal ? "

" Yes and no. This one, that one and the other
one. He can't let well alone. He never could. Oh,
your miserable Cobalts are all right. I didn't mean
them particularly."

" You've got some too."

" Axel's Christmas present to me. He's a very dear

fellow, Malcolm. There's nothing I wouldn't do for him. There isn't much I haven't done, for that matter, in the course of my long life."

" What have you done for him ? " I asked, profiting by this mood of apparent expansiveness.

He chuckled.

" I've mended a broken nose for him among other things."

" Oh," I said simply. " So that's why his nose has a kink in it."

He looked at me with sudden sharpness.

" I wonder if you really are about half as clever as you think you are—that's to say, about as clever as I think you ? "

" Probably. Have I annoyed you ? "

He did not reply, but rubbed my wrist and arm up and down, making the hissing noise of a groom attending to a horse. For a while I shut my eyes and enjoyed the sensation. Then I looked at him suddenly and said: " Have you seen the nurse yet ? "

His fingers tightened on my arm.

" So you've been having naughty thoughts! Why did you ask me that ? "

" I don't know. I saw her this afternoon; but I assure you——"

" Oh, come, come. There's no need to be prudish with me. I'm the little father-confessor of all the world. If you knew all I know about human nature with its twists and turns and kinks—you'd find most people very easy to understand."

" I dare say. I think I should enjoy a long talk with you—if you'd let yourself go."

Evidently, as I came to know him better, my boldness with him was growing.

" Well," he said, " perhaps some day we'll have a long talk, and I shall let myself go, and you'll feel what a very dull little person you are beside the great-souled and heroic Martin Green. But not to-night. To-night we must go to sleep early. There, that should do."

He replaced the bandage, but much more loosely than the night before.

" Are you going to give me a sleeping draught ? "

" Am I going to give you a good-night kiss! " he said violently. " No, you won't need one. However, it's nice of you to suggest it. Sign of trust, perhaps."

" What do you mean ? "

" Nothing. Well, your toilet to-morrow should be an easier matter than it was to-day. Edwins can help you if necessary, and I'll have a look at you after breakfast, if I've got time. How do you like the blind ? "

" Let it up, will you ? And would you mind opening the window ? "

" Wide, like this ? "

" Yes, it's such a warm night."

" Now, is there any other service I can render ? "

" No—except let me thank you—"

" For my great kindness, etc. Well, as a patient I don't find you distasteful. Sweet dreams."

" Good night, Doctor."

Almost as soon as he left me I fell asleep, but had a long spell of intermittent wakefulness between one

and three. It was during that time that I heard
the return of Amabel and Dixon—first, the car
in the drive, and then, when they had put it
away in the garage and stood by the porch, their
voices.

" I don't care what happens," Dixon said in a
thick voice. " I know you'll stand by me. Let's
celebrate again, shall we ? It's been a good evening.
Where are they, old girl ? "

" What do you mean ? " she asked, and then,
when presumably he had explained himself by a
gesture, she went on, " Oh, they're in the shed behind
the garage. But, we can't to-night. Remember, it's
a house of mourning."

She giggled in exasperating fashion.

" Now, old girl, give in to little Lennie for this
once."

" You'll wake them all up."

" No, I won't. It didn't last night. Besides, we're
awake. Why shouldn't they wake too ? "

" Now come in, you great bear with a sore head.
You'll disturb Sheila. Oh, I forgot, Master Malcolm
Warren is in her room to-night. I don't mean what
you mean! "

" He's a rotter, anyway. What do I care ? "

" Well, I do. In you go."

" Oh, no you don't. All right, but you must be
punished first."

At this there was the sound of a little scuffle,
followed by resounding kisses. Then the front door
slammed.

So that accounted for Amabel and Dixon, I mused

lazily, without trying to fathom what they had been arguing about. Was Clarence in ? And what about the nurse ? Did nurses use front or back doors ? And how long would it be before Dr. Green came in and broke my nose ?

So did my waking life mingle with dreams.

IX. TULIPS IN BOWLS

Boxing Day—8.30 a.m.

BOXING DAY. My wrist. Harrington Cobalts—
(rather piano this time). The death of Mrs. Harley.
Amabel and Dixon at breakfast. (What was it they
had been saying in the porch ?) Amabel with her
short and fluffy hair, Amabel with her assumed
Oxford drawl, Dixon with his scowls and pugnacious
rudeness, Sheila the taciturn, Clarence the difficult,
Harley the pitiable—how could I face them at
breakfast, with the prospect of seeing them all day ?
Why begin the battle before I must ? I would
breakfast in bed, and stay there for a long time.

I rang the bell.

"Good morning, Edwins. Yes, much better
to-day, thank you, but could I have breakfast in
bed ? "

It was again a lovely day, and, while I ate my
breakfast, I looked with delight at the trees which I
could see from my window. Surely spring could not
be very far away. By way of contrast to my inquisi-
tiveness of the previous evening, I felt detached from
the household and disinterested in its woes and
perplexities. Beyond making myself as agreeable as I

could, why should I not just lazily enjoy the fine
weather and the comforts of the house, behaving as
if I were spending a short holiday in a well-managed
hotel ? It was a form of cowardice, I suppose, a
reaction from nervous strain. Memories of Quisberg's interview with the stranger, and of Amabel's
incomprehensible conversation with Dixon, came
over me from time to time, but I brushed them
aside, and deliberately tried to turn my thoughts to
themes quite unconnected with my unfortunate
visit to Beresford Lodge. How delightful the sunshine was! Next year I would really try to enjoy the
spring and summer. I would fill my rooms with
spring flowers. (I could buy hyacinths and tulips
growing in fibre quite cheaply from a nursery, and
transplant them in my own bowls.) I would have
my sitting-room repainted. I would go for a short
motor trip at Easter. For the summer, I might even
take a little cottage on the river where I could have
my friends to stay at week-ends. We would have
bathing parties, and floodlit games of bridge on the
lawn. I might even buy a little cottage—if these
Harrington Cobalts. . . . No, I refused to think of
Harrington Cobalts or the ill-omened Christmas
Eve on which I had bought them. I must escape,
mentally, at least, from the deadness of the year,
and the deadness of the big padded house, surrounded by so many other houses no less big and
padded, in which, for a few dreary days more, I was
to be a most unwilling guest. Escape! This really
was the wish that drove my imagination over these
extravagant fields. It was not that I had any grounds

for anticipating disaster; for whenever I tried to look " facts " in the face, the " facts " receded from my view and became silly inventions of my own, scraps of conversation misheard and misinterpreted, mystifications without motive, puzzles unworthy of solution. But the whole atmosphere of that house, as I lay in bed trying to contemplate nothing but the sunshine, dwarfed and distorted me, making me a puny pantomime puppet whom some horse-play or other might lead into a nasty accident, if I were not continually on my guard. The sunshine, spring, tulips and hyacinths in countless bowls, a country cottage and moonlight on the river—these were the prospects in which I should find myself again, when I emerged, reduced but not extinguished, from the ordeal of the next few days.

" Come in! "

" So there you are, tucked up in your little pig-sty. Show me the wrist! "

Dr. Green put my breakfast-tray on the floor, and bent over me. His words were in his usual idiom, but his expression was strangely joyless. Was it simply exasperation at having to hunt me out in my retreat ? Why should that make him look as if he hadn't had any sleep ?

" How did you sleep ? " he went on.

" Only fairly well, thank you. And you ? "

" I always sleep well. I had to get up and see to Axel, as a matter of fact. He was fretting again. Oh, nothing. I shall keep him in bed till dinner time, and he'll be all right again."

" Have you seen the others ? "

" Sheila only—and Clarence tramping miserably up and down the terrace with a face like a dry toadstool. You're all right."

" Do you mean I'm quite cured ? "

" You will be, by to-morrow morning. Nature can do the rest, now."

" Don't I need any more massage ? "

" No, no more massage."

He spoke the words almost wearily, and turning his back on me, went to the window, where he stood for a few moments, whistling softly.

" Well, then," I said, " I suppose I'd better get up. Will you come for a walk with me over the Heath ? "

" No."

He paused ungraciously and continued, " I'm much too busy. To-morrow, perhaps—to-morrow and to-morrow and to-morrow. Is that Shakespeare ? "

" Yes. Were you awakened by Amabel and Dixon coming in late last night ? "

" No. Did they come in late ? "

" Yes, very. They were talking about rousing the whole house with something kept in a shed behind the garage. I heard them through my window. What could it have been, do you think ? A new kind of motor-horn ? "

He turned round, and surveyed me with distaste for a moment before answering.

" Probably. Anything brazen, vulgar and noisy would certainly commend itself to their shoddy little souls ! "

"Well, they didn't do it, whatever it was. I feel rather worried about you, Doctor. You've lost your bedside manner. Has anything awful happened in the night? Harley hasn't followed his poor mother, has he?"

"Nothing of the slightest importance, even to the most inquisitive, has happened during the night," he rapped out. Then, surprisingly and suddenly, he broke into loud laughter and came over to my bed. "Come, come, my young friend," he said, "what is it? Out with it! You seem to be suffering from a mental costiveness. I've been busy with Axel during the night, and I'm too busy to-day to go a walk with you, though the prospect of doing so would in happier circumstances delight me. I shan't be in to luncheon and I very probably shan't be in for tea. I've some business to do for Axel in London—in or near Baker Street, as the house agents would say. So much for me. Now you?"

I crumpled up completely. "I've got an attack of nerves. Before you came I was thinking of tulips in bowls, so as to distract myself. I feel as if I've been here six weeks. I want to go away. I never knew time could pass so slowly. Every minute I'm downstairs I seem to be fighting in a battle—as you would say, resisting a mental toothache. I'm really dreading the time when I shall have to leave this room and meet the others."

I had let myself become so carried away that I hardly cared whether he laughed at me or scolded me. Instead he surprised me by doing neither, and saying very calmly, "Malcolm, I'm sorry. It's the shock of your tumble, and on the top of that, the shock of the sad discovery you made yesterday morning. Well, as I told you, during the day I have to go about other people's business. But to-night I'll order you to bed early and prick these psychological blisters of yours. Oh yes, I'm just as good a psychiatrist as I am a bone-setter. And I cure just as quickly."

" But," I said weakly, " what are you going to the West End for ? The shops aren't open to-day."

" Of that I am well aware. None the less I shall be able to transact my business. Now get up and go out in the fresh air, and be nice, polite, clean and good till dinner's over."

He made an absurd little face at me and went out.

I felt better for my outburst, and relieved to think that in a few hours I should be able to pour out my worries—vague though they were—into an intelligent and sympathetic ear. I rang the bell and Edwins, who presumably had been told by my kind hostess that my calls on him had precedence over all ordinary duties, insisted on ministering to my toilet, though now there were few things which I could not have done without help. We talked, of course, while I was dressing, but beyond saying that Mr. Clarence had eaten no breakfast, he had no news for me. This mention of Clarence reminded me that I possessed his poem—or the poem in his writing—and I resolved to give it to him as soon as I could find him. The poem for Clarence, a walk on the Heath, and, if the coast should be clear, a little visit to

Amabel's " shed behind the garage," formed my programme for the morning.

After a short greeting to Sheila, who was playing the piano, I went into the garden and found Clarence walking up and down near the rock-garden. He gave me a black look when I said " Good morning," and showed no wish at all to talk to me. However, whether it was my talk with Dr. Green, or the sight of someone more wretched than myself that emboldened me, I came quickly to the point.

" I'm afraid, James," I said—we called one another by our surnames—" I've got something that belongs to you. This."

I handed him the poem, which he took with an air of angry bewilderment.

" I'm sorry to say I had to read it," I went on. " If I hadn't, Amabel would have passed it on to Dixon, and I thought you would rather trust me than him with your private affairs."

" Oh, that," he said, with a show of indifference. " So Amabel got hold of it."

" You left it in a book, she said."

" Yes. As the people in this house can't read, I thought a book was a safe place to leave it in."

" Are you the author ? " I asked unpardonably.

" As a matter of fact I am. Do you like it ? "

" Yes -in its way——"

" Well, I don't," he said, and tore the paper into small scraps and flung them in the pond.

I gasped.

" Are you protesting," he asked, " against the

destruction of so valuable a poem, or my choice of a wastepaper basket ? "

" Both."

" Well, I don't think you need trouble."

Evidently he hoped to drive me away, but I refused to accept dismissal.

" I wasn't," I said, " prying into your affairs."

" Of course not."

" How about going for a walk ? " I asked, irrelevantly.

" I don't feel like one, I'm afraid."

" Well, I think I ought to take one. Do you recommend your yesterday's route ? "

" Yesterday ? Oh—I don't know. It was very muddy."

He looked contemptuously at the new pair of shoes I was wearing.

" Then," I said, " I must find my own road."

He said nothing till I was about to turn away, when his expression altered for the better.

" I really am frightfully sorry, Warren, that we're all socially so hopeless. I have, as a matter of fact, a reason for not wanting to go too far from the house this morning. But the others might do something. No wonder you're bored to death with your visit."

" Oh, but——"

" Please, don't be polite to me. I'm very much an outsider in this *ménage*, as no doubt you have gathered, and it isn't my place to entertain you."

" I was trying to entertain you."

" That's not so easy, I'm afraid. I'm perfectly

sincere in what I'm saying. I do apologize for this
household. If I were you, I should get out of it
as soon as you can. For your own sake, I mean.
Speaking personally, I'd far rather have you than
many people here."

This, I felt, was the limit of his graciousness.

" Well," I said, " I shall go for a walk somewhere
or other. I wish it weren't quite such a Protestant
Sunday kind of day. However——"

In despair of finding a cliché with which to close
the wretched conversation, I simply turned my back
on him and walked down the path, and read once
more the labels in the beds: Primula Denticulata
Superba, Primula Florindæ. Then, further on,
Phlox Le Mahdi, Delphinium Mrs. Townley Parker,
Pæonia Albert Crousse. Yes, when the days length-
ened I would go to the river, take my own cottage
and grow my own phloxes, delphiniums and
peonies. I should have to learn to row a little better,
of course, and my swimming was not all that it
might be, and river water, in England, was usually
far from warm. Still, my own cottage, my own lawn,
my own herbaceous border. When the days length-
ened, how pleasant life could be. Till then, I must
content myself with tulips in bowls. Meanwhile,
where were the tulips at Beresford Lodge ?

I had reached the end of the walk on the south-
west side of the garden. Of course, the tulips were
all at the foot of the terrace, where a strip of bare but
immaculate earth, about ten feet broad, showed a
fine crop of labels. But instead of turning to the left
and examining the names, I found myself walking

up some rough stone steps on my right, which led, through a thick shrubbery, to the incinerator and potting-sheds. It was a part of the garden to which visitors were not conducted, unless they wished to see the greenhouses, and even these could be reached by a more impressive route. One would only pass the potting-sheds if one were going to the green-houses straight from the garage. Immediately behind the garage stood a little shed—and as I saw it, the memory of Amabel's talk with Dixon on the steps of the porch came back to me—if really it had ever been very far away—quite ousting all thoughts of tulips whether in bowls or beds.

"They're in the shed behind the garage!" Amabel had said. There was the shed. What was inside it?

Then, stupidly, I hesitated. The very fact that I very much wanted to look inside the shed made me feel guilty. What should I say if someone saw me? "I was only exploring. It looked such an interesting shed!" On the contrary, it was a most ordinary shed. I might as well say that the housemaid's closet looked interesting. Still, nothing very terrible could happen to me if I were discovered taking a peep. There would be no headline in the papers, "Stockbroker expelled from Hampstead Mansion. Guest goes in disgrace." Perhaps, in retrospect, I am exaggerating my timidity, but I know that I hung about shiftily for a quarter of an hour, walking past the potting-sheds towards the greenhouses and back again, before making up my mind. Then, when I had made up my mind and was advancing towards the door, this time with the definite intention of opening it, a man, whom I took to be a gardener, suddenly appeared, carrying something in a basket, and went into one of the potting-sheds, where I could see him through the window. He could also see me, but, strange to say, this fact, which made it impossible for me to loiter any more, gave me the courage I needed. Never again, perhaps, would such a chance come my way. As if I carried on my person the written authority of the shed's owner, I went boldly to the door and opened it.

The shed contained a carpenter's bench, two or three spades, a few thin wooden planks, some pea-sticks, some green dahlia stakes, sheets of corrugated iron, bales of netting, a barrel full of vegetable roots, and three broken basket-chairs. On the bench was a large brown-paper parcel, half unwrapped, containing fireworks. The first and only one which I examined had round its conical top a pink label bearing the words, " The Jubilee Flash. Novelty. Price 2s. 6d.," and instructions for use. Almost mechanically I put my hand into my overcoat pocket and pulled out the empty firework-case which I had found, about twenty-four hours before, in the pond of the rock-garden. There was no question but that the two fireworks were twins.

Two other objects in the parcel interested me. The first was a detonating pistol, which had clearly been used. The second was an invoice, dated December 23rd, which informed me that Miss Amabel Thurston had spent some five pounds on fireworks. The

account included six Jubilee Flashes and one detonating pistol. So much, then, for the mystery of the
shed. Amabel and Dixon had let off one " flash "
on the night of Christmas Eve. When they came
home on the night of Christmas Day, Dixon would
have liked to let off another. That was all. I could,
indeed, hardly credit him with so innocent a caprice.

X. INVASION

It was now a quarter past twelve. I had forgotten all about my proposed walk and went indoors to the terrace room, where I heard voices. There I found Amabel, Sheila and Dixon. But a new blow was in store. Mrs. Quisberg was in bed, and had been told by Dr. McKenzie to stay there all day.

"He says it's 'flu," said Amabel not unpleasantly. "I didn't know there was any about, but doctors always have it ready, don't they? Mother's sure it's only a chill and is terribly fretty about you, Malcolm. I'm sure she'd like you to look in on her afterwards, even though she says you must keep away in case she's infectious. Daddy's in bed, too. Why, I can't think. Harley has gone to a married cousin's for the day. Dr. Green is out to lunch. So you'll have to make do with Leonard, Sheila and me—and Clarence, if he's about. A cocktail may help you to bear it. Help yourself—and give me one."

I did so. Indeed, I repeated my excesses of Christmas Day, and when luncheon came, after nearly an hour's uninstructive and unamusing conversation, I was almost tottering as I walked into the dining-room. "Mrs. Quisberg ill," I kept thinking. "Really, I can't stay here if that is so.

125

All the cocktails in the world won't keep me buoyed up."

Amabel sat at the end of the table facing the garden and Sheila at the other end. I was on Amabel's right and Dixon on her left. A place was laid for Clarence between me and Sheila. Nobody had thought of waiting for him, or seemed in any way surprised when he came in gloomily after the first course and sat down without a word. Dixon and Amabel tried to rally him for a while, but soon desisted, and conversation became duller and more spasmodic than ever. Only one interesting thing happened during the meal, and that came at the end while we were drinking our coffee and nibbling at *marrons déguisés*. Dixon, who had got up to help himself to a cigar, suddenly paused by the french window looking on to the terrace, and said:

" Well, I'm damned! What infernal sauce! Look here, Amabel. What do you make of that ? "

With the exception of Clarence we all joined him by the window.

" Look there," he said, and pointed to the far wall that separated the garden of Beresford Lodge from the garden of Paragon House. About a dozen youths were sitting perkily on the top and gesticulating in the direction of our windows.

" What can they be doing ? " asked Sheila, a little slow, as usual, to put two and two together.

" It's got round the neighbourhood, evidently," her sister answered. " I suppose we shall have bands of louts swarming up from West Hampstead all the afternoon to see the scene of the accident."

Her voice drawled a little over the journalese.

" I suppose you want it stopped ? " Dixon asked.

" I should think we do! "

" Let's turn the hose on 'em! "

" It won't reach anything like so far."

" How do you fill the rock-garden pond then ? "

" With water from the bodge—the water-carrier," Sheila explained informatively.

Dixon was not impressed by the horticultural term. " Do you want me to ring up the police ? " he asked Amabel.

" We certainly can't stand it all day," she said. " Suppose Harley came back and saw them all gloating——"

At that moment, whether it was the outcome of high spirits or because the intruders had caught sight of us at the window, some horse-play seemed to begin, and two of the lads fell on our side of the wall, where the shrubs hid them from view. This was too much for Dixon.

" That's plain trespassing," he said. " Lord knows what damage they won't do to Mr. Quisberg's choice plants. I'll show them. Just let me get that stick of mine! "

In one moment he had worked himself up into a brutal frenzy and rushed from the room before any of us could speak. Amabel made no attempt to interfere. Perhaps she enjoyed the prospect of her hero pitting himself against superior numbers. In another minute we saw Dixon on the terrace, which he had reached by one of the terrace room windows, carrying a thick weighted stick which I remembered noticing in the stand in the lobby. Then he ran down the Louis Quinze staircase and straight across the lawn.

" I hope he doesn't hit any of them too hard," I said. " It looks rather a dangerous weapon."

Then Clarence, with an expression of disgust on his face, got up from the table and went to the door.

" I'm afraid I don't get any satisfaction," he said as he passed me, " in watching our bull-like friend attacking a few half-starved youths."

" At any rate," Amabel began angrily, " he's more use than you are . . ."

But Clarence was out of the room before she had time to finish.

Perhaps because he was out of breath, Dixon moderated his pace as he reached the end of the lawn, and completed the last part of his journey through the rock-garden and the shrubbery behind, in a dignified walk. Then the shrubs hid him from view, but great excitement was evidently produced among the little figures on the wall. One or two of them jumped down into the Paragon House garden, while others clung aggressively to their positions. I saw one of them take a catapult out of his pocket and aim with it. I thought, too, that I heard a faint sound of shouting, but this may have been imagination, as the window was shut and the scene of the fight a long distance away. Amabel looked at me questioningly, as if she thought that I should go as a reinforcement. I had, of course, no intention of doing so and was about to draw a shamefaced attention to my wrist, when George, the butler, came in to say that Dr. Green wished to speak to Mr. Dixon on the telephone.

" Dr. Green! " Amabel exclaimed. " What can he want with Leonard ? All right, George, I'll go and have a word with Dr. Green myself."

She went out. Now was my opportunity to slip away.

" I think," I said to Sheila, " I shall go upstairs and pay my respects to your mother before she has her rest. I shouldn't be any use helping Dixon, though I expect he'll be all right. Will you excuse me ? "

" Yes, of course," she answered. " I shall stay here and see the fun, if there's any more to be seen."

I reached the shelter of my bedroom before Amabel came out of the telephone-room. I had now had a good innings with the younger members of the party and felt entitled to an hour's privacy. But before settling down it was only right that I should see if Mrs. Quisberg would receive me. Besides, on Mrs. Quisberg's floor, I might again meet the nurse— that interesting character whom I had forgotten all the morning. Accordingly I took my miserable Christmas gift, which I had not been able to bestow the evening before, and went up another flight of stairs to Mrs. Quisberg's bedroom. I did not meet the nurse, but as I was about to knock at the door I heard a laugh, faint, silvery and provocative, coming from the top landing, followed incongruously by the angry slamming of a door.

" Come in! "

" It's Malcolm. May I ? "

" Oh, Malcolm. I'm so glad to see you—but mind you don't come near me. No, I won't even shake hands with you. Sit down right over there, by the window."

" I am most sorry to hear you aren't well. You look as delightful as ever. Don't you think it's just a chill ? "

" Yes, I think so really. I felt seedy and shivery before breakfast, and took my temperature. It was just over a hundred. I had Dr. McKenzie in when he came to see Cyril, and he insisted on my staying in bed."

" Have you a headache ? "

" Yes, a little. It's rather better now. No, don't be in any hurry to go. It's so nice and refreshing to talk to you."

" I was only going to give you this, with my love. But what can one give—except one's love—to those who have everything ? "

I approached the bed with my little parcel.

" No, no. Keep away. Put it on that table, and I'll get Flora to give it to me later. Now, Malcolm, it is most naughty and kind of you. I warned you specially we weren't a Christmas-present-giving family. As a matter of fact, you'll find a tiny memento from me when you get back to your flat— that picture we saw together at the French Painters' Exhibition."

I was thrilled.

" Oh, that is really too generous. I don't know what to say. Do you really mean you are giving me that exquisite Paul Dubois ? But it's worthy of an art collector. You must keep it yourself. It would look lovely here in that panel over the mantelpiece."

" No, it would be wasted on me. I don't understand these modern things. I like simple paintings, like that flower-piece there. This is a pretty room, isn't it ? "

I sat in my chair and looked round, while she talked. It certainly was a pretty room, especially if one compared it with the other rooms in the house. The walls, which would have been improved if they had been stripped of a late Victorian panelling, were painted a buff-stone colour. The curtains, the valances of the two kidney-shaped dressing-tables, the eiderdown and the upholstery of the chairs, were a semi-glazed chintz with minute clusters of snow-drops on a yellow ground. The furniture itself was a bright satin-wood, such as was sold very expensively just before and just after the war. Fortunately there was not very much of it, as the wardrobe had been replaced by a built-in cupboard, and the washstand was behind a Chinese screen. The room, as I think I have mentioned, faced north-east over the glass roof of the aviary. My chair had its back to a big bay window, and by turning my head to the right I could see right down the garden, although the corner of the house cut off most of the view.

My thoughts were wandering, I am afraid, while Mrs. Quisberg talked on, and I kept looking towards the small patch of garden wall that was visible to me, hoping to catch a glimpse of Dixon doing battle with the louts. I thought it better to say nothing to

Mrs. Quisberg about the invasion, for fear it should distress her. However, except for three or four yards of the wall and a very thin slice of Paragon House beyond, there was nothing to be seen. Either Dixon had been successful, or the fray was further to the left. As I gazed out of the window, and replied mechanically to my hostess' many questions as to my welfare, I felt a great distaste growing within me for Paragon House, its garden and its structure. The few feet that were visible to me looked mouldy and repellent. It was a most unpleasant house, I thought, an evil and a cruel house, even more horrible in its solidity than it would have been in ruins. I could imagine snakes writhing in the basement, vampires fluttering in the attics, while its walls exuded through strips of damp wallpaper all the diseases and disasters of its previous owners. It would, indeed, be a mercy, I thought (looking, by way of contrast, round the bright bedroom in which I was sitting), if Mr. Quisberg could buy it and pull it down. Standing where it did, it was a monstrous neighbour, almost purposeful in its offensiveness. I could not help feeling, either, when I recalled the gesticulating figures on the wall, that somehow the hated building had still an ominous function to perform—as if, moved to vindictive envy by the peace and prosperity of Beresford Lodge, it were only waiting to visit us with calamity.

Despite my absorption in this fantastic reverie, I luckily remembered that, as a visitor in a sick room, I had almost overstayed my welcome. My hostess, who had been telling me about the shop where she bought her carpet, was clearly tired and made little effort to keep me when I rose to go.

" Are you sure," I asked, " that you wouldn't feel relieved if I went back to my flat ? "

" On the contrary, Malcolm, I should be most grieved. I love to think of you here, even though I can do so little to amuse you. Besides, I hope to be down again to-morrow, if not for dinner to-day. Dr. McKenzie's coming again at half past five and I'm sure he'll find me ever so much better than I was this morning. Now what are you going to do ? "

" I really think I shall have a nap, and perhaps go for a walk afterwards. I'm afraid I've had too many cocktails again to-day. I feel so sleepy. Aren't you ashamed of me ? "

" Not at all, Malcolm. Get all the rest you can. You looked so tired when you came here on Christmas Eve. Perhaps you'll look in again if I'm not down this evening? "

" Of course I will. *Au revoir*."

It was now nearly a quarter to three. It'll have to be a very short nap, I thought, as I reached my bedroom, if I am to get a walk by daylight. No doubt a walk would do me good, but the prospect of dozing in a chair by my fire, which must have been lit during luncheon, was irresistible. It was a shame to waste the daylight, but still greater shame to waste the fire.

Giving way to my sloth, I was going to the arm-chair when I saw through the window two figures walking down the drive. They were Dr. Green, in a thick overcoat, and Dixon, swinging his heavy stick in his right hand. I could not see their faces, but a jerky and petulant movement of Dixon's shoulders gave me the impression that he was not likely to enjoy the walk. What can they have to say to one another, I wondered, as they turned to the left in Lyon Avenue and went towards the Heath ? Then I remembered that Dr. Green had telephoned to Dixon when the watchers on the wall were engaging our attention. Well, it was another little problem to think out. . . . During my walk, perhaps, I would give my mind to it. And that very evening Dr. Green had promised to have a talk with me. He was one in whose presence I could think aloud. Meanwhile, I could think of nothing but my sleepiness, the warmth of the fire and the softness of the armchair. Deliciously I abandoned myself to their charms.

XI. SERENADE

I AWOKE at half past three and roused myself with a great effort. The sun, I knew from my diary, would set at 3.55. (I always take great interest in the times of sunset in winter, and gloat over every minute gained by the afternoon sun.) If I did not set out at once I should barely have time to see the Heath by daylight. I was resolved to have my walk, even if it meant my being late for tea. After all, the other members of the party had put in the most irregular attendances at meals. Surely I was entitled to miss one.

It was indeed a lovely evening, a real foretaste of spring. As I walked up Lyon Avenue I smelt in imagination the lilac and may trees that some day would flower again by the road, the wallflowers, as yet only six inches high in the trim borders. There were may trees on the Heath, too, I noticed, when I had turned to the right up West Heath Road—may trees, silver birches and patches of gorse. Five minutes left of daylight. I had to hurry if I was to see the sunset from the top of the hill.

For a while I stood on the highest ground, watching the sky. The sun, which in summer would bury itself in the glittering waters of the Welsh Harp, was

already on that winter day hidden behind the
buildings on the slopes of the Finchley Road. The
sky above the roofs and trees was mistily pink and
gold, turning to yellowish-green as the horizon ran
farther from the central point of the sunset. Here
and there, in the vague landscape spread out before
me, a pond or sheet of metal or window caught the
glow, while one by one the innumerable lamps—
white, orange, green and red—of the outer suburbs
filled the valley and the more distant hills with
points of light. Behind me—and as I thought of it
I turned round and walked across the ridge to the
other and more precipitous slope of the Heath—lay
the City. Somewhere in that growing darkness were
my office, the Stock Exchange, the place where I had
my midday meal—the tedious yet romantic streets
which I crossed and re-crossed, and should cross and
re-cross many times a day, spending my life—to
what essential purpose ?

It was strange how this bird's-eye view of the dark
town—for already the dying light and a rising mist
had obliterated all landmarks—made me feel as if I
were seeing not only a map of London but also a map
of my own life, with its course leading obscurely and
crazily from one event to another. I had set out on
my stroll partly to get some fresh air and partly to
think over all the little episodes of the last forty-eight
hours which had made me uneasy or curious. But
now, as I walked up and down the steep slope of the
hill, I was unable to give my mind to them. Instead
it was the larger issues of life (and death) at Beresford
Lodge which claimed an emotional attention from

me—as if I were contemplating them blurred by a lapse of years. " I used to know the Quisbergs," I could imagine myself saying a little wistfully to a friend. " They lived in a big house near Hampstead Heath—an ill-assorted family. The husband was a nervy little man, a mixture of shrewdness and gross ignorance. His wife was, even then, a very pretty woman. Now, of course. . . . And there was a daughter Amabel, egotistical and strong-minded, obviously heading for some sort of a crash. I was staying with them when the mother of the resident secretary was killed. Let me see, I think it was I who actually found the body. . . ."

It was strange, I thought, following the lead of my last imaginary sentence, how suddenly a physical event can give a twist to a whole lifetime. Suppose Dixon, that very afternoon, had struck one of the boys on the wall just a little too hard and killed him ? What a difference there would have been not only to Dixon's life, but to his mother's, if he had a mother, and to Amabel's. Take my fall during musical chairs. Had it been a little more severe, I should have spent a month with a broken wrist. Why must it be that the blessings of life—health, wealth, and friendship—are as a rule so slow and uncertain in their coming ?

I had now completed a circular zigzag walk on the south-east side of the Heath, and climbed up to the top of the ridge again. The evening was still very mild, and I sat down on one of the seats on the West Heath a little way below the crown of the hill. The whole place was deserted except for a man and

a woman who were walking away from me to the
left towards West Heath Road. All at once the man
stopped, while the woman walked on with self-
conscious steps. Then the man ran after her and
seemed to catch her by the wrist, and for the second
time that day I heard the laugh, faint, silvery and
provocative, which had echoed from the top floor of
Beresford Lodge when I was going to Mrs. Quisberg's
room. Was it the nurse ? And who was her companion ? Both the figures had seemed not unfamiliar
when first I saw them, though it was not till the little
scene began that I gave them any conscious attention. While I was wondering about them, they
paused again and then moved off the road on to the
grass, where they became vague shapes in the darkness. Then, as if in ironical accompaniment to the
lovers' quarrel (if such it was), there suddenly came
out of the depths of the black distance the sound of a
flute or a reed-pipe. The notes were exquisite in
tone, though very soft, and I was enraptured by the
surprising melody. The two figures in which I was
interested apparently heard it, too; for they walked
back to the road and stood together for a while, as if
listening. Then, with another laugh, the woman ran
straight forward down the grassy side of the hill,
while the man, irresolute as before, took a few slow
steps down the road and then suddenly gave chase.
In a moment they were both out of sight.

Was it the nurse, and who was her companion ?
I still could not be sure. The woman was not in
nurse's uniform, but no doubt a nurse off duty
would not wear one. The man was lithe and active,

and reminded me of Edwins, the footman at Beresford Lodge, whose services to me would shortly
demand a huge reward. It was quite possible that
Edwins had become infatuated with the nurse, and
that she had given him a perverse encouragement.
Yet, surely it could not have been the prospect of
meeting him which, when I saw her on the afternoon
of Christmas Day, had seemed to fill her with so
mysterious a joy.

Meanwhile, the flute or reed-pipe still played and
(as always when I hear music outside a concert hall)
my emotions responded at once. It was indeed
delightful to sit on that winter's night by the hilltop
and watch the many coloured lights twinkling across
the great valley, while such sweet music played.
For once, the feeling of suppressed apprehension,
that was hardly ever very far from my thoughts,
left me and gave place to a mood of rare and perfect
calm. No matter if such calm were but the prelude
to a storm. For once I would accept the present and
enjoy it, neither hoping nor fearing, looking neither
forwards nor backwards. If only, I thought, I could
give but a little twist to my nature how happy I
might be. If only I could take what life offered me
instead of desiring precisely that which it withheld!
If only instead of looking to yesterday or to-morrow
I could grasp the joys lying hidden in to-day!

Ah! Moon of my delight, that knowst no wane!

I even recalled Clarence's borrowed line with a
certain pleasure, and from his sonnet my mind
strayed luxuriantly over fragments of verse by more

celebrated poets, and lingered with peculiar satisfaction on the first quatrain of Donne's famous sonnet:

> At the round earth's imagined corners, blow
> Your trumpets, Angels, and arise, arise
> From death, you numberless infinities
> Of souls, and to your scattered bodies go. . . .

How enchanting poetry could be, I thought! Why did I spend so little of my time reading it and laying in a store of mental treasure?

Then the music stopped in the middle of a phrase, as suddenly as it had begun, and with contrasting sound a clock far on my left struck the first quarter of the hour. I had missed tea. The thought of my truancy from Beresford Lodge and all its vexations gave me satisfaction. It was my own life that I was living now. Why should I hurry back to those padded rooms and stifling radiators, the drawling Amabel, the swaggering Dixon, and all the petty difficulties which, when I was amongst them, seemed to claim all my forces? For another half-hour at least I would hold myself free to wander over the West Heath and find, perhaps, the musician who had given me so much pleasure.

For some distance the ground ran steeply downhill, and the worn patches of grass, where the crowds sat on summer afternoons, gleamed white in the darkness. Then, when I had passed the line of gardens that filled the narrow area between the Heath and North End Road, the slope became more gradual, and the bare expanse gave place to clumps of trees and bushes, which grew thicker and thicker till it seemed as if I were lost in a little forest. I was walking slowly, for there were many pitfalls—rabbit holes, curved roots projecting from the earth, and low branches stretching across the winding path. Here, somewhere in the thicket, the flute player must be—unless I was deceived and the sound had come from one of the heath-side gardens I had left behind on my right. What kind of man, I wondered, had made the evening lovely with his serenade? Somehow, I felt sure it was a man. Perhaps I had in the back of my mind a classical legend of some goddess who destroyed a flute and its inventor, declaring, when she saw her puffed-out cheeks reflected in a mirror, that the instrument was quite unsuited to her sex.

I was still wandering among the trees and bushes when I heard swift footfalls approaching me. The sound startled me, and I felt none too happy at the thought of meeting a stranger in that dark labyrinth. But even while I was wondering whether I had not better retrace my steps, if I could, to the more open ground, the stranger's steps came nearer and nearer, till suddenly I saw the figure of Clarence James emerging from a little clearing. When he recognized me he stood quite still, panting, and with an expression of horror on his face. Then, stretching out a shaky hand and pointing to the bushes behind him, he gasped: " There's a friend of yours down there— Dr. Green. Dead! " And before I could answer, or even absorb the full force of what he had said, he swept past me like a ghost and disappeared in the darkness.

" James! James! " I shouted, and made as if to pursue him. But the sound of his running feet grew fainter, and I felt that it was my first duty to go where he had pointed, and see if there were any truth in what he had said. Besides, if, as it seemed, he was intent to escape from me, I could never catch him on that treacherous ground.

My first act, which I still think most creditable in a person so unpractical as myself, was to tie my white silk muffler to the branch of a hawthorn bush near which I had been standing when Clarence first came upon me. This, I thought, would give me a starting point for my search in case I went too far and had to begin it again. Then I moved slowly forward, peering into the undergrowth on either side of the narrow path. It was so dark beneath the bushes that I was almost despairing of finding anything without an electric torch, when my eyes caught a silvery glint behind some brambles. Forcing my way through them, I found myself in a small clearing almost completely shut in on every side. A tree was growing in the middle, and by the tree, in sprawling attitude, was the body of Dr. Green.

No doubt the fact that Clarence had warned me of the dead man's identity helped me to recognize the body, but a gap in the close branches overhead let in sufficient light from the clear sky to remove all my doubts. " This," I thought as the horrifying implications of the event began to dawn on me, " this cannot be accident. This is either suicide or murder —that is to say, if the man is really dead."

I had no torch, no matches, and my cigarette

lighter would not work. Perhaps there was some illuminant in the doctor's clothing. I searched him with my trembling left hand, and found in a trouser pocket a box of matches, which luckily was nearly full. With some difficulty, because I had to do the striking with my left hand, I struck a light. The cause of injury seemed obvious—a wound on the right temple, which was covered with blood. I next unbuttoned the doctor's coat and shirt and felt the heart, but could detect no beat. The flesh, however, was quite warm. In my search for the matches I came across two objects which I thought I ought to take into my charge—one, a leather notecase with some loose papers inside it, and the other a heavy gold cigarette-case. These I put into the pocket of my overcoat. I then struck a few more matches and looked round. A weighted cane, which reminded me exactly of that with which Dixon had threatened the young spies on the wall, was lying a few feet from the body. The silvery glint, which I had seen first, came from the metal studs of a small flute-like instrument. I left the stick and the flute where they were, and was walking round the clearing once more before going for help, when I tripped and fell among the bushes. Luckily the ground was soft—indeed, I seemed to have alighted on a kind of mud-heap—and I picked myself up, dazed but uninjured except for a few scratches on my face and left hand. Then I lit another match and saw that I had stumbled over a piece of board, apparently fixed in the earth and projecting a few inches at one end. I was already so shocked by what I had found, that this last discovery of mine did not strike me as being anything very unusual. My one desire was now to get back to Beresford Lodge and entrust whatever had to be done to other hands.

It was fortunate that I knew that part of the Heath fairly well. Otherwise, despite the Great Bear and the Pole Star, which were shining overhead, it might have been a long time before I reached civilization. As it was, I judged that my easiest route was to push on in the direction I had been taking when I found the body, in the hope of striking either West Heath Road or the by-road at right angles to it, which separates the West Heath from the public garden known as Golders Hill Park. I emerged on this by-road in about five minutes' time and followed it to the left till it joined West Heath Road, which was brightly lit as usual. In another five minutes I reached the junction of West Heath Road and Lyon Avenue, turned to the right down the Avenue and to the right again into the drive of Beresford Lodge. I was about to ring for admittance, when the door was opened from within and I saw Dr. McKenzie, with one hand on the latch, talking to the nurse, who was standing by him in the lobby. I was still breathless with nervous shock and my hurried walk home, and, making no attempt to draw the doctor aside, I blurted out, very much in the words Clarence had used to me: " I've just found Dr. Green lying dead on the Heath." Then, as Dr. McKenzie gazed at me with a look of bewilderment not unmixed with a professional disapproval which exasperated me, I added: "What are you going to do about it? It's your affair, not mine!"

Before he had time to reply or turn round, the nurse tottered and fell heavily on the floor, and I, as if such fits were infectious, felt my own head swimming and reeled dizzily by the wall.

XII. SEARCH PARTY

Boxing Day—6.10 p.m.

THE next hour or so lives in my memory like a
nightmare. I remember leaning limply against the
wall of the lobby while Dr. McKenzie tried in vain
to find the bell—one never can find bells in halls or
passages—and finally went out on to the steps and
rang that by the front door. It was answered by
Edwins, to whom the doctor gave a multitude of
orders. Two maids soon appeared and busied themselves with the nurse, while Edwins and the doctor
piloted me upstairs to my room and put me on my
bed, where they left me. I was still so stupefied that
the passing of time meant nothing to me. I think
I really did faint at one moment, though a self-
protective instinct may have prompted me to make
the most of the attack. My one desire was to be left
undisturbed, and to have all responsibility taken
from me.

I suppose it was about seven o'clock when Dr.
McKenzie came back to my room, with two policemen whose names I never learnt. He first gave me a
kind of medicinal cocktail which certainly made me
feel better, and then told me that I must accompany
him and the two policemen to the place where I had
found the body.

" We won't bother you with any questions yet," he said. " Just take us to the place and you shall be brought back and put to bed and given your dinner. There's a good fellow."

It was not unpleasant to be treated as if I were in a state of dangerous collapse. The doctor himself escorted me downstairs and into a motor which was waiting by the front door.

" Now, sir, do your best for us, won't you ? " said one of the policemen—a superintendent, I think. " Where's the nearest point we can drive to ? "

" If you go into West Heath Road and turn to the left," I said feebly, " and then stop about three hundred yards before that other road which goes along by Golders Hill Park, I think I can take you to the place."

" Why, that's quite near ! "

" We'll have to look," I said, " for a tree with a silk muffler tied round it."

They stared at me with amazement.

" It's my muffler," I said. " I tied it to mark the place."

" Now that was really sensible of you, Mr. Warren," said the Superintendent, as we all got into the car, which was driven off by the other policeman.

" I don't mean," I continued wearily, " the place where I found the body, but the place where I began to look for it."

This remark caused another sensation. Dr. McKenzie gazed at me with apprehension, as if I were light-headed.

" Began to look for it ? " the Superintendent asked. " What made you do that, now ? "

" Come, come, Superintendent," said the doctor. " You promised me you wouldn't ask my patient any questions for at least a couple of hours."

" But, Doctor," he protested, " when it's a case of something which the whole affair may hinge on— surely you can't expect me not to clear up this one point ? "

" I was walking in the wooded part of the Heath," I said in a colourless voice, " when I met Mr. James. . . ."

Out came notebook and fountain-pen.

" Mr. James ? "

" Mr. Clarence James," put in the doctor testily. " Mrs. Quisberg's eldest son by her first husband. I can put you straight as to the family."

" Thank you, Doctor. Now, Mr. Warren, you were walking in the wooded part of the Heath when you met Mr. James. About what time was that ? "

" About half past five, I suppose. Mr. James was running. He said: ' You'll find Dr. Green's dead body down there! '—or something like that—and ran away."

" And what did you do ? "

" I couldn't catch Mr. James, so I simply started to look for the body. I tied my muffler to a tree in case I got lost."

The driver was now slowing down and looking at us for instructions. I judged that we must have gone a sufficient distance along the road, and

suggested that we should stop. We got out of
the car, and I led the way over the Heath, with
the Superintendent holding me tightly by the
left arm.

"I can't promise to take you straight to the
spot," I said, "though this is the right direction.
You see how these paths twist about among the
trees."

"All right, sir," he said with bluff reassurance,
"you take it as easy as you like. There's no use
making more haste and less speed."

Both the policemen had electric torches, and our
progress through the undergrowth was quicker
than mine had been when I had to grope my
way without a light. It was not long before
we came to the muffler hanging where I had
left it.

"This," I said, "is where I met Mr. James. I was
standing—here—and he pointed down there. If you
follow that little track and look into the bushes on
the left, you ought to find the little clearing where
the body lies."

"All right, sir. You stay here with the doctor, will
you? and we'll search. How far down the track do
you think the place is?"

"I should say not more than forty yards."

At this the two policemen went forward, flashing
their torches to the left. I could still see the beams of
light playing among the bushes, when the junior
officer shouted: "Look there, sir. . . . Why, it's a
kind of whistle!" A moment later they must have
penetrated into the clearing and found the body;

for after a short pause the junior officer came running back to us and asked the doctor to join the Superintendent.

"Certainly," said Dr. McKenzie. "I presume the Superintendent doesn't require Mr. Warren here any more."

"No, sir."

"Well, then, you must take Mr. Warren back to Beresford Lodge and put him safely into the hands of the footman. Mind, Mr. Warren, you must go to bed as soon as you arrive and have your dinner sent up to your room. I shouldn't see any member of the household if I were you, except Edwins, of course, whom I've had to take into our confidence a little. You must say, if necessary, that you're under my orders. I expect some member of the Force will have a great many questions to ask you later in the evening and you will need all your strength for that. So go to bed at once, and rest while you can. Otherwise you may have a serious breakdown."

"Serious fiddlesticks," I nearly said—not because I wasn't still feeling very much shaken, but because I resented the way in which the doctor seemed to take me for granted as a patient.

"All right, sir," said the policeman. "I'll look after Mr. Warren for you. Just let me have a word with the Superintendent first."

"Very well," the doctor answered, "I'll come with you," and, giving me a look of grave solicitude, he followed the policeman down the track. Meanwhile, I untied my muffler from the tree and put it round my neck; for a breeze was rising and I felt damp and chilly. Let them make their own landmarks, I thought. There was a faint murmur of voices in the bushes, and a continual flashing of lamps. Then my escort, the junior officer, came back, and taking my arm in imitation of his superior's action, led me out of the wood and across the open Heath to the car.

" I'm afraid all this is a bit of a strain on you, sir," he said, as he put the rug round my knees. " You'll soon feel better when you've got a cup of something nice and warm inside you."

It was strange, I thought, when we drove off, how both the policemen seemed to imagine that I had been through a physical ordeal. Perhaps they did not believe that a mental shock could produce such a bodily reaction. Or perhaps the doctor, in his self-important way, had exaggerated the slenderness of my hold on life. When we reached Beresford Lodge I noticed another policeman standing by the gate in the Avenue. Evidently the house was under surveillance. Leaving me in the car, the policeman who was driving me got out and rang the front door bell. It was answered very promptly by Edwins, who looked self-possessed, but pale. Then the policeman opened the door of the car and helped me to get out.

" Now," he said to Edwins, " you take the gentleman straight to bed, and don't let anyone come bothering him. Those are the doctor's orders—and the Superintendent's. One of us will be back before long. Meanwhile, if you're in any trouble, there's

Bill there in the road, looking after you. Good night to you—and to you, sir."

He saluted, got in the car and drove off. Edwins took my coat and hung it up in the lobby, and then went upstairs with me to my bedroom.

" I should have a stiff whisky and soda if I was you, sir," he said as he helped me off with my clothes and into bed. " Terrible goings-on they are. The master and the mistress in bed, and only Miss Amabel and Miss Sheila in. I don't know whether I oughtn't to speak to Miss Amabel."

" I should leave that to Dr. McKenzie or the police," I said. " They're in charge now, and the best we can do at this stage is to say as little as possible."

" Quite so, sir. Dinner was to have been at half past seven, though I expect Miss Amabel will put it off till Mr. Dixon comes back. But I can get you something now, sir, if you feel faint."

" I haven't any appetite at all. Just bring me something when the others have their meal. Meanwhile, I think I'll take your advice about a glass of whisky."

" Certainly, sir."

He poured one out for me, gave the fire a poke, and went out.

Peace—for how long ? As I lay back in bed, rising on my elbow from time to time to take a sip of my drink, I began first of all to take stock of my own condition rather than the events which had produced it. Was I really ill, or unstrung? Or had I been shamming? There is no doubt that, however calm I was when I found Dr. Green's body, the responsibility thrust on me by the discovery, and the further shock caused by the sudden fainting of the nurse at the horrible moment when I was imparting my news to Dr. McKenzie, produced a sensation of utter feebleness in me which had not yet worn off. "For God's sake," I would have said if I could have uttered my thoughts aloud, "leave me alone! Don't ask me any questions. Don't expect me to help you. Let me get out of this business." It was this revulsion which led me, perhaps, to make the most of my physical frailty, to let policemen take me by the arm and help me in and out of the motor without demur, to follow Dr. McKenzie's dismal lead and suppress my impulse of contrariness when he talked about the danger of my having a serious breakdown.

Yet there was another and more commendable cause for such little malingering as I practised. I was most anxious not in any way to commit myself by making any statement till I had time to think carefully over the whole problem. This may sound surprising, and I can well imagine someone, with a more direct mind than mine, reproaching me with the words, "What have you to conceal? If you tell the truth, the whole truth, and nothing but the truth, you'll be all right." But really, the situation was not so simple. I had had enough experience in the case of my aunt's death to know—even if I was not aware of it before that—that the whole truth may be told in

many ways. The disclosure of actual facts might be
harmless enough, but even in the baldest narrative
facts must be given some sort of a setting, and it was
this setting that was liable to infinite misconception.
That very afternoon I had transgressed a little,
though very pardonably. In talking to the Superintendent I had referred to " the place where I had
started to look for the body," and the use of this
unguarded phrase made it inevitable that I should
reveal my meeting with Clarence James, which put
him at once on the list of suspects. It is true that
both for my own sake and in the interests of justice—
and how much this abstract conception of justice
really weighs with me I shall never know—I should
have been bound to mention this meeting sooner or
later. But there were other matters which might or
might not be relevant. How was I to treat them ?
Should I declare, for example, that the woman I had
seen on the Heath reminded me, at least when I
heard her laugh, of the nurse ? Should I say, on
slenderer grounds still, that the man resembled
Edwins ? As to this, I made up my mind at once. I
was quite unjustified in mentioning Edwins at all.
Most probably I should find that he had been on
duty all the afternoon. He was at Beresford
Lodge, in his uniform, when I returned. So, for
that matter, was the nurse. But the nurse had
fainted. Besides, there was that characteristic
laugh. And what of the weighted stick which I
had seen near the body ? Should I say that I
had seen Dixon carrying a similar stick that very
afternoon when he set out on his walk with the

murdered man ? If I were asked, yes. But if I were not asked ?

" Your duty," my imaginary monitor will say, " is to tell the police everything you think relevant." I was not—and still am not—so sure. There is, to my mind, no guarantee that suspicion will not fall upon the innocent, and even if the truth triumphs in the end, the unfortunate suspect may have to suffer great misery in the meanwhile. Besides, there is always the risk that by indiscriminate probing one will drag to light some secret which were better unrevealed. Most of us have our secrets. Suppose, for example, I told the police that Dixon and Amabel had come in very late on the night of Christmas Day, it might easily come out that their friendship was unpardonably close. Such a dis-closure might do them and their relations incal-culable harm.

But even granting that my duty is to practise no discretion or reticence at all, how should I know, how should the police know, what is relevant and what is not ? In order to acquaint them with all the facts in my possession, should I not have to go back to the death of Mrs. Harley—even farther, perhaps, to my very arrival at Beresford Lodge on Christmas Eve, telling them in detail my whole story up to date in a dozen chapters ? Indeed it might well be that in some of the dullest passages of my narrative—accounts of my rising and my going to bed, my move-ments about the house, the openings and shuttings of doors—the most important clues would be contained.

My ideas on this subject—my duty to the police and my duty to the innocent—were no doubt the result of instinctive feeling rather than of any rational process. In as far as I came to any decision, it was to speak the truth, to answer " Yes " or " No " with as little embroidery as possible. My experience, however, had taught me that " Yes " or " No " did not always satisfy the questioner.

I remembered the Superintendent with whom I had had dealings after the death of my Aunt Catherine. I know I quickly rubbed him up the wrong way, but the fault was largely his for exasperating me by his continued scepticism as to the facts.

" What! " he or one of his kidney might have said. " You saw Mr. A. give his nephew a pound ? " " Yes." " Did it not strike you as very strange that he should make so large a gift to such a small boy ? " " No." " Yet Mr. A. is not at all well off ? " " No." " While the boy's parents are known to be very rich ? " " Yes." " Are you sure, then, that it was a pound note which passed between uncle and nephew? Might it not have been a cigarette picture ? " And so on.

This is an imaginary conversation, but it illustrates the kind of interrogation which the " Yes " or " No " system of answering produces. It also illustrates the psychological narrowness with which I had had to contend, as exemplified by the questioner's inability to believe that a poor uncle would give a rich nephew a pound note. What kind of a man would my questioner prove to be in this instance, I wondered ? The Superintendent whom I had taken to the body on the Heath was quite a pleasant fellow, but it would not be easy to steer him through the cross-currents at Beresford Lodge. If only I were able to consult someone first, both for my own guidance and for my peace of mind! If only Dr. Green were still living and able to come to my aid! And now for the first time since my discovery, I thought of him not as a corpse, but as a man, as a friend whom I had lost. Who was there now, in that household, to whom I could turn in my distress ? Who else would massage my wrist with such gentleness and sureness ? With these selfish regrets were mingled others of a more generous nature. I had only known him for forty-eight hours, but his strange and lively personality, the intuitive sympathy which underlay his rudest remarks, had even in that short time made it seem unbearable that he should be taken from us, without a word of warning or farewell. I shut my eyes as I thought of him to keep back my tears, and a feeling of such wretchedness came over me that when Edwins brought me up my dinner I could hardly touch it, and pushed the tray aside after swallowing a few mouthfuls.

A few minutes after I had abandoned my dinner, there was a knock at the door and to my great surprise Amabel came in. She was pale and most agitated.

" You must excuse this intrusion, Malcolm," she

said, assuming her drawl to begin with. " I haven't come to vamp you. . . ."

" No, do stay," I said, " though both the police and Dr. McKenzie said I wasn't to see anyone yet."

She sat down nervously, and continued, in her normal voice.

" I simply don't know what to do. I've seen Dr. McKenzie, and he told me about your finding Dr. Green's body. What's bothering me is Leonard. He went out with Dr. Green, you know, and he hasn't come back yet. Do you think we shall have to tell the police that they went out together ? Are you going to tell them ? "

" I shall have to, if they ask me. So will you. There's no use concealing that kind of thing from them. They'd be sure to find it out. Besides, there's nothing in it, of course."

She played nervously with her handkerchief.

" Of course not, only . . ."

" If you're worried about Leonard," I said, " the best thing you can do is to tell the police at once. Meanwhile, you and Sheila must have something to eat."

" Sheila's having something. I'm not hungry."

" Then there's Clarence," I said, unguardedly perhaps. " Has he come in yet ? "

" No. Why ? "

" Well, I saw him," I said gently but ambiguously, " just before I found the body."

" Oh Lord ! Malcolm, you're not suggesting that . . . ? "

" No, no. But I think you've just as much cause
to worry about him as about Leonard."

" I see."

She seemed, on the whole, somewhat relieved by
this thought.

" Now what about your mother, Amabel ? How
is she, first ? "

" I heard she was better after tea. I haven't been
to see her since I saw Dr. McKenzie."

" Then I think you ought to go and see her.
Remember, she's got to break the news to Mr.
Quisberg. It would be far better if she did than if
Dr. McKenzie did."

" Yes. I'm afraid Daddy will feel it dreadfully.
It'll break him up completely. Malcolm, you've
been in a murder case before. Is it very awful ? Do
they ferret everything out ? "

" That's the trouble," I said. " They do. And if
you try to hide anything it's all the worse when they
get to know. I was made to look very small myself
after Aunt Catherine died."

" Life isn't going to be exactly gay, then, for the
next few days."

" No, it isn't—for any of us. Do you know, I've
somehow felt this coming on—ever since Mrs.
Harley died! "

It was a piece of frankness on my part difficult to
account for, but it seemed to win her sympathy.

" Then I've been very blind," she said, " and so
wrapped up in—my own affairs. I know what you
mean, though. I wonder. . . ."

At this point, I felt that the sharing of such

conjectures was altogether too intimate. Besides, I heard steps in the passage.

" Well, I really think you'd better go and see your mother. If the police hear we've been talking together, they may get some silly ideas in their heads. That's the thing to avoid if we can."

" Good night, Malcolm. And thank you. . . ."

She went out just as Edwins came in to take my tray away. Well, if he reported that we had been conferring together, it couldn't be helped. There were worse secrets than that, probably, which would have to be revealed.

When Edwins had gone, I lay down and went over my old thoughts again, adding one new one to them —was Mrs. Harley's death an accident ? I had no real grounds at all for thinking that it was not, except that the occurrence of two violent deaths, the second one being manifestly a murder, in the same household within forty-eight hours, was a startling coincidence. What really perplexed me, however, and had perplexed me the whole time, was the strained atmosphere at Beresford Lodge. This I had noticed almost as soon as I arrived on Christmas Eve. Had I not seen Quisberg and Dr. Green talking together with more than ordinary intentness as my taxi turned into the drive ? And the dinner party on Christmas Eve, even making full allowance for the incompatibility of the guests, had hardly been a normal meal. No, the whole time I had been aware of what I have called " undercurrents," swirling round us and hiding heaven only knew what perilous rocks below. I had been " jumpy " and " on edge " during the visit, not only because I found the party, as a whole, uncongenial to me, but because—and here I was beginning laboriously to re-examine all the " sore places " in my mind, when the door opened and Edwins announced Detective-Inspector Parris of Scotland Yard.

XIII. QUESTION AND ANSWER

Boxing Day—9.15 p.m.

INSPECTOR PARRIS was a tall and very good-looking man of about forty. Had he been a little thinner, he might have been a male film star. He had thick, rather greasy, light brown hair, large blue eyes, a strong though slightly snub nose, and a large but not unpleasant mouth and jaw. He came straight to my bed and held out his hand.

" Mr. Warren, I'm more than sorry to have to bother you at such a time. But no doubt you were expecting one of us. Of course, if you feel really too done up, I'll put off my talk with you till to-morrow, though naturally——"

" Not at all," I said, as he shrugged his shoulders elegantly. " I'm better now, though still a bit feeble, and shall be very glad to get this over to-night. I shall sleep better."

" I expect you will," he said sympathetically. " May I sit down ? "

" Of course, and won't you have a drink ? "

" Not yet, thank you very much. Later, perhaps."

He sat down in an armchair near the fire, drawing it up at an angle, as if to avoid confronting me too directly, and went on:

" Well, Mr. Warren, before I begin to ask you all

my wearisome questions, I want to make a little speech myself. In the first place I know all about you. Oh, you needn't blush. I mean, I know all about the sad experience you had when your aunt, Mrs. Cartwright, died. As a matter of fact, the papers relating to that case were sent up to us for perusal, and I had to make a report on them. I want to tell you, too, how much I sympathize with you for being involved in another such affair—though, happily, this case cannot cause you the same personal distress."

Looking up and seeing that I was smoking, he lit a cigarette, and continued.

"What I'm getting at is this. (I'm saying things I shouldn't, perhaps, but I rely on you.) In your poor aunt's case, your relations with the police were a little unfortunate. You found yourself, through no fault of your own, on the other side. No doubt they antagonized you quite unnecessarily. Their handling of the trouble was not all it should have been. Of course, our provincial police are excellent fellows—it was in the Midlands, I think?"

"Yes, at Macebury."

"Oh, yes, of course! As I was going to say, their methods are very rough and ready. They're quite hopeless, many of them, when it comes to dealing with—shall we say?—men and women of the world. After all, poor fellows, they don't get much experience of crime amongst the—er—well-to-do classes. So, you see, I'm going to ask you, if you can, to wash out all your preconceived notions of us, and to give me a fair chance. Don't let my questions, when they come, upset you or prejudice you against me. I'm quite human—as a matter of fact, I was once a theological student, but circumstances made me give up the Church—and I'm doing this, often odious, task, for my living. You taxpayers are paying for me. We are not—I certainly am not—in any way vindictive. No doubt I shall unearth many secrets, but I will treat them with all respect. I may also—in my blundering way—offend many susceptibilities. For this I ask your forgiveness in advance. So do, please, try to think of me neither as an enemy nor a busybody, but as a friend. Give me, as far as you can, your full confidence, and, as far as I can, I on my side will give you mine, and, if it interests you, will let you in a little farther ' behind the scenes ' than is perhaps quite usual—to make amends for our *gaucherie* on a previous occasion."

He put his head on one side and smiled at me.

" You certainly are," I said, " a great improvement on Superintendent Glaize." (This was the officer who had investigated my aunt's death.)

" Thank you. I rather thought I was. Well, now we'd better begin. Do we need this bright centre light ? That's better, isn't it ? Now you lie down comfortably and tell me all about things. Imagine you're being psycho-analysed, if you like, and look the other way. I believe psycho-analysts usually talk to their patients in the dark so as to spare the blushes on both sides. I had a psycho-analytical case once—but I must tell you about that some other day. We'll start first, please, with the chain of events immediately leading up to your discovery. You were taking a walk on the Heath, I gather ? Were you alone ? ''

" Yes. I had finished my walk and was sitting on a seat about fifty or sixty yards below the hilltop when I suddenly heard the sound of a wind instrument coming from the dark space below me."

" Why do you mention the wind instrument ? Don't be alarmed. I'm only trying clumsily to deduce how your mind works."

" I mention it," I said drily, " partly because it seems to me somehow to be a link in the chain of events you talked about just now, and partly because it made a great impression on me. The sound, in such a setting, really was most beautiful— and moving."

" I quite understand."

" When the music stopped, which it did quite suddenly, in the middle of a phrase, I had an impulse to look for the musician. By the way, a clock struck a quarter past five the moment the music had finished."

" I wonder why you noticed that."

" Partly through the contrast of sound, I suppose, and partly because I had dared to be late for tea here. I started to go down the slope by the extreme right-hand edge of that part of the Heath. Do you know it ? There are a number of gardens backing directly on to the Heath. The houses are all called Heath Brow, Heath View, Heathlands, or Heath something. The entrances are, I suppose, in North End Road—a road which meets the Finchley Road at Golders Green."

" I know it."

" I followed the line of these gardens for a time, and then struck out to the left into the middle of the wooded patch. You know there is a big undulating stretch, covered with trees, mostly thorn and silver birch, and overgrown with clumps of gorse, brambles and bracken. I wandered in this thicket for some time, bearing on the whole to the left and still downhill, when all at once I heard footsteps—running steps—quite close to me. Then someone came running towards me, and I recognized Mrs. Quisberg's son, Clarence James."

Inspector Parris drew a piece of paper from his pocket and studied it.

" Clarence James. The son by her first husband ? "

" Yes. He seemed quite distracted and said: ' You'll find a friend of yours down there. Dr. Green. Dead! ' and pointed down a track between the bushes. I shouted to him, but he hurried off, and I thought I ought to disregard him and look for Dr. Green, in case there was anything to be done."

" Most wise."

" Then I tied my silk muffler to a tree, in case I got lost, and began the search. You have probably heard the rest of my story from your superintendent. Would you like me to go on ? "

" I'll take you through it with questions, if I may. How did you find the little clearing where the body lay ? It was pitch dark, wasn't it ? "

" The sun had set, of course, but the sky was extraordinarily clear and light. If it hadn't been, I should never have recognized Clarence James. It was an intermittent darkness. Under some of those thick thorn trees, and among the bushes, one could see practically nothing, but whenever there was an opening in the vegetation, the darkness was by no means complete. As a matter of fact, I think there must have been a moon, though I don't remember noticing it."

" Yes, there was."

" Before I found the body I saw something glittering on the ground, and finding that the glitter came from a wind instrument—I don't know if I'm entitled to say *the* wind instrument, meaning the one I heard played . . ."

" Nor do I, yet. But I think probably you are."

" . . . I wormed my way into the clearing and discovered the body. I searched it for a light and found a box of matches. Oh, I had quite forgotten! I also found a notecase and a gold cigarette-case, which I thought I had better remove."

" That was a little naughty. No, perhaps it wasn't. Where are they ? "

" I'm ashamed to say they're still in the pockets of my overcoat, which is hanging in the lobby down-stairs. Would you like me to ring for it ? "

" I'll get it myself now. No, it's no trouble. I want in any case to have a word with one of my men. Perhaps you'll be so kind as to pour me out a drink, will you—a weak one—and, I hope, one for your-self ? "

He left the room and I did as he suggested. On the whole I was not dissatisfied with the interview as far as it had gone. The Inspector was a most

agreeable man. Film star, shopwalker or clergyman
—which became him best? I was beginning
fatuously to compliment myself on the way I had
played up to him, when he returned and handed me
my coat.

" Perhaps you'll be kind enough to give me the
two articles now," he said, " before we forget."

' Shopwalker,' I thought, and, fumbling in the
two outside pockets, produced from one of them the
notecase and from the other the cigarette-case. He
studied the latter for a few moments.

" A fine piece of work. Feel the weight of it," he
said. " Price—about eighty pounds, Bond Street,
and would cost nearly thirty to make. And there's
an inscription, too. ' M.G. from A.Q. Dec. 1922.'
Is A.Q. Mr. Quisberg, I wonder ? "

" Probably. His name is Axel."

" They've been friends for some years, evidently.
Well, we must resume, as they say. (I don't quite
know where they say it, but no matter.) You
searched the body and found a box of matches.
Were you sure that you were dealing with a dead
man, or did you just go by what Clarence James had
told you ? "

He put the cigarette-case and the notecase in his
coat pocket, took his glass of whisky and sat down.

" I felt for the heart underneath the shirt," I said,
" and couldn't feel any movement. And I saw the
wound on the side of the head which had stopped
bleeding. I gather from the detective stories I have
read that bodies don't bleed after death. I haven't
any medical knowledge, of course."

"Oh, detective stories have their uses. Most people rely on them for practical hints when they come into contact with crime—and crimes themselves tend to imitate the detective story. It's another case of Nature imitating Art. . . . And when you'd satisfied yourself that Dr. Green was dead, what did you do ? "

"I set off for Beresford Lodge as quickly as I could, struck the ride at the end of the Heath and followed it till I came to West Heath Road. Then I found Dr. McKenzie talking to the nurse by the front door, told him my news, and more or less collapsed."

"Yes. . . . Suppose Dr. McKenzie hadn't been here, whom would you have told ? "

"That's a hard question. I suppose I ought to have told Mr. Quisberg, but as far as I knew he was in bed. I think I should have told Miss Thurston— that's Mrs. Quisberg's eldest daughter by her second husband—and telephoned myself to the police station. Or if I'd been feeling too ill myself, I might have tried to get Dr. McKenzie on the telephone."

"Thank you. Just let me think for a moment. Oh, there are three things connected with what we may call the scene of the crime that I should like to ask you about. First, the wind instrument that first caught your eye. Did you pick it up ? "

"Yes, but I put it down again almost exactly where I found it."

"How far was that from the body ? "

"Say six or seven feet."

" Was Dr. Green a musician ? "

" Not to my knowledge. I never heard him play any instrument. I heard him whistling once."

" Any special air ? "

" No—a kind of coloratura passage not unlike flute-music. He was a man, I should say, of many varied accomplishments."

" Yes, we'll return to him later. Second point—did you notice a cane—a kind of life-preserver—in the clearing ? "

" Yes."

" Had you seen it, or one like it, before—I mean, since your visit here ? "

" Yes. There was one in the umbrella stand in the lobby here."

" Do you know whose it was ? "

" I think it was Leonard Dixon's. He's Miss Thurston's friend, you know."

The Inspector consulted his paper again.

" Are they engaged ? "

" Not officially, but I think they would like to be."

" Did you ever see Dixon using such a stick ? "

" Yes. He took it with him when he drove away some youths who had climbed on to the wall separating this garden from Paragon House, the property behind. He even referred to the stick as his, before he went out to chase them."

" When you came back after finding the body and had your little scene with Dr. McKenzie in the lobby, did you notice if the stick was in the umbrella stand ? "

" No. I was much too upset."

"Of course. Now the third point. Did you happen to notice a hole in the clearing, with a plank projecting from it?"

"Yes. I tripped over the plank and fell into the bushes."

"Did you examine the hole at all?"

"No. Was there anything odd about it?"

He looked at me for a moment and smiled.

"It was a very big hole, and there was a spade inside it. The earth had evidently been newly dug. There, I've been most unprofessional. Let's hurry to another subject. When did you last see Dr. Green—before you found his body?"

"I saw him from the window of this room shortly before three this afternoon. He was going for a walk."

"Was he alone?"

"No. Dixon was with him."

"Was Dixon carrying his stick?"

"Yes."

"Was Dr. Green carrying anything?"

"No. He had, as far as I remember, his hands in his overcoat pockets."

"What was the relationship between Dr. Green and Dixon?"

"Do you mean blood relationship?"

"No. By the way, that's a possibility that hadn't struck me. No, I mean were they friendly? Did they see much of one another? How did they get on?"

"I shouldn't have said they had any relationship. I don't think Dr. Green cared for Dixon at all. He hardly ever troubled to speak to him. It was a great surprise to me when, shortly after luncheon, just as Dixon was launching his attack on the youths on the wall, the butler came in and said that Dr. Green wanted Dixon on the telephone."

" Who answered the call ? "

" Miss Thurston. She was using the telephone when I came upstairs to pay my respects to Mrs. Quisberg and have a doze before going out."

" What time, roughly, was this telephone call announced ? "

" Soon after two. We were in the dining-room."

The Inspector took out a notebook and a pencil.

" Now," he said, " let's see what kind of a time-table we can construct. How does this do for a beginning ?

Telephone-call for Dixon ..	2–2.15 p.m.
Dr. Green and Dixon start for their walk	2.45–3 p.m.
Music heard on the Heath..	5–5.15 p.m.
Music stops	5.15 p.m. precisely.

Warren meets Clarence James in wooded part of the Heath—what time do you think that was ? This really may be important, though I don't suppose you'll be able to help me much. No more convenient clocks striking ? "

" I'm afraid not. Now, let me think. I didn't go down the slope to search for the flute player immediately the music stopped. I was in meditative mood. Say I was five minutes before stirring. That takes us to 5.20. Then there's my walk down the side of the Heath, past the gardens. I wasn't hurrying. Still, it was very much downhill, and there was no difficulty in seeing one's way. Say three minutes— 5.23. Then there's my walk through the dark and wooded part. I may easily have been ten minutes over that."

" Could you have been fifteen ? "

" I hardly think so."

" Well, then, if we say that this rather vague stage of your journey took not less than eight and not more than fifteen minutes, you must have met Clarence James between 5.31 and 5.38. I shall put down 5.35 in my time-table. It can't be far wrong. Now at what time do you suppose you found the body ? "

" Within five minutes of my meeting with James."

" 5.40, then. And your arrival at this house ? "

" About 6.10, I should say. It's only a ten minutes' walk from here to the point where I struck the ride. I dare say I was about eight minutes finding the ride."

" That's to say, you were probably in the immediate neighbourhood of the body between 5.40 and 5.52—twelve minutes. However, I don't think that's very important. What I should like to fix, of course, is the interval between the cessation of the music and your meeting with James. We've done our best, but we can't get it closer than from sixteen to twenty-three minutes. Well, much can happen in twenty minutes."

He paused reflectively and took a drink.

" Now," he said at length, " for a few isolated questions. Don't ask me why I ask them, because

I'm not sure if I know. Number One: What do you really know of Quisberg ? "

" Nothing—except that he's Mrs. Quisberg's husband and a good client of my firm's. I know, as a matter of fact, some details of a rather ambitious financial transaction in which he is involved. Do you want to hear them ? "

" Not at present, thank you. Is it, however, a life-and-death matter ? If this transaction went wrong, would it ruin him ? "

" Oh, far from it. At least, I don't think so. I even doubt whether it would make any serious difference to his way of living. My firm is a very cautious one, and before we began to act for him we naturally took up references and so on. They were entirely satisfactory, and all the time he has been our client he has never caused us the slightest uneasiness. I have often felt that his operations are more a hobby than a necessity."

" And Clarence James ? "

" He's the awkward one of the family. I suppose he takes after his father, he's so different from the other children. He doesn't fit in with this household at all."

" Do you like him ? "

" Yes and no. I should like him better if he liked me better. He's much involved with what I believe is called a very highbrow circle. I've been in and out of the fringe of it myself. The fact that I came to this house as a friend of his mother's made him regard me at once as a person of no interest. Besides, being a stockbroker is not a passport to the world of art and letters—unless you are a potential buyer of pictures."

" He's intolerant, I suppose ? "

" Very, of the things most people tolerate. I dare say in other ways he might shock us by his broad-mindedness."

" Free love, and so on ? "

" Oh, I expect so. He's also extremely sensitive and highly strung. His mood changes from hour to hour."

" I wonder if you could give me a kind of tempera-ture chart of these moods of his ? Not now, but when I've ceased to torment you, perhaps you would think over his behaviour during this Christmas gathering and jot down for me the periods of his different moods."

" That's rather a responsibility, isn't it ? "

" Not too great for you, I think. You're so clearly a person of perception. And now disjointed question Number Three. This may startle you. Do you, or do you not, think there is any connection between the death of Dr. Green and the death of Mrs. Harley ? "

He smiled half at me and half to himself and lit a cigarette. For a time words failed me. His question had so suddenly probed a sore place in my mind from which I had been suffering long before the death of Dr. Green. To suppose any connection between the two deaths could only imply that Mrs. Harley's death was not an accident. But what grounds had I for thinking that it was not ? As in my previous meditations, I did all I could to curb the melodramatic instinct which raised a doubt over such a point. Mrs. Harley's death was so easily explained by natural causes. Why should I have been disquieted about it? I could think of two reasons only. My first was that, ever since my aunt's death, I had been prone to regard all apparent accidents in a sinister light, just as the valetudinarian regards every stomach-ache as an attack of appendicitis, every cough as the onset of consumption. My second reason, the more legitimate of the two, was the atmosphere of suppressed turmoil which had prevailed at Beresford Lodge since my arrival. How was I to reply?

" I have no grounds—no real grounds," I began.

" None the less," he said, interrupting me, " you have considered the possibility?"

" Yes, in a sense. If two people caught measles within a few hours of each other you would say that the source of infection was the same."

" But did you diagnose the first as a case of measles before the second case occurred?"

He was clearly pleased at the use he had made of my simile, and looked at me almost as if hoping for applause.

" Not exactly as measles," I answered. " As German measles, perhaps!"

At this point any further attempt at repartee was prevented by Edwins, who came in to say that a constable wished urgently to have a word with the Inspector.

" That means good night, I fear," he said when Edwins had gone out. " It has been, as far as I'm concerned, a most pleasant conversation. I wish I could think that all the interviews I'm going to have will be so lucid and harmonious. I should like to see you to-morrow morning if I may. Will you breakfast in bed ? "

" Yes, I think I shall."

" Then I'll visit you again at half past nine, here, if that's not too early. One irksome little piece of routine. I have to ask all of you not to leave the house or garden without permission from the constable at the gate."

" And what about taking my finger-prints ? "

He laughed loudly and put out his hand.

" Oh, if I wanted those I should take them without your knowing it. Quite a technique has been developed for that. Now, good night. You don't want to see the doctor—I mean, Dr. McKenzie— again, do you ? "

" Not in the least."

" I thought not. I told him I'd let him know if he was needed. Good night again, and I do hope you'll sleep well."

He gave me another smile, and a little bow, went out and shut the door.

XIV. NOCTURNE

Boxing Day—10 p.m.

THEN began a long and painful night. My " interrogation " was over—at least, the first instalment was
—but there were many things I had not confessed to
the Inspector. I had made no mention of the two
figures on the Heath, Dr. Green's errand to the
purlieus of Baker Street that morning, Mr. Quisberg's interview with the stranger on the evening of
Christmas Day, his fainting fit when he heard the
news of Mrs. Harley's death, and his agitated
conversation with Dr. Green at the moment of my
arrival on Christmas Eve, which now seemed to have
been a sinister prelude to the whole of my miserable
visit. No doubt, in due time these things would be
revealed, but I trembled for the manner and the
consequences of their revelation.

Meanwhile, there was nothing to be done, except
to sleep. But this was not easy. I turned out my
light and tried desperately to calm myself. Busy
thoughts raced round my head incessantly, while my
heart beat an excited accompaniment. In vain I
counted sheep, imagined myself carried over a
mountain landscape in a sedan-chair, played an
imaginary harmonium, and recited to myself fragments of poetry—among which I remember the

following couplet echoing for a long time in my
mind:

> Alma quies, optata, veni! Nam sic sine vita
>   Vivere, quam suave est, sic sine morte mori!

and my attempt to translate it into English:

> Come, kindly sleep! How sweet thy mystery—
> Lifeless to live, and deathlessly to die!

Needless to say, I was far from satisfied with my
version, and strove so hard to mould it into better
shape that I became even more wakeful than before.
" This is too awful," I thought. " Even if I am
destined not to sleep at all to-night, I shall survive
somehow. Enough of this! "

I sat up in bed and turned on the light. A quarter
to twelve. What should I do ? Then I remembered
that the Inspector had asked me to jot down the
varying moods of Clarence James, and to make, if I
could, a chart of his emotional temperature. The
task was less wretched than my undirected reverie,
and it was with some relief that I took a pencil and
piece of paper from the table beside my bed, and
made these notes:—

> *Christmas Eve*. C. J. at dinner. Bored with the
> party. Deliberately irritating to Miss Thurston.
> Played bridge as if to oblige, but not entirely without
> pleasure.
> *Christmas Day*. Comes in shortly before luncheon
> radiant from a long walk on the Heath. Full of noble
> sentiments and altruism. Almost the little friend of
> all the world. Disappears after luncheon and not
> home for dinner.

Boxing Day. Tragic in the morning. (" With a face like a dry toadstool "—Dr. G.) Bored and miserable when I talk to him by the rock-garden. Unbends a little towards the end. Says he has a special reason for not wanting to leave the house that morning. Harmless at luncheon, but expresses disgust with Dixon's brutal attitude towards the boys on the wall. Disappears. Next seen by me, tragic again and scared, on the Heath. Directs me vaguely to the body and runs away. Not seen by me since then.

Once more I turned out the light and lay down. My nerves were less on edge, but sleep was still far away. Had I, perhaps, yielded a little too readily to the Inspector's blandishments ? Was it quite fair of me to make so free with the spiritual vagaries of Clarence James ? At least, I had suppressed all mention of the poem, which seemed to be a sore point with him. The poem could not possibly be relevant. Or was it ? . . .

Oh, for sleep and peace from these worries ! Had the nightmare no end ? Would the day ever come when I could (as in my imagination on the Heath that very afternoon) refer to the whole tangle in the past tense ? Why could I not be a passive spectator, like George the butler, or Edwins. Edwins ! Had I really seen him on the Heath that afternoon ? Was it my duty to drag him in, too ? How could I bear to see him bringing up my breakfast, if it was I who gathered him into the net ?

' I am being carried in a sedan-chair,' I thought, ' over the mountains of Thibet. Enormous peaks of bluish-white snow are towering above me. Here is one, and there, on the left, cut in half by a cotton-wool cloud, is another. There is a sound of water rushing downward over the rocks. The torrent strikes the stones on the mountain side and the air is filled with a fresh, bubbling spray. Up in the air, almost as high as the highest peak, is a hawk. It has seen a brightly coloured bird hopping among the primulas in the valley ten miles below. It swoops, falling and falling, one mile, then another mile, with the cold air whistling between its outer feathers. . . .'

There was a muffled knock on my door, and almost before I was roused from the dream in which I was at last losing myself, the door opened and shut, and a husky voice beside me said: " It's Dixon. I've got to have a talk with you."

I switched on the light. He was standing beside me, with a cut on his cheek and a black eye, scared, pale and enormous.

" Sit down, then," I said resentfully. " When did you come in ? "

" About two hours ago. I've just been put through it by that Inspector bloke."

" I hope you made yourself pleasant."

He looked at me angrily, then no doubt realizing that he must be conciliatory, sat down in the chair by the fire and began to talk. At first, with incredible perversity, I felt so sleepy that I hardly listened to what he was saying. I remember phrases such as " pulling together," " all in the same boat," " rotten affair," " sake of Amabel," " sake of ' Mrs. Q.,' "

" sake of the family," appearing and reappearing in his monologue, till finally I interrupted him impatiently with the words:

" Look here, what exactly can I do for you ? "

Again he repressed a movement of hostility.

" Well, in the first place," he said, " you might ask me how I got my face in such a mess."

" I was wondering."

" That was thanks to those damned hooligans on the wall this afternoon. There were about twenty of them. One hit me in the eye with a stone from his catapult. Of course, they'd no idea of fighting fair. Oh, I got rid of them all right, though it took me some time. Then I came back to the house and found that Green had rung up for me, asking me if I'd be ready to go for a walk with him when he got back here. He was telephoning from somewhere near Marble Arch, Amabel said—she took the message. I thought this a bit queer. However, he said it was urgent and all that sort of thing, and I hung about downstairs till he came back, which was about three, when we started our walk together."

" Which way did you go ? "

" Over the Heath. Not the part near here, but the other side, more in the Highgate direction—along Spaniards Road, you know, and down to the right. Well, I oughtn't to tell you what we were talking about, but I suppose I've got to. It seems that the doctor had got up some kind of a syndicate that was interested in tea-planting. You know, I did a bit in Ceylon a couple of years ago. He began by asking me a lot of questions about my work and the

fellows I was working with, and I'm afraid I told
him things I oughtn't to have—details of costs and
profits and so on, which I shouldn't have given
away, because the other fellows are still out there
working the estate and I hadn't really any right to
give the game away like that. Of course, he's no
fool, and I didn't see what he was up to. Well, we
sat down on a seat, and he took down everything I
told him on a piece of paper and put it in his notecase. Then he went on asking me for more details,
figures and so on, that I couldn't remember offhand.
So I told him I had a pal in Finchley who used to
work with me, except that he was more on the
clerical side, and that this fellow would be much
more use to him than I was. Then he asked me if I
would go at once and see this friend and bring back
some special information to-night. He gave me half
a promise that he would let us in this syndicate of
his, and promised to pay us both well in any case.
Well, we've none of us got too much of this world's
goods, have we, and in any case I knew my friend—
his name is Charlesworth—was in pretty low water.
So I thought it would be a decent thing to do, to
give him the chance of making a bit, and agreed
with the doctor to go and visit him there and then.
After all, it isn't so far from Highgate to Finchley.
The doctor was awfully bucked at the idea, and
promised to tell Amabel where I'd gone, when he
got back, in case I was late. I hadn't seen Charlesworth for some time, and I thought it might mean
staying to supper with him. Some fellows are rather
touchy, you know, about things like that. So off I

went. Oh, one rather queer thing happened when I left the doc. He asked me to lend him my stick. He said he was going to walk back right round the Heath, and didn't care to be out there after dark without a stick. Evidently the old fellow was a bit jumpy, and as I didn't want the damned thing I said he was welcome to it."

" What time was that ? " I asked.

" Fourish. By the way, the doc. said at the beginning of our talk that it was to be absolutely confidential. He made me promise not to let on to old Q., who, it seems, doesn't take to tea as readily as he takes to cobalt, and wouldn't have anything to do with the doc.'s syndicate. Well, I gave the doc. my stick and went off to Finchley. It took me some time, as I went to the wrong part first. Finchley's a huge place, you know, and the Charlesworths live right at the north end. I found quite a beano going on—Bobby Charlesworth, my pal, his mother, and two cousins and an aunt. Of course, they asked me to stay to supper, and I had to, as otherwise I shouldn't have been able to get my pal alone. We had a bit of a talk afterwards, but he didn't take it quite as I expected. In fact, he got quite ratty, and said I'd no business to give the firm's secrets away without making sure what use the information would be put to. He suggested he should see Green himself and find out how the land lay. I felt rather nettled at first, specially as I'd hoped to do Charlesworth a good turn, but in the end I'm bound to say I saw he was right and wished I hadn't spoken so freely myself. So I said I'd fix things up, and got back here about two hours ago—finding all this business going on, with a policeman on sentry-go by the gate."

He paused, and as I looked at him, with his black eye and strong hands which he kept clenching and unclenching, I felt somewhat uneasy. Suppose he really were the murderer of Dr. Green and Mrs. Harley! At all costs I must not show any suspicion of him, still less any timidity in his presence. The bell-switch was hanging near my pillow. I could ring for help if the worst came to the worst. But why should it—unless the fellow were a homicidal maniac? He looked so repulsive in his nervous state that I almost thought he might be.

" Well," I asked, " what's really worrying you? The stick? "

" Oh, no," he said, " though it's a beastly nuisance."

" I suppose," I said unwisely, " you can get your friend Charlesworth to come and support your story? "

" You suppose so, do you! " he replied angrily. " What does that mean? You think I'm a liar, do you, and have made the whole business up? I'd have you know I'm not used to being called a liar! "

" For God's sake be sensible! " I said. " I'm only trying to help you—if you want help. I don't really know why you've told me all this yet. I'm very tired and not at all at my brightest. I wish you'd get to the point."

" Sorry, Warren. I suppose I'm a bit upset too.

This is the point. I'm worried about those notes the doctor made when I was talking to him on the Heath —all the figures he jotted down and certain names and so on. I see now I was a B.F. to gas away like that. He folded up the paper and put it in the note-case. What I want to do is to get hold of the paper —nothing else, mind—before any harm's done. The Inspector was as close as an oyster with me. He got me talking all right, but he wasn't giving anything away. Now, you've been a bit behind the scenes. Did you see or hear anything of the notecase ? "

" Yes, I did. When I left the body on the Heath I took the notecase with me, for fear it should be stolen. I gave it to the Inspector afterwards."

" Damn! If I'd only reached home sooner instead of jawing away to Ma Charlesworth I'd have got it by now! "

I felt somewhat annoyed by his assumption that it would have been quite easy to make me part with the paper. However, nothing was to be gained by showing my resentment.

" I suppose," I said with docility, " you didn't mention the notecase to the Inspector ? "

" Of course I didn't, directly, but I led him up to the subject rather smartly I thought."

(" You poor boob! " I said to myself).

" I asked him," he went on, " whether robbery could have been the motive, and he said he couldn't say, but that it rather looked, when the police found the body, as if the pockets had been gone through. The old devil! And you'd given him back the note-case the whole time! "

" There may have been other things missing apart from the notecase," I said. " A watch and chain, perhaps, or loose money."

"Anyhow," he answered savagely, " I'm in a rotten hole if the Inspector's got the notecase."

" Come, come," I said, in rather an unnatural voice, I fear, " things aren't so bad as all that. You haven't done anything so very dreadful. We all become a little unguarded sometimes. I dare say once or twice I've let out things about my clients' investments that I ought to have kept to myself. If I were you, I should speak quite frankly to the Inspector, and I've no doubt he'll see that your indiscretion doesn't lead to any harm."

My observations, somehow, seemed neither to satisfy him nor to comfort him. Then what did he expect me to say, I wondered ? Did he think I had the notecase somewhere in the room ? Again I became nervous of a violent outbreak. How could I get rid of him ?

" I'm sorry I can't say any more," I went on, as he made no reply. " We must have a talk to-morrow if you still feel uneasy. Meanwhile, I think I ought to go to sleep. So ought you."

He walked up and down the room with his hands in his pockets. Then suddenly he came to the bed and said ungraciously: " Well, many thanks for listening to my story and all that. You might keep it to yourself, will you ? I don't want to worry Amabel about it. Good night."

He went out before I had time to answer.

It was a quarter past one. For a time I sat, propped up against the pillow, with my light burning. Why had Dixon come to see me? Quite probably, because he wanted to let off steam and talk to someone. Did he really imagine that I shoud be able to help him to get the notecase? Did he think, making a lucky guess, that I had been through the pockets of the corpse? I felt thankful, indeed, that he had not come in a few hours earlier while I still had the notecase in my keeping—even if it was in the pocket of my overcoat downstairs. And what did he really want with the notecase? What really was this paper of which he was making so much fuss? I could not believe his story to be entirely false. It contained too many circumstantial details. Yet if it were true, why so much ado about nothing? The one point which had struck me as being rather grave was the finding of his stick by the body. And that hadn't seemed to distress him much. The fact that he was comparatively light-hearted about this, made me tend to absolve him from any major share in the crime; for he was clearly not clever and not a good actor. My thoughts turned once more to the notecase. How lucky I had given it to the Inspector, though I could not help wishing I had taken a glance at its contents. Then suddenly I remembered that, when I had taken the case out of the breast pocket of the dead man's coat, it had bulged with papers not properly stowed away in the compartments. When I took it out of my overcoat pocket it was relatively slim, and I could not recall any loose papers protruding from it.

What had happened to these papers ? Unless they were entirely the product of my imagination they must still be in my overcoat pocket.

I jumped out of bed, locked the door, took my overcoat from the chair where the Inspector had laid it, turned out the left-hand pocket and found amongst a débris of bus tickets, concert programmes, receipts and fluff, two clean sheets of typewritten paper folded into four. I venture to say I should not have been human if I had not read them.

A. B. Detective Agency,
33 Baring Street,
Baker Street, W.1.

Re L. D.

Probably the illegitimate son of Admiral Nether-field. Brought up by Miss Purvis (? his mother) at 99 d'Avigdor Road, Panham, near Gosport.

Educated at local grammar school. Expelled for gross bullying.

Joined Littlewood & Sons, big firm of horse-dealers.

Served with distinction during the War (M.C. and bar).

Shortly after the War went to Ceylon in employ-ment of Messrs. Watts & Wisney. Lived with native woman, who had a child by him. Scandal. Intemperate in habits. Struck one of the firm's agents and dismissed.

Returned to England three years ago. Became traveller for a firm manufacturing wireless com-ponents. Dismissed after six months. Had serious breakdown (drink) and was sent to institution.

Discharged, cured, two years ago and obtained

re-engagement with firm of horse-dealers. No trace
since then of relapse into intemperance.

Affairs, locally, with girl in sweet-shop, governess
and chemist's daughter.

Kept in touch with War friends, among them being
Captain Drew of Hampstead. Since leaving institution has paid several visits to London.

Admiral Netherfield died last April, and it is
thought that he left Miss Purvis a legacy of two
thousand pounds. He had almost certainly been
paying her an annuity for some years past.

So that was Dixon's dossier, I thought. In the face
of such a testimonial, would Mr. Quisberg consider
him a fit husband for Amabel ? No wonder Dixon
had been eager to secure the paper in the notecase.
Indeed, for a man of his temperament, it was almost
a motive for murder. But there was his unconcern
over the stick. Unless assumed, this did much to
show him innocent. Had he assumed it ? Again, I
felt sure he had not. Though, no doubt, he had told
me many lies, he had small gift for deception.
Indeed, it was strange to find so crooked a nature
accompanied by so small a gift for self-protection.

I unlocked the door, put the document under my
pillow, and turned out the light for the third time
that night. Now should I sleep ?

' I am being carried,' I began, ' in a sedan-chair
over the mountains of Thibet. Amongst the primulas
in the valley is a snake, which coils its sleek body in
and out of the green shoots, towards the edge of the
cataract. All I can see is a waving of the golden
flower-heads and a streak of dark blue passing,

passing and repassing—for the snake has reached
the cataract, quivers, and turns again—passing
right down to the depths of that far valley. . . .'

But though I slept at last, the night was not yet
over. I awoke, quite suddenly, about four—that
dismal hour when all the horrors of life and death
crowd to the bedside—with a feeling of panic.
Suppose, I thought, with a flash of instantaneous
lucidity, Clarence James denies my story altogether.
Suppose he declares that he was miles away from the
Heath all the afternoon and produces a perfect alibi.
What will happen to me then ? Shall I not be the
chief suspect—I, who led the police to the body in
the traditional manner, with a trumped-up story ?
Suppose I never really saw Clarence at all, mistook a
stranger for him, had a hallucination! Even if I
were not convicted on the score of my extraordinary
evidence, what kind of figure should I cut in after-
life when it became known that I had tried, quite
wantonly, to implicate my hostess' son in the crime ?
I felt hot with horror. It seemed impossible that
when Clarence had his interview with the Inspector,
he would say: " Yes, Warren is quite right. I
directed him to the body." That was altogether too
simple, too easy an escape for me. Would the
morning never come ? In my desperate agitation, I
even thought of wandering about the house in my
dressing-gown and trying to find Clarence's room on
the top floor. " You were there, weren't you ? " I
would say to him. " Promise me that you were and
will tell the Inspector." He would think me mad.

Or he might murder me, concealing crime with crime—for there was no doubt he was the murderer. Had he come in yet ? Or was he hiding, still running wildly to Chinatown or the Docks ? Gradually, as I thought of him in mad career through narrow streets and over riverside quays, he became a dark blue snake gliding among the primulas of Thibetan valleys. Fearfully, from my sedan-chair, I watched the wavy line of its curved progress, while the golden flower-heads bent and recovered in the bright mountain sunshine, and the cataract roaring over the crag drenched me with its clear spray.

XV. WHITEWASHED WINDOWS

Sunday—8 a.m.

At eight Edwins brought me a cup of tea. I drank it, fell asleep and woke again three-quarters of an hour later, when he appeared with my breakfast.

" Is Mr. Clarence in ? " I asked, after I had said something about the weather.

" No, sir. He never came home last night."

" And Mr. Harley ? "

" Mr. Harley got back about eleven, sir."

" And how is Mrs. Quisberg ? "

" I'm told she's no worse, sir. At least, I hope not. She was up with the master half the night, I hear."

" Oh, dear! I'm afraid that means he must be ill."

" I think it's more worry and nerves than illness, sir, if you know what I mean."

" Well, I mustn't keep you any longer, Edwins. I really think I shall be able to manage for myself this morning. My wrist seems almost well again. I shall be quite ready for the Inspector if he wants to see me."

" Very good, sir. I'll bring him up as soon as he asks for you."

The sobering influence of morning had routed some of my more fantastic nightmares, and I ate my breakfast not without pleasure. Indeed, now that I thought the crisis near at hand, I felt detached from it as if I were following it in the newspapers. As to my own position, I felt more assured. The fact that Clarence James had been away all night seemed to show that my meeting with him on the Heath was not a hallucination on my part. Yet, if he confirmed my story, would he be suspect? Murderers, we are told, often have charming characters. I was not very sensible to the charm of Clarence James, but I could not conceive him as a murderer, and was even distressed at the thought of his being one. Then there was Dixon. My imagination was again becoming unpleasantly feverish when the Inspector came in.

" Good morning," he said urbanely. " I do hope you slept well."

" Not at all well," I answered. " I'm a mass of nerves. I look to you to soothe me."

He smiled.

" I'll try, though my time is terribly short. In fact, you may find me almost brusque. Perhaps, in order to emphasize the confidential relations that I want to exist between us, I may begin by giving you a piece of news. For the time being, it must go no further. If you tell anyone, I shall know! It's about Mrs. Harley. I had the body re-examined last night, and it is now quite established that she sustained injuries which could not have been caused only by her fall."

I can't whistle, but I made as if to do so.

" What injuries were these? "

" Her neck was broken, but not by impact on the balcony or balcony railing."

" You mean, it was broken before she fell ? "

" Yes. Unless someone chose to break it for her afterwards—but that is hardly reasonable, is it ? "

" Then she was murdered ? "

" That is what I am indicating."

" But why ? What motive ? Of all the innocent and nondescript persons. . . . Does Harley inherit anything on her death ? "

" How wicked you are! I don't know, but I shouldn't think it would be very much. Her life, of course, might have been insured. But surely Harley was away in London during the whole night ? "

" Yes, but it's almost a rule to suspect all alibis, isn't it ? "

The Inspector laughed, and then went on seriously: " You were present, weren't you, when he heard the news ? "

" Yes, it was a painful scene."

" Did his grief strike you as assumed ? "

" Far from it."

" Then I think we can take it as genuine. I refuse to believe that ordinary people can simulate really deep emotions—at all events, before an intelligent audience. No, I don't fancy somehow that Mrs. Harley's little savings, or her insurance money, were the motive of this crime."

" Then what could it have been ? "

" I don't know yet. It's not impossible that you will discover it yourself. If so, I rely on you to confide in me."

" Me ? I ? "

" Yes—with your quickness of perception and your close relations with this family, you have chances that I haven't got."

" I'm a bad spy."

He laughed, perhaps to hide a momentary annoyance.

" Oh dear, this *amour-propre* of yours! However, I am quite content to leave it to your conscience—or, if you're too modern to have a conscience, to your good taste and sense of propriety. So much for that. Now what secrets have you to tell me ? "

" When you had gone last night I remembered that when I gave you Dr. Green's notecase it was quite thin, while, when I took it from the body, it had bulged with some loose papers. I searched in my overcoat pocket and found this document."

I took the folded sheets from under my pillow and gave them to the Inspector, who read them without comment.

" Thank you. Anything more ? "

" No other papers. I had a visitor during the night—Leonard Dixon. He gave me a long account of his doings from the time he set off for his walk with Dr. Green, and seemed most anxious to get possession of some private memoranda which the doctor had made as a result of their talk."

" Well, that's plain sailing, isn't it, in view of the contents of this letter ? "

I felt grateful to him for assuming that it had been quite proper for me to read through the document before handing it over.

" Yes," I said. " Dixon had a strong motive. . . ."

" For murder ? "

" I meant for trying to get the paper back."

" And for murder ? "

" Not strong enough for murder in cold blood, perhaps, but——"

" For a sudden blow with that heavy stick of his, you mean ? "

" I suppose so."

" Don't worry. You're not convicting any fellow creature. My own mind is not entirely without agility. Well, I must leave you, refreshing though this conversation is."

" One little point, Inspector. Suppose Clarence James does not corroborate my story ? "

" Oh, but he will! Don't distress yourself about that."

" I'm told he didn't come back here last night."

" No. We know where he is, though. He spent the night with an artist friend in Bloomsbury. The friend rang us up. I'm going to pay them a visit soon. Now, I should get up if I were you, and take a stroll in the garden. Don't worry, but think intelligently. We'll have another talk later on. Good-bye."

By the time I had bathed, shaved and dressed, it was half past ten. As I crossed the landing to go downstairs, I heard loud voices in the drawing-room and, quite shamelessly, did my best to overhear. The first words I caught were spoken by Amabel.

" You," she shouted, " calling yourself a nurse! You're nothing but a common little gold-digger! "

There was such an ill-bred anger in the reply that I could hardly believe it was the nurse who spoke.

" Who are you, Miss Amabel, to talk like that, I should like to know ? What about the stick that was found by the body ? Whose was that ? You ask your precious boy friend! A fine pair you are, the two of you, racketing about together all night, coming home drunk and letting off fireworks at two in the morning, with illness in the house! You'll cut a pretty figure in the witness-box, you will."

" At any rate," began the answer, " I'm not a common——" The rest was, perhaps, luckily, drowned, for the nurse interrupted, and for a moment or two the whole house seemed to be filled with recriminations. Then suddenly the door opened and the nurse, pale with rage, rushed on to the landing and upstairs, without seeing me, while from the drawing-room came the sound of angry sobs.

Reflectively I made my way down to the hall, took my hat from a peg in the lobby, and went out through the front door into the garden.

The fine weather of Boxing Day had not lasted. The garden was wet with a recent shower, and a dark sky, full of clouds hurrying from the north-west, promised more rain. I circled round the side of the house, and strolled for a while up and down the paths on the north-east side of the big lawn.

My thoughts were busy, but I could find no one object on which to concentrate them.

The Inspector had by now almost succeeded in making me a wholehearted ally. The murder of Dr. Green had struck me with a sense of personal loss, and I was quite ready to help, if I could, to find his murderer—unless the murderer turned out to be Mrs. Quisberg. But this seemed most unlikely; for I shared the Inspector's view that very few people can entirely mislead one as to their real natures. I was prepared to admit that the murderer might be a person of great charm and even virtue—for example, Dr. Green's character, which I admired, was to my mind in no way inconsistent with murder—but I could not bring myself to associate the character of Mrs. Quisberg with any kind of crime. It was different with her husband, Dixon, Clarence James, Amabel, the nurse and Edwins. Any of these might, I thought, in certain circumstances have been guilty. Mrs. Quisberg, Sheila and George, the butler, I definitely ruled out.

I still found it hard to realize, despite the shadowy suspicions which had been troubling me for a long time, that we were also investigating the murder of Mrs. Harley. It was possible, of course, that she and Dr. Green were not killed by the same person. It was even possible that the two crimes were not connected in any way, and that the unfortunate household had been visited by two separate disasters within forty-eight hours of one another. But this was altogether too much of a coincidence to be credible. I was convinced that there must be some link between the two deaths, and that the discovery of this link was bound to provide a valuable clue.

How, then, should I set about this task ? As at the time of my Aunt Catherine's death, I was sure that any skill I might have, lay, not in collecting evidence, but in making psychological deductions. I had some talent, I felt, at guessing luckily. There might, it was true, be a few points on which I should need precise information in order to verify a theory, but it was useless for me to examine the house and garden with a microscope, or analyse the fluff in Dr. Green's waistcoat pockets. For this kind of research I had no facilities. Besides, the police were, no doubt, conducting it with great efficiency.

By way of self-discipline I began, while still strolling through the more secluded parts of the garden, to consider the whereabouts at that particular time of each member of the house-party. Mr. Quisberg was probably in bed, muttering miserably to himself. Mrs. Quisberg would also be in bed, or she might, poor soul, be tottering into Cyril's room, or trying to comfort her husband. Clarence, the unaccountable, was in Bloomsbury, confined there, no doubt, till the Inspector had been to see him. Probably he was reading poetry, or discussing, somewhat nervously, with his friend the iniquity of all bourgeois institutions. Amabel was drying her eyes in the drawing-room—or she might, by now, have flounced downstairs in search of Dixon, whom I pictured as biting his nails gloomily in the terrace room. Sheila was with her mother or Cyril, or reading or writing in her bedroom. The nurse was

upstairs, packing feverishly and planning new
taunts with which to goad the young lady of the
house. It would be interesting, I thought, to know
the nurse's movements from the time when she
fainted in the hall. Presumably a housemaid had
attended to her. She would revive quickly, I
surmised, and excuse herself to Dr. McKenzie as
best she could. There was no need, she would assure
him, for her to rest. Cyril was convalescent, and she
could do everything that was necessary for him. She
knew the household, and with Mrs. Quisberg unwell
it was far better that she should stay on duty. She
had probably had a long talk with Dr. McKenzie
late on the previous night. Perhaps it had been he
who had told her about the finding of Dixon's stick.
Or she might have been eavesdropping. She had, up
to a point, a privileged position and sources of
information which were denied to others. But why
had she fainted ? Was it possible that she and Dr.
Green . . . ? This conjecture left me rather dazed,
and I passed on deliberately to Harley, that moth-
eaten little sphinx whom we had all, except Mrs.
Quisberg, seemed to ignore. Sooner or later he
would have to be told that his mother had not died a
natural death. Perhaps by now he had been told,
and was sitting in his bedroom thinking and suspect-
ing. Would he, I wondered, suddenly give vent to
some amazing disclosure ? Apart from the uninter-
esting members of the staff and the sedate George,
there remained Edwins, who was probably pressing
Mr. Quisberg's trousers. Or doesn't one press
trousers on Sunday ? Had it been Edwins I had

seen on the Heath at the time of the flute playing ?
By fainting, the nurse had made me almost sure that
she was the woman I had seen. Were there two such
melodious laughers in Hampstead ?   If the woman
had been the nurse and the man Edwins, was it
possible that Dr. Green had caused the lovers'
quarrel ?   One could then perhaps conceive the
murder as the outcome of Edwins' jealousy of the
doctor. Yet Edwins, that very morning, had seemed
so satisfied with himself—and, in any event, how
could a row between two men over a pretty woman
be connected with the death of Mrs. Harley ?

Coming to a halt in my unprofitable survey, I
found I had absentmindedly walked along the path
at the bottom of the terrace to the sheds and green-
houses behind the garage. As I approached, a
young gardener, who had been stoking the fire of
the vinery, walked, rather ostentatiously I thought,
to the shed in which I had found the packet of
fireworks. It occurred to me to wonder if the fireworks were still there, and if they could have any
possible bearing on the mystery which I was trying
to fathom. I would look later, I decided, when the
coast was clear. But as I turned away I saw such an
expression of disappointment on the gardener's face
that I felt bound to speak to him. (Oh dear, did he
expect a Christmas box ?)

" Good morning," I said. " A great change in the
weather from yesterday, isn't it ? "

The remark was more than usually flat; for at
that very moment the sun began to shine through

the clouds, and the whole garden regained much of the spring-like air it had worn on Boxing Day.

" Yes, sir," he replied without interest. Then, his eyes brightening, he added, " You didn't take a spade from here yesterday, by any chance, sir, I suppose ? "

" No," I said. " Why ? Are you missing one ? "

" Yes, sir. There's four spades kept in that shed as a rule, and there's only three now."

" When did you last see all four ? " I asked.

He hesitated a moment before answering.

" I suppose it would be Christmas Eve, sir, or maybe the day before that. You see, it's been holiday lately, and in any case there isn't much digging to be done at this time of year."

" And when did you first notice that a spade was missing ? "

Again he hesitated.

" This morning, sir. Mr. Smith, the head gardener here, said all the gardening tools should be kept together in the tool shed over there, and I was tidying out this shed, like, when I found we was one short."

He shifted his feet uncomfortably, and I felt sure he was trying to deceive me.

" Well," I said, " I expect you'll find it somewhere about. It isn't the kind of thing that's any use to most people, is it ? I seem to be spending a good deal of my time in the garden. If I see a spade lying about, I'll let you know."

" Thank you, sir. Mr. Smith's a terror if there's anything missing."

I smiled, gave him a nod, and walked away, past the greenhouses towards the rock garden. So, a spade was missing from a shed at Beresford Lodge. And a spade, the Inspector had told me, had been found in the newly dug trench in the clearing on the Heath by Dr. Green's body. No doubt the Inspector had questioned the gardeners, and the man I had just spoken to was trying to do a little detective work on his own. This sinister misplacement of a spade seemed definitely to link Dr. Green's death with the household of Beresford Lodge. Also it implied a degree of premeditation in the crime, which did much to demolish my fanciful notion of a quarrel between Dr. Green and another man (possibly Edwins), for the favours of the nurse. The shadowy figure I had seen on the Heath, talking to the woman with the melodious laugh, was certainly not carrying a spade. I had little doubt that the trench in the clearing had been dug some time previously, for the concealment of the body. Perhaps the experts could tell from the state of the excavated earth exactly when the spade was used. Such accuracy was naturally beyond my powers, and I had only the gardener's vague statement to guide me as to the period in which the trench could have been dug.

Now, I thought daringly, I will try to reconstruct the crime. By this I meant the second crime, for the first crime, the murder of Mrs. Harley, still seemed to me so motiveless and purposeless that I felt my only approach to it lay through investigation of Dr. Green's murder. In my eagerness to gain complete seclusion for my thoughts, I had walked down the south-west side of the garden and taken the path which lay on the far side of the shrubbery behind the rock garden, where the ill-omened bulk of Paragon House frowned at me through the bare trees. As my gaze wandered over its dilapidated surface, my former feeling of repulsion for the building returned to me, and I was about to walk on to a less depressing spot when I noticed a man standing inside one of the upper windows, rubbing the glass with a sponge. From the opaque look of some of the panes on which he was working, I judged him to be applying a kind of whitewash. Evidently he saw me staring at him, for he pulled up the lower half of the window and leaned out. He was a big fellow with a large, square head, a sallow complexion and features so devoid of any expression that I was reminded of an Oriental. Yet at the same time I had the impression that I had seen him before, not so long ago. Before I could study him further, he startled me by shouting, " Come to see the job done, have you ? " His loud voice, echoing suddenly across the quiet garden, so amazed me that I continued to stare at him in surprise. Then, although I had an impulse to retreat, I shouted back: " What job ? Do you mean the white-washing ? "

" What else should I mean ? " he replied. " Well, you can tell the guv'nor that I'm carrying out instructions all right! "

" What guv'nor ? " I asked stupidly.

" You know all right," he said, jerking his thumb

towards Beresford Lodge. " Him that owns the property you're on now—the foreign gent. You can tell him from me that I know it ain't nice to be overlooked, and that if he'll stump up for the whitewash we'll call it quits."

" I don't quite understand," I said. " Do you want me to give Mr. Quisberg a message ? "

" Ain't I just told you so ? " he said, and then as if exasperated by my slowness, he quickly jerked his head and shoulders back through the window and disappeared from view.

" So that," I thought, as I walked back towards Beresford Lodge, " is the caretaker of Paragon House. Not a very prepossessing person ! " No wonder, if heads like his were liable to pop out of the window at any moment, that Mr. Quisberg disliked being overlooked, and in default of buying the building and pulling it down had arranged for the windows to be whitewashed. Meanwhile, I had achieved nothing at all in the way of constructive thought during my stroll in the garden. It was essential for me to have privacy and free use of pencil and paper if I was to make any real headway as detective. I wondered very much how we should manage to exist during the remainder of the day, unless we all stayed in our separate rooms. There was not one of us, except Sheila and the little patient upstairs, whose nerves would not be strained almost to danger-point. I pictured interviews with Mr. Quisberg, with his wife, with Amabel, with Clarence—had he yet returned ?—with Dixon, with

Harley and with the nurse, and foresaw in each of them possibilities of a hideous emotional tension. It should be a well-recognized convention, I thought, that when a house is afflicted with murder, the members of the household should be segregated from one another. I had already had two interviews in the garden which had disturbed the systematic working of my thoughts. Henceforth, I decided, I would cling to my bedroom like an oyster to its shell. I little dreamt as I made my way down the path on the north-east side of the garden that a third interview was at hand, in comparison with which the other two would seem colourless indeed.

XVI. THE DROPPED PIPE

Sunday—11.45 a.m.

I MOUNTED the terrace by the north-east wing of the Louis Quinze staircase, and was surprised to see Mr. Quisberg, wrapped up in rugs and sitting in a chair outside the terrace room. His back was set at a slight angle to me, but I had a good view of his profile, the long forehead, the strange nose which was both arched and snub, the bulging cheeks, and the slit of his tormented mouth, which moved now and again with a nervous twitch. What strange caprice, I wondered, had brought him downstairs ? He was indeed a pitiable figure as he sat there this wintry noon, shrunken, ill and miserable. Yet, as I stood by the french window of the dining-room and surveyed him more closely, I was surprised at the essential fineness of his features, and felt that somehow there were about them the elements of nobility, and even—despite their superficial ugliness—of a kind of beauty.

My impulse, naturally, was to creep away unseen, but recollecting the caretaker's message I resolved to approach him. After all, he was my host, and little though he might wish to talk to me, it seemed hardly right to disappear without a word. Accordingly, I walked slowly and quietly towards him—with a most astonishing result; for my coming so startled him that he jerked backwards in his chair and dropped the pipe, with which he had been fiddling, on to the stone floor. And at the same moment as he turned round and stared at me with frightened eyes, I had a vision which blotted out, for a few seconds, Mr. Quisberg, Beresford Lodge, and six and a half years of my life.

I have often wondered what it is that provokes those sudden memories which arise for no apparent reason in the least imaginative of us. Why is it, for example, that a musical phrase, perhaps from a piece learned in childhood and long since forgotten, should leap into one's brain during a game of bridge ? Or why, to take another example, should I suddenly be reminded, when walking in the park, of a day twenty years before when my mother took me and my two sisters to have tea in Dinard, by ferry from St. Malo ? Nothing very memorable had happened on that afternoon. It was only one of many such little excursions, an afternoon without elation or catas-trophe. Yet, for some reason, my mind had chosen to store up this most unimportant episode and have it ready to flash upon me, perhaps once in every eighteen months. No doubt psychologists have their theories and might, if they took the trouble to examine one's reactions, discover some association of impressions—the tint, perhaps, of a stone wall or the peculiar barking of a dog—to account for the purposeless invasion of the present by the remote past. Or is it, as the new school of physicists seem sometimes to hint, that past, present and future are all equally real, and that on occasion we have the gift (or disability) of slipping backwards or forwards through the time-dimension ?

The episode which Mr. Quisberg's dropped pipe brought suddenly to my mind was, in itself, less remarkable even than our family tea in Dinard, though dating back, as I have said, only six and a half years, it was less deeply buried in the past. It had taken place on a stifling afternoon in July. (Was it the contrast in weathers which helped to suggest it to me ? My mind is largely moved by contraries. Were I a poet I should write odes to spring in late October.) The day, I remember, had been so hot that even the little walk from my office to the Stock Exchange (which I had then newly joined) seemed hardly bearable. Business had almost been at a complete standstill, not only because it was the slack season, but also because we were in the backwash of a big financial failure which for a few days paralyzed all the markets. The " crash," as it was called, was my first experience of anything of the kind. I had felt as if the end of my little world were at hand and —such is a novice's enthusiasm—could talk of nothing else. When Jack Slicer, the then junior partner in my firm, suggested that we should leave the office early and take a taxi to Hampstead Heath so as to get a breath of fresh air, I was surprised at his composure. However, I was glad enough to escape from the exhausting heat of the City and much enjoyed sitting on the top of the hill by the flagstaff, (it was my first visit to Hampstead), watching the people and trying to imagine that there was a faint breeze blowing towards us from the Harrow ridge.

As was too much my habit in those days, I quickly brought the conversation round to " shop," and in the end, I think, my companion must have found me rather tedious. " Oh," he said, " this affair's nothing new. You'll get used to these panics in time. Look at the Cabal crash. Though I don't suppose it was quite so big as this one, it made much more of a scare at the time."

" The Cabal crash ? " I asked. " When was that ? "

" It was in 1904. I know a good deal about it, because my father lost thirty thousand pounds in it, and if my unmarried uncle hadn't come to the rescue, I should probably have been taken away from my bad but expensive preparatory school."

" Do tell me about it," I asked him, " if it doesn't bore you. I know the name, of course, but it means rather less to me even than the South Sea Bubble."

" The Cabal Trust," he said, " was a progressive finance company—something rather new in those days, I believe. I don't know when it was formed or what it specialized in—as a matter of fact it had a go at nearly everything—but it was, or seemed to be, astonishingly successful. The preference shares were considered a first-class investment for the widow and the orphan. The ordinary shares were nearly all privately held, though a few of them were doled out from time to time at a big premium in return for services rendered. My father got hold of a few—I

think he paid four pounds ten per pound share—and
he put a good deal of money into a subsidiary
company managed by the Cabal. For a while
everything went well. The Cabal paid thirty or
forty per cent. and enlarged its scope about twice a
year by the issue of debentures at a low rate of
interest, and people used to say that it was only a
matter of time before it bought up the Bank of
England. Then, quite suddenly, in 1904, the crash
came during the Easter holidays. On the Thursday
before Good Friday markets were oddly depressed.
There were never any dealings on the Stock
Exchange in Cabal ordinary shares but the preference shares, of which there were about three million,
used to change hands very freely. They had been
weak for two or three days, but the usual story of
liquidation of a deceased account was put about,
and nobody thought very much of it. Then quite
suddenly, about midday on the Thursday, they
became unsaleable. Even then most people only
thought that a large holder must have got into
difficulties, and went away for their holidays without
feeling uneasy. The real news didn't come out till
the Saturday morning."

" What was that ? " I asked.

" The vice-chairman, a baronet by the way, was
found shot in his study—obviously suicide—with a
letter of apology to his wife and friends on the desk
beside his body. The chairman more or less gave
himself up to the police. Two guinea-pig directors,
a peer and a general, declared they knew nothing at
all about the workings of the company or indeed any

other company, which was probably only too true. It didn't save them from appearing in the dock, however. The chairman got a big term of imprisonment and died a year later while serving his sentence. The company's auditors were not only ruined financially, but had to appear in Court with the other defendants. I think one partner in the firm of auditors was actually found guilty of fraud, while the others escaped gaol with a severe caution. The real villain of the piece was the vice-chairman, who shot himself."

" Where did all the money go ? "

" That's what's always so mysterious in these cases. A lot of it, of course, was never really there except on paper. Some was spent by the guilty parties. Some was lost in a series of wild-cat schemes in Africa, and it was said that the President of a South American republic got a good deal in return for dud concessions which, anyhow, he hadn't any power to grant. Of course, there were some assets, but they were only sufficient to pay the creditors about four bob in the pound. The whole business was terribly involved and took a long time to straighten out. Oh, I forgot to mention that the youngest director, a Swede or Dane, I think, did a bolt and got clean away and has never been heard of since. It was said that about a quarter of a million in high-class foreign bonds vanished at the same time."

As my friend spoke the last two sentences, a middle-aged man, whom I had vaguely noticed as sitting on a seat a yard or two in front of us, rose with a jerk, dropped his pipe on to the grass, picked

it up with a shaky hand, and walked away. But so
indifferent was I to his going, that I did not even
observe in which direction he went.

This was the memory which swept over me six and
a half years later, while I stood on the terrace of
Beresford Lodge a few feet away from its owner. It
did not, of course, come upon me *seriatim*, as I have
recounted it, but instantaneously and with a
pictorial vividness that is altogether lost in narrative.
When, after what seemed an age, my wits returned
to me, I tried with all my force to make a remark
which would disguise the wandering of my mind. I
did, I believe, stammer a few words of apology to my
host for startling him, and was continuing with some
poor phrase of sympathy, when his tired eyes filled
with tears and he made a sign for me to go away.

Presumably I obeyed, though so absorbed was I
in the new thoughts which now beseiged me, that I
cannot remember where I went. It may have been
to my bedroom, or into the garden again. Nor can
I remember where I was, when twenty minutes later
I saw the Inspector and Clarence James walking
towards the front steps. All I know is that somehow
I contrived to catch the Inspector as he was going
out of the front gate, and asked him in trembling
voice if I might leave the garden for a few moments
and use a public telephone.

He gathered at once that I was in a state of
excitement.

" But," he said, " you can use the instrument in
the telephone room. We haven't cut the wires."

" I can't risk that," I answered. " I might be overheard by the household."

" Whom are you going to ring up ? "

" A friend of mine who's on a newspaper. No, don't be alarmed. I'm not going to give him information. I want him to give some to me."

" Perhaps I can help you ? "

" Now, please, Inspector," I begged, " do let me have my own way over this. I may really be able to help you later on."

He laughed.

" Very well, then. We'll defy routine for once. Why shouldn't we ? I'll tell my watch-dog that you'll be away for half an hour. But I must have your word that you won't give anything away to your man."

" I promise. I suppose I may tell him that I'm in what I believe is called a house of crime, mayn't I ? I shall have to give some reason for my urgency. And if I can persuade him to send me what I want by special messenger, you'll let the messenger deliver the letter into my own hands, won't you ? "

" All right. I'll mention that to the bobby, too. I shall be here again after tea when I may have a surprise for you. By the way, you must be pretty hot on this new scent of yours, because you haven't asked me the question I was expecting."

" What question is that ? "

" Whether Clarence James confirms your story. Don't worry. He has."

" Are you thinking of arresting—— "

" I shan't arrest anybody for some hours."

I went indoors to get my hat—(we must, I think, have been walking about on the little front lawn)—and when I came out again I found the Inspector talking to the policeman in the road. The Inspector waved genially and the policeman saluted as I passed them. Luckily I knew where the nearest telephone box was, because once, when I was spending an afternoon at Beresford Lodge, I had slipped out to have a word with my bookmaker. I am still young enough to feel a certain shame in my small betting transactions, and had not wanted my conversation to be overheard.

I should perhaps explain that the friend whose help I was seeking was on the literary side of his paper, and that he felt both indifference and contempt for the sensational aspect of journalism. I knew him to be utterly reliable, and had no fear that he would lead me into breaking the promise I had given to the Inspector.

When I got through to him, he seemed rather cross.

" Hullo, Malcolm. I thought you were spending the holidays somewhere in the country."

" I'm in Hampstead," I answered. " At Beresford Lodge. Doesn't that convey anything to you ? "

" It sounds very grand, but I'm afraid it doesn't."

" Two—I mean, a member of the house-party was found dead on the Heath yesterday."

" Good lord ! You're not getting mixed up in another murder case, are you ? Why can't you leave all this crime alone ? "

" You might say, why can't it leave me alone!

We're all practically prisoners for the time being, and I'm afraid I can't give you any inside news——"

"For God's sake, don't begin to do that. The great news for to-morrow is that a live turkey is loose on the Underground. The whole policy of the paper—photographs, news, leader, correspondence and cartoon—are based on that. We really can't bother with anything else now."

"I don't want you to. I shall love reading you on the turkey. I'm ringing you up because I really want your help very badly indeed. You'll think what I want quite mad, but please don't ask any questions for the time being. Later, perhaps, if you want to pacify the news editor, I might be able to give you a 'scoop' for him—or do you call it 'coup'? You told me once that your paper has a very fine library of pictures since about 1900. I wonder if you could possibly get hold of all the pictures of the Cabal crash and send them to me, *at once*, by special messenger in a taxi. I'll pay all expenses, of course. You remember the Cabal crash, don't you? I believe it was in 1904."

"I hadn't even gone to Oxford then," was the indignant reply.

"I mean, you remember hearing about it. I believe it made a great sensation at the time. You're sure to have some pictures of the people concerned. And if you could get me any Press cuttings about it, I should be most grateful. You will send me *all* your pictures, won't you? What I want may not be in the most important ones."

"Very well. What will you be asking for next, I

wonder ? The pictures will be very bad if they date from 1904. And if I do send you any cuttings, for goodness sake don't take them too seriously. You know how full of lies our news always is. If we say a queue of a million people besieged the abandoned office, it means that half a dozen reporters and two errand boys were there, talking about the Test Match. However, I'll do my best. Where do you want me to send the messenger ? "

" Will you take the address down ? Beresford Lodge, Lyon Avenue, Hampstead. The messenger will find a policeman on duty outside the house, but the policeman has instructions to let him deliver the goods straight to me—which is what I'm anxious for him to do. I don't want to risk anyone else opening the package."

" All right. Really, I can't think what you'll be up to next. Please don't let me hear that you're being held to ransom by Chinese bandits. That would be too much to bear. Well, I suppose you want me to start ferreting out our photographs. Take care of yourself now. If there's a murderer in the house, stay in your bedroom and lock the door. Good-bye."

" Thank you so much. Good-bye."

It was almost time for luncheon when I reached Beresford Lodge again. As I crossed the hall I saw Sheila talking to a new nurse—a very different creature from the smiling sylph who had caused such a flutter in the household. I loitered about for a moment or two and caught Sheila when the nurse had gone upstairs.

" I hope it doesn't mean," I said, " that your mother is worse."

" Oh no. Dr. McKenzie insists that she shall stay in bed, but I think she's getting on all right. Why do you ask ? "

" I felt a little uneasy when I saw you'd got a second nurse."

" Oh, she's come instead of the other one. Nurse Moon left this morning. She had a scene with Amabel, I believe, and another one with Dr. McKenzie."

" What did you say her name was ? "

" Nurse Moon. M—double O—N. You know, ' Moon, moon, serenely shining.' I think she shone a little too serenely, don't you ? "

" I dare say she did," I answered. " And what is the new nurse's name ? "

" Nurse Phillips. She seems a sensible old body. Lord, there's the gong! I must go and wash."

I was not in the least interested in the name of Nurse Phillips. But Nurse Moon's had immediately brought to my mind the borrowed line which opened Clarence's poem:

" Ah! Moon of my delight, that knowst no wane! "

I had been so busy during the morning that luckily I had had no time in which to dread the publicity of luncheon. It was, after all, my first meeting with the house-party since my discovery of Dr. Green's body. However, feeling myself to be no longer a timorous spectator but a leading character in the plot, I was filled with a new sense of bravado and decided that, however rude, inquisitive or menacing my companions might be, I would take no notice of them, and eat and drink—especially the latter—to the full.

We were a subdued little party. Amabel sat at the head of the table, with me on her right and Dixon on her left. Clarence sat at the other end, flanked by Harley, who was on my right, and Sheila. Mrs. Quisberg was still in bed, and Mr. Quisberg, I gathered, was having a meal in his study. Rather wisely we made no attempt at all at conversation beyond a few half-hearted preliminary greetings. Amabel was white and far too heavily powdered. Dixon had gone sallow and looked both cowed and dangerous. Harley was, as always, mouse-like and minute. The rings under Clarence's eyes were deeper than ever and his expression, when in repose, had a look of misery and wounded pride. Sheila alone was fairly normal, and even she was pasty-faced. If a picture had been painted of the meal, it might have been called " A Study in Bad Complexions."

My only fear was that, when we had finished, some one would draw me aside for a heart-to-heart talk. Although on general grounds the more confidences I received, the more material I should have to work upon, I felt quite unable to deal with them until I had made some headway with my great idea. Accordingly, almost as soon as coffee was served, I murmured a word of excuse to Amabel and went straight up to my bedroom. There I settled in an armchair by the window, through which I should have an excellent view of anyone coming to the house. Even if the special messenger from Fleet Street came in by the back door, I should be bound to see the taxi as it passed the front gate in Lyon Avenue.

My mind was too full of the tidings the messenger might bring for me to accomplish any constructive thinking. I did, however, so as to make the time pass more quickly, write down certain headings for later consideration. I kept the paper and reproduce its contents now, because, though by no means an exhaustive summary of " clues," they had (I was glad to find later) a real bearing on the problem.

1. Conversation, hurried and agitated, between Dr. Green and Quisberg on the front lawn as I first arrived.
2. Did I really smell antaronyl in Mrs. Harley's bedroom ?
3. The cardboard firework-case, which I found in the rock-garden pond. The fireworks which I found in the shed from which a spade was missing. The drunken talk on the front steps between Amabel and Dixon.
4. Clarence's poem. " Ah! Moon of my delight, that knowst no wane," etc.
5. Nurse Moon. Her rapture on the afternoon of Boxing Day when I saw her, lost in a romantic reverie on the landing. Her fainting fit when I arrived from the Heath with my grim news. Her tiff with Amabel. Her departure.
6. Mr. Quisberg's visitor on Christmas Night. The talk in the study, of which I only caught one

phrase—" Why, in that light I saw it as plain as I can see you! " In what light ? What was so plainly seen ? And where was it seen from ?

7. The music on the Heath, intended for whose ears ?

8. The " lovers " I saw quarrelling on the Heath. Whom, in this house-party, could I mistake for Edwins ? Certainly not Dr. Green or, for that matter, Dixon. Possibly Clarence James.

9. Dixon's stick found by Dr. Green's body. Dixon's black eye. His elaborate alibi. Had his visit to North Finchley been confirmed ?

10. My meeting with Clarence James in the under-growth of the Heath. His panic and flight.

11. Dixon's midnight visit to my bedroom. What did he really hope to gain ?

12. The under-gardener and his news that a spade was missing from the shed. The spade and trench in the clearing beside Dr. Green's body, which ill accord with any theory that the murderer struck the doctor down in the heat of the moment.

13. The slight mystery surrounding the whitewashing of the windows of Paragon House. The caretaker's message to Quisberg. My sensation that I had somewhere seen the caretaker before.
    [NOTE.—My ears serve me better than my eyes. I am always sure of what I hear, less sure of what I see.]

14. Who was Mrs. Harley ? When did she arrive ? Had Quisberg ever seen her before ?

15. Was it essential for Quisberg to spend the night of Christmas Eve in London ? Did he really spend the *whole* night there ?

Once or twice I read my headings through, giving each one a quick consideration. Little did I realize at the time, how proud I should afterwards be of one short sentence! Then, still with one eye on the window, I added another point:

   16. Who was Quisberg?

Hardly had I written these words when, to my great relief, a taxi stopped by the gate and a commission-aire got out, and after a few words with the police-man walked up to the front door. My messenger from Fleet Street had arrived.

XVII. THE PHOTOGRAPHS

Sunday—3 p.m.

INSIDE the little package were some photographs, some Press cuttings and a covering letter. The letter ran as follows:

1001A Fleet Street,
E.C.

Dear Malcolm,

Herewith this rubbish. You must return everything, especially the photos, as soon as you can. We don't seem to have been very much on the spot with the Cabal crash. Probably we were devoting all our intelligence to a marmoset in the crypt of St. Paul's. Don't believe a word of the letterpress. Quite possibly we have even got the names wrong. Now, as I said over the telephone, do take care of yourself. Why must you always be mixing with sensational people ?

Ever yours,
N. A.

Then I looked at the photographs. The first was a picture of the Vice-Chairman at the theatrical garden-party, sleek, jaunty and debonair. The second was the Vice-Chairman's " palatial residence " in Wimbledon. The third was the Vice-Chairman's study with an X in the middle of the

floor, " marking the spot where the body was found
in tragic circumstances." The fourth showed the
wife of the Vice-Chairman talking to the wife of the
Chairman—two expensively dressed figures with
utterly expressionless faces. The fifth showed the
Chairman in the dock, tall and imposing, with a
look of conscious virtue. Three accountants were
inset, and named from left to right. The sixth was a
magnificent picture of the Director who was a
General, riding in Rotten Row, while the seventh
displayed the head and shoulders of his colleague
who was a peer, an unimpressive elderly man of non-
conformist appearance. The seventh and eighth
were more pictures of the Chairman. The ninth
picture held my attention at once. It bore the
legend:

> Mr. Löwenstjierna (the missing Director) making
> a speech at a recent dinner given by the North
> European Chamber of Commerce. Inset: Mr.
> Löwenstjierna's pretty secretary, Maud Johnson,
> who gave sensational evidence at yesterday's hearing
> of the case.

Mr. Löwenstjierna, " the missing Director," had
been photographed by flashlight, and the result was
not too good. He was tall, slim, good-looking and
probably a little over thirty. His evening clothes
were admirably cut. His long forehead was well
covered with dark hair. The nose was well formed
and aquiline, the cheeks were slightly indrawn and
cadaverous and the lips thin and ascetic. The chin
was covered by a small pointed beard which gave

the whole face the look of an artist rather than a business man. The " inset " Maud Johnson was a very pretty young woman of about twenty-three or four.

The two remaining pictures were both of the Vice-Chairman and did not interest me. I studied Mr. Löwenstjierna's photograph for a while, and then moved to the little writing-desk, where I wrote the following note:

> Dear Harley,
>
> I wonder if you would have the great kindness to write down your mother's Christian name and her surname before she married, and send them to me by the bearer of this letter. (I enclose a spare envelope and piece of paper in case you haven't writing materials at hand.)
>
> You must try to forgive my strange request. I really have a most urgent reason for wanting the information, and I assure you that my inquiry is anything but impertinent. I shall be grateful, too, if you will, for the time being, tell no one the contents of this letter.
>
> When one feels real sympathy, it is almost impossible to convey it by word of mouth. May I therefore now tell you how very sorry I have been for you, and how glad I should be if I could do anything to help you ?
>
> > Yours very sincerely,
> > > MALCOLM WARREN.

After sealing up the letter in an envelope, which I addressed:

> > H. Harley, Esq.,
> > > Beresford Lodge.

I rang the bell. It was answered, somewhat to my relief, not by the astute Edwins but by a housemaid.

"Do you know," I asked, "if Mr. Harley is in?"

"I'm not quite sure, sir," she said, "but I dare say he's in his room."

"Well, if you can find him I should be most grateful if you'd give him this note. If there's an answer, perhaps you'll bring it back to me here. And if you can't find Mr. Harley, perhaps you'll bring my note back, will you? Then I shall be able to send it to him later, if I want to."

She was a little surprised, I think, but took the letter without question and went out. When she had gone, I turned to the photograph of Mr. Löwenstjierna once more, and wrote the following observations on a sheet of notepaper:

QUISBERG	LÖWENSTJIERNA
Long sloping forehead. Bald.	Long sloping forehead, partly covered with luxuriant hair.
Eyes wide apart.	Eyes wide apart.
Nose, bent and snub.	Nose, shapely and aquiline.
Cheeks, bulging and somehow crinkled.	Cheeks, spare and indrawn.
Lips, thin.	Lips, thin.
Chin, pointed.	Chin, covered by beard.

My two difficulties were the nose and the cheeks. Was it possible, I wondered, for age to alter their contours so completely? Noses, of course, are sometimes broken and reset. Then, suddenly, I remembered a phrase used by Dr. Green when he was talking to me in my bedroom. "There's nothing," he had said, "I wouldn't do for Axel. I once even mended a broken nose." Excellent! Had the breakage been quite accidental, though? And was it necessary, in resetting the nose, to make such a change in its shape? Dr. Green, I felt sure, was not a clumsy operator. As for the cheeks—but at that moment the housemaid brought me the answer to my note.

> Dear Mr. Warren,
>   My mother's name before she married was Maud Johnson. Thank you very much indeed for your kind sympathy.
> Yours sincerely,
ERNEST HARLEY.

I sighed with relief and pride. Indeed, my vision had led me to the truth, and my excitement now was the excitement not so much of discovery (which I had really made with instantaneous clairvoyance on the terrace that morning), but of a successful verification. What, then, was I to do with these new facts? How work them into the pattern? Mrs. Harley had been Mr. Quisberg's secretary. Mr. Quisberg had, to say the least, left England under a cloud at the time of the Cabal crash. (Had not a quarter of a million pounds vanished with him?) Twenty years later he returned not only older but physically changed, a rich man, a model husband, a conscientious stepfather to his new wife's children. How was he to know when he engaged Harley that he was engaging Maud Johnson's son? It was a cruel coincidence, and more cruel still that he should ever have been brought face to face with Maud Johnson herself. If only the Quisbergs had not been so kind to their dependents, or if Mrs. Harley had not elected to come to London just at the time when her son could not be given a holiday to look after her—if the Harrington Cobalt crisis had occurred a week earlier or a week later—in short, if nothing unforeseen had happened, he would never have been unmasked. But unmasked he clearly was. Mrs. Harley recognized him at first sight, he recognized her, and they both knew it. The same night, while Quisberg was staying at the Carlton, Mrs. Harley was murdered.

Again, I asked myself, as in my list of ' clues,' what of this alibi ? How could I possibly test it ? I might, to be sure, have a long talk with Harley and try to get his account of Quisberg's movements on Christmas Eve. But any information he could give me was bound to be inconclusive by itself. I might even ask the Inspector's leave and go to the Carlton and, as in detective stories, by judicious largess of ten-shilling notes, try to collect evidence from waiters, valets, porters, chambermaids and liftboys. But this task I really felt to be beyond me, apart from the distastefulness of it. Suppose, for the moment, that Quisberg had no alibi. Then I must assume that he visited Beresford Lodge, silently and unobserved, during the small hours, murdered Mrs. Harley, threw her body out of the window and crept away back to the Carlton so as to be ready for the early morning conference with G——. Such an

escapade would have been both difficult and
dangerous; for there was always the risk that our
Christmas Eve tomfoolery might have continued
till any hour. Indeed, Amabel, Dixon and their
friends, the Drews, were in such high spirits that we
probably should have been up most of the night if I
had not interrupted the party by straining my wrist.

Another point. What, if anything, did Dr. Green
know of Mrs. Harley? How far was he in the
secret? Was he even an accomplice? But people
do not murder their accomplices—unless, perhaps,
there is a threat of blackmail. I was rather startled
by this thought, which seemed to give me a new line
on which to work. Suppose Dr. Green knew too
much, and it was essential to get rid of him? Had
Quisberg a perfect alibi at the time when Dr. Green
was murdered? So far as I knew, he was in bed, a
sick man. But what if the sickness was mental rather
than bodily? Had not the shrewd Edwins hinted to
me that his master's illness was "worry and
nerves"? If this were so, there was no reason why
Quisberg should not have been able to slip out and
commit his second crime.

Then I remembered the spade and the trench
already dug to contain the body. There must have
been a previous "slipping out" to make these pre-
parations. Could Quisberg twice have eluded all
those, including his wife, who were devoting themselves to his illness? It would have been difficult, I
thought, though I could not say it was impossible.
And what of Dixon's stick, which was found by the
body? Was it a fact that the blow which caused

Dr. Green's death was actually made by the stick? Was
Dixon's story more or less true, and did the doctor
really borrow his stick when taking a last walk over
the Heath ? If so, Dixon was merely the victim of a
coincidence, and the murderer had provided himself
with another weapon; for he could not have known
that the stick would be available.

Then I had an idea, of which at the time I was
quite proud. Suppose the injury to Dr. Green's
head had been caused by the spade—not the metal
part, but the wooden handle ? No doubt, medical
evidence on this point would be forthcoming, but
the theory had the merit of making it possible for the
murderer to have set out without carrying either a
duplicate stick or any other weapon. It implied, of
course, a pre-arranged rendezvous—but so, in any
case, did the digging of the trench. What pretext
was used to entice the doctor to the chosen spot, I
could not guess, unless perhaps the nurse were used
as a decoy. This showed the laughing lady in a very
sinister light, though she need not, necessarily, have
been cognisant of the whole plot. " I want you,"
the murderer might have said, " to have Dr. Green
at such a place at such a time. This thousand-pound
note will make it worth your while." No wonder
the poor woman had fainted when she heard that
her charms had led to such a fatal result.

As I proceeded with my theory, I kept remembering small disconnected sayings and events with which
to give it confirmation. Yet, even then, I knew I was
ignoring other memories which were in apparent
conflict with it. Why, for example, had Quisberg

fainted when he and Harley returned from the
Carlton on Christmas morning ? If he was the
murderer of Mrs. Harley, he should certainly have
assumed a look of consternation, but there was no
need for him to faint. Of course, it might have been
a faint induced by several hours of acute nervous
strain, or by relief at finding that his crime was
generally accepted as an accident. But this explanation did not altogether satisfy me. Indeed, as the
reader may have gathered, all the time I was working on the supposition that Quisberg was guilty, I
was distracted by another problem—a problem of
ethics rather than detection. Now that I was sure
that Quisberg was Löwenstjierna and that Mrs.
Harley had been Maud Johnson of the Cabal case,
what was I to do ? Ought I to go at once to the
Inspector, or ought I to say nothing ? There was a
third course open to me also. I could demand an
interview with Quisberg and threaten that, unless he
cleared himself to my satisfaction, I should have to
tell the police what I knew. This course appealed
to my romantic instincts as being the most heroic,
but at the same time I viewed it with apprehension.
Suppose Quisberg were the murderer. He had
already got rid of Dr. Green who was too danger-
ously in the know. How would he deal with me ?
It would not be pleasant to sit facing him and
wonder every minute whether he was going to whip
out a knife or a revolver. True, my death in such
circumstances would very probably lead to his
conviction, but there was no knowing what he might
do, if pressed too far.

I sat for about half an hour by the window, watching the daylight yield to the early darkness and trying to make up my mind. If I had been certain that Quisberg had killed either Mrs. Harley or Dr. Green, I should not have hesitated, but without this certainty I felt strongly that I had no right to make free with his past life—however full it was of financial knavery—and bring him and Mrs. Quisberg to ruin. Even my wish to be fair to the Inspector was out-weighed by these qualms. So great, indeed, was my perplexity that I began to regret my clairvoyant access of memory and the responsibility which my zeal had thrust upon me. It had been very pleasant to probe the minor secrets, to learn that Amabel was in the habit of letting off fireworks with Dixon, and that Clarence had addressed a sonnet to Nurse Moon, but it was not a little harassing to make a big discovery.

Try as I would, I could only find one line of action which was not repugnant to me. I must see Quisberg and tell him openly that I knew his secret and how strong a motive he had for wishing to murder Mrs. Harley. If he cleared himself, I would suspend sentence. If he did not—but just as I was making these somewhat presumptuous decisions, there was a knock at the door, and I had barely time to hide my photographs before the Inspector came in.

" I've taken a great liberty," he said. " I'm dying for some tea, and I've asked them to serve it in here —for two. Do you mind ? "

" Not at all," I answered. " I'm delighted."

" You see," he went on, " I think we really have a good deal to talk about. I've taken you very much into my confidence, and I'm sure that by now you have a lot to tell me in return. Haven't you ? "

I blushed.

" I'm trying to develop my ideas," I said. " You must give me time."

" Oh, I've no doubt," he answered with disconcerting acumen, " that you intend to find the murderer yourself first, and then give me his name, or her name, if you think I ought to know. I don't blame you. But I may perhaps warn you that I already know one or two things which you may think I don't. You yourself have given me some useful help. Won't you give me some more ? Hello—here's tea."

We made conversation till Edwins, who had brought up our tea, was safely out of the room. Then the Inspector turned to me and said, with a smile:

" So as to pile up your indebtedness to me still further, I'm going very shortly to give you the chance of seeing an interesting experiment. Don't ask me now what it is. I think it'll surprise you. It may even be slightly dangerous—but not really to you, or I shouldn't let you come."

" That's very kind of you."

" I hope you think it is. Now won't you help me in return ? "

" You mean, you want to know why I telephoned to Fleet Street this morning ? "

" No, not yet. I can see that you're all agog with

some discovery or other, and positively refuse to confide it to me. I won't press you then for the time being. What I want you to do, is to give me some of the details—isolated details, if you like—which you've been going over in your mind and have either fitted in, or been unable to fit in, to your theory. Not the theory itself, mind you. Won't you help me like this ? You won't be able to reproach yourself afterwards, even if I arrest—Amabel. . . . No ? That prospect doesn't seem to harass you very much. Shall I say Mrs. Quisberg ? "

I hesitated for a minute. Though I was still resolved to tell him nothing about Quisberg's alias, I felt it really might be my duty to give him some of the subsidiary facts which had come to my notice. Perhaps the man had hypnotized me a little. At all events, I pulled out of my pocket the list of headings I had made while waiting for the messenger from Fleet Street.

" If you like," I said, " I'll read you some of the memoranda I have prepared for myself. They're incomplete, of course—and probably irrelevant——"

" Never mind about that. Can I see the paper ? "

" I'm afraid not, because it contains a reference to what I still——"

" Want to hide from me, you mean," he said with a smile. " Well, I shall be most grateful for any crumb that falls from your table. And I'm not at all sure that a crumb won't be more useful to me than a whole loaf of bread."

I then read to the Inspector the first thirteen points on my list, suppressing the last three, because they tended to draw too much attention to Quisberg. The Inspector listened to me with a concentration which was both flattering and alarming, and asked me many a quick question, the import of which I could not always follow.

" I really am pleased with myself," he said when I had finished. " It shows what an excellent judge of character I must be. I thought you were a person of great intuition and perception, and find myself admirably justified. The way you've put your finger on many of the key-spots, without any technical practice or assistance, is quite amazing. And what a keen sense of hearing! Well, I must go and make myself very busy now—arranging the party I promised you. Will you meet me in the hall in half an hour—that is to say, at twenty to six, wearing your hat and coat—and umbrella, if you like ? "

" I shall be most delighted. But what are we going to do ? "

" That you will learn very soon. Now be good and don't go downstairs till you come to meet me in the hall."

" One question, Inspector. I can't keep it back. Have you really solved the mystery ? "

" In a sense, yes. That is to say, I am sure I understand its broad outlines. I realize all the principal motives, the characters on which those motives acted, and the main opportunities presented to those characters for criminal behaviour. I am still in the dark as to some of the mechanism—perhaps, indeed, some of these details will never be fully known— and I still have some tests to make in the hope of strengthening the weaker links in my chain of evidence. But, taken as a whole, the case is over."

" Will the result, when I come to learn it, be a great shock to me ? "

" That depends on what you are really thinking— and how shockable you are! "

He smiled again, with his sweet, rather shop-walkerish smile, and went out before I had time to reply.

XVIII. HOUSE-HUNTING

Sunday—5.40 p.m.

"Come outside," said the Inspector, " and I will introduce you to Mr. Edwards. I, by the way, am Mr. Rogers for the time being. You are still Mr. Warren."

He was wearing a brown mackintosh, with the high collar turned up over his chin. I wore the only overcoat I had with me—my dark " City " overcoat —and carried an umbrella. It was as well I did, for when the Inspector had shepherded me through the lobby and down the front steps, I found that a fine but very wetting rain was falling.

A man, wearing a mackintosh somewhat like the Inspector's, was standing by the gate.

" Mr. Edwards—Mr. Warren," said the Inspector. " By the way, Mr. Warren, for your own sake, I think it will be as well if you will maintain complete silence during this expedition of ours—even should anyone speak to you. If that happens you must let me answer for you. Do you mind ? "

" Not at all," I replied. " But where are we going ? "

" To Paragon House."

He said no more, and we all walked in silence down Lyon Avenue to the right—the direction which led away from the Heath. Though the road in which Paragon House stood was parallel to Lyon Avenue, it did not give access, like the latter, to West Heath Road, and in order to reach Paragon House we had to go round three sides of a square. It was perhaps the strangest little walk I have ever made, lying as it did in such very respectable thoroughfares, all of them flanked with large quiet houses and gardens, and leading to what I could not possibly guess. With an odd sense of contrast, as I saw the familiar glare of the arc lamps on the wet roads and our three shadows now lengthening in front of us and now suddenly dropping diminutively behind, I felt that we might all have been going to evening service in a suburban church. Indeed, when we made our second right turn, we did pass a church. The bell was tolling, and through the open door I caught the muffled sound of the organist practising his voluntary, and a whiff of ecclesiastical odours.

But this mood of calm was not to last, for it occurred to me quite suddenly to wonder if the Inspector had not been deceiving me with his confidential affability. Was there a chain of evidence of which I knew nothing, implicating me ? Had I really been under suspicion the whole time ? After all, it was I who, in the fullest sense, discovered both the corpses. Was I now, in the gloom of Paragon House, to be faced with an ordeal or kind of third degree ? I could almost imagine apparitions of Mrs. Harley and Dr. Green arising in front of me with accusing fingers and saying in sepulchral unison: " You did it, Malcolm ! " Nor did it add to my peace

of mind to know that if I were subjected to any such
bogy trick, however innocent I was, I should act
guiltily. Much as I disliked my last few days at
Beresford Lodge, I would have given anything to be
back within its comfortable walls.

Too late. We had already reached the iron gate-
way bounding what used to be the short carriage
drive to the front door of Paragon House. The
Inspector led the way up the front steps and rang
the bell. It was the old-fashioned kind which one
pulls and emitted what, I believe, is often described
as an " eerie peal " in the basement. Two minutes
passed and there was no answer. The Inspector
rang again, with greater violence. Then we heard
heavy steps approaching the door and the sound of
rusty bolts being withdrawn. When, after what
seemed a very long time, the door was opened, I saw
the caretaker, whom I had seen that morning from the
garden, standing pugnaciously in the aperture. He
was in his shirt-sleeves, and such expression as there
was on his large inscrutable face was certainly not
one of welcome.

" Well, what d'you want ? " he asked.

" We have an order to view the house," said the
Inspector quickly, " from Lanchester & Co., who,
I understand, are the agents who employ you. My
name is Rogers. This is Mr. Warren, my wife's
brother-in-law, and this is Mr. Edwards, who will
advise us as to any repairs we might have to make if
we considered taking the house."

While the Inspector was speaking, the caretaker
flashed his electric torch on each of us in turn. I

fancied he let the beam fall on me longer than on the others. However, his only comment was, " Well, if the agent says you can see over the house, I suppose you can. But it's a dam' fool time to send visitors, on a Sunday and after dark. There ain't no electric light on, you know."

" You have your torch," was the reply, " and Mr. Edwards and I have ours. You often find, don't you, Edwards, that owners cut off the light when a house takes a long time to sell. A very false economy, as a matter of fact. Well, we'd better make a start. Will you lead the way, Mr. Caretaker ? "

" You don't want to see the basement, do you ? "

" Of course we do, cellars and all."

The caretaker muttered something, and led the way down a long passage, past a door that was almost off its hinges, to a flight of very worn stone steps, which he went down, flashing the torch in front of him. When he reached the basement, my two companions looked into every door and cupboard, and kept up a steady flow of domestic patter. Had the place been properly illuminated, I think my impression of its squalor would have been greater than it was. Almost everything that could be broken was broken, and the general filth was lamentable. Only one room showed any sign of attention, and that was a large one on the road side of the house which had probably been the servants' hall—or as we are now told to call it, the " staff sitting-room." It contained an iron bedstead, a table, a broken cane chair and a broken armchair, a tin trunk and some cooking utensils—in fact, the maximum furniture which the law allows to remain in a house if it is to be exempt from rates.

" This, I suppose, is where you shake down," said the Inspector in a hearty voice. " I should have thought you'd have found the kitchen more convenient."

" You wouldn't, if you knew the kitchen. It's through here."

He opened a door, and the survey continued. The kitchen was frightful and the scullery unbelievable. In one corner of it there grew a clump of huge and smelly toadstools.

" Well, I think that's enough for this floor," said the Inspector at length. " Now for the floor above. Will you go first, please, Mr. Caretaker ? "

The ground floor comprised a large double dining-room (the walls of which were " enriched " with a plaster ornamentation in the worst taste of 1850), a study, a pantry and an entrance hall. The house-hunters spent less time over it than they had over the basement and, after a glance at the strangest of bathrooms on the half-landing, we reached the first floor. At the back of the house was a large double drawing-room, and on the road side were three or four small rooms. There was also a box-room without windows or fireplace, the atmosphere of which was horrible.

" Well, Edwards," the Inspector said, flashing his torch on his wrist-watch as he spoke, " in view of the general conditions of the place, I think the owner's asking exactly three times what the house is worth.

In fact, I hardly think we need go any further. However, I suppose my wife will say I'm shirking my job, if I don't look at the next floor."

The caretaker looked round hopefully when the Inspector spoke of abandoning the investigation, but the Inspector drove him towards the next flight of stairs and then turned round and said casually to Edwards: " By the way, you might examine the fireplaces on the ground floor, will you ? I don't think there'll be anything new for you to criticize up above, apart from the usual squalor."

Edwards said, " Righto! " and ran downstairs. The caretaker, who was half-way up to the next floor, looked down apprehensively and hesitated, but the Inspector, signing to me to follow him, walked quickly upstairs, driving the man ahead of him.

" We'll have a look at the main back bedroom first, please," he said.

" It's just like the bedroom underneath," the caretaker murmured, as we followed him in. " Ceiling's a bit lower, that's all."

" It isn't so much the bedroom I'm interested in, as the view," the Inspector answered. " I suppose the windows open all right ? "

As the Inspector flashed his torch on to the panes, I noticed that they were opaque with whitewash. This, I think, was the window out of which the caretaker had leant to speak to me that morning, when I was walking in the garden of Beresford Lodge.

" The windows open all right," the caretaker said,

with a trace of aggressiveness, " but it seems a queer time to look for a view—six o'clock on a Sunday night, when it's pitch dark."

" I only want to see," the Inspector replied docilely, " whether the garden at the back is private or not. Down in London you expect to be overlooked, but up here, especially in a house of this price, you don't want to be bothered with neighbours."

As he spoke, the caretaker raised the lower halves of the three big windows to their full height. A delicious freshness filled the room.

" Look, Malcolm," said the Inspector. " I'm afraid there's one house that we can see all too plainly."

Again I saw him glance furtively at his wristwatch. I was a little surprised at his calling me Malcolm, till I remembered that I was supposed to be his brother-in-law. Clearly, I thought, as I went to the window, something was going to happen. The caretaker, too, seemed uneasy; for he kept turning his head to the door and then toward us and shifting from one foot to the other, till the Inspector took him by the elbow and led him, with strange deliberateness, to the middle window.

" Look," he said, " through those trees. You see the whole side of that enormous house. There isn't a window that doesn't overlook us."

I followed his gaze through the bare branches of the plane trees. It was quite true. The whole façade of Beresford Lodge was revealed. Despite the drawn curtains, there were chinks of light in the french window at the end of the dining-room, the windows of the terrace room, the drawing-room, two rooms on the second floor and two rooms on the third floor. It only needed, I felt, the slightest stirring of the curtains, the momentary flapping of a blind in the wind, for any of those lighted rooms to give up its secret. There was a fascination in watching the big house, unobserved, and for a moment I ceased to wonder why I was where I was, and gave myself up to the contemplation of those many windows—as if I could gather from them material for a play or a novel, or even an emotional experience of my own. Should I see Amabel locked passionately in Dixon's arms, Clarence crumpling up the failure of a sonnet, or Quisberg desperately turning out a secret drawer and burning the evidences of his former life ? Had Nurse Moon been in the house I felt sure she would have appeared at an open window, or on the balcony perhaps, and smiled across the dark lawn to a lover hidden below.

The Inspector, too, seemed absorbed by the view; for he stood motionless by the middle window and said nothing, while the caretaker beside him moved his feet restlessly. Yet even he seemed to share our interest, and made no attempt to speak or walk away.

Then suddenly the whole sky was illuminated by a dazzling light which appeared to rise somehow from behind Beresford Lodge and then hovered in the air over the middle of the garden, directing a powerful searchlight on to the whole side of the house. And at that moment a tall figure leant out of the window of the room where Mrs. Harley had slept, and flung a great whitish bundle, which might have been a woman in a nightdress, over the sill. Horrified, I watched the body, if it was one, fall down the house side till it struck the spiked railing of the balcony below—the balcony on to which my bedroom of Christmas Eve had access. Then, before I had time to look again at the figure by the window of the room above, the light failed, and a thin rain of silver sparks drifted downwards to the earth. I turned round and, as I did so, heard footsteps creeping stealthily to the door. The Inspector remained where he was, apparently oblivious of everything, but I could no longer see the dim outline of the caretaker beside him.

" Inspector," I whispered, but he turned his face towards me, put his finger to his lips, and shook his head. Then after what seemed a very long time I heard the sounds of a short scuffle below, followed by two quick blasts on a police whistle. At that the Inspector relaxed, took my arm and flashed his torch towards the door.

" Did that frighten you ? " he asked pleasantly.

" Yes," I said. " It did. But the caretaker ? . . . "

" Oh, they've got him all right! Now quickly back to Beresford Lodge."

" Do you mean," I asked obstinately, " that you've had the caretaker arrested ? Was he the murderer ? "

The Inspector laughed not without bitterness, I thought.

" I've had him arrested," he said, " but I don't think I can quite call him a murderer."

We walked together in silence back to Beresford Lodge. My thoughts came and went at great speed, but left me little the wiser.

XIX. CONCLAVE AND CIGARETTES

Sunday—6.30 p.m.

DESPITE the Inspector's enigmatic words after the arrest of the caretaker, I could not help hoping that when I reached Beresford Lodge I should find the whole mystery at an end—that we should all wake up, as it were, from the long nightmare of suspicion and mutual hostility, and spend the last evening of the Christmas holiday in an atmosphere of relief and sympathetic friendliness. The caretaker seemed so convenient a culprit on whom to thrust the troubles of the house, that I almost forgot the irregularities of Quisberg's past life, Dixon's bad record, the dubious position of Clarence James, and the possible complicity of Nurse Moon. But I was destined to be gravely disappointed; for the hour which followed was perhaps the most harassing period in my whole visit.

When the Inspector and I had taken off our coats in the lobby, he turned to me and broke his long silence by saying, " I shall probably see you again quite soon. You'd better go into the terrace room for a bit now. I dare say you'll find some of the others there. If you want to tell them about Paragon House, I don't really mind." Then he walked abruptly to the stairs, leaving me in the hall. I did

as I was told, and went into the terrace room, where
I found Amabel, Dixon and Clarence. Amabel and
Dixon were sitting by a table loaded with drinks.
Clarence sprawled, with his eyes shut, on a sofa at
the far end of the room, where he twitched rest-
lessly.

" Hello," said Amabel miserably, " so the little
wanderer is back! Help yourself."

I did, while Dixon glared at me and said nothing.

For a while, as so often during the past three days,
I searched desperately for something to say—something which without being too commonplace could
wound nobody's susceptibilities. But this time I
could think of nothing and stood there inanely, glass
in hand, looking at Amabel, till finally I felt I had to
blurt out my story or sink through the floor.

" Something extraordinary," I said, " has just
happened in Paragon House."

" Really ? " she drawled.

" Yes. I've been there with the Inspector."

Dixon looked at me sharply, and said to Amabel
" I think we might hear about this, don't you ? "

She nodded to him, and pointed to a seat.

" Make yourself comfy," she said, " and tell us all
about it. It's rather a relief to see someone who
seems quite pleased with life."

" Are you being polite ? " I asked.

" Not at all. Couldn't be if I tried. I shall adore
hearing the worst. Do begin."

I began—baldly and self-consciously. But my two
listeners seemed interested, and my narrative
improved a little. Apparently they heard or saw

nothing of the firework which had suddenly illuminated the house—after all, the curtains had been
closely drawn—but they recognized it, from my
description, as being similar to the one which they
had let off together on the night of Christmas Eve.
Amabel began to explain this escapade of theirs to
me, but I unfortunately allowed her to realize that I
already knew all about it.

" So you know that, too," she said, while Dixon
glowered suspiciously at me. " It seems to me we're
the only transparent people in this affair. But don't
stop now. The flash lit up the whole garden—I
quite believe that."

I continued. When I reached the climax, she
whistled and said: " No wonder we were warned off
the upper floors this afternoon and herded in here.
They must have stage-managed the show pretty
well. What do you think of it, Len ? "

Dixon had been drinking almost ever since my
arrival (and probably before it), and when he spoke,
his voice was thick and hoarse.

" I think," he said slowly, " that it's a great pity
Mrs. Quisberg ever asked such a skunk to join her
party."

I was so dazed by the sudden rudeness that I said
nothing, while Amabel put her hand on his arm and
whispered to him.

" No, leave me alone," he went on. " It's time we
had a little plain speaking. This has been a bloody
affair for everybody, but it has been a thousand
times bloodier than it need have been, because one
of the party has been behaving like a police spy."

I looked at him as courageously as I could, and said with an attempt at dignity: " Are you by any chance referring to me ? Because if you are——"

" I am," he said, rising unsteadily from his chair. " What else are you but a dirty little copper's nark ? Who's always been on the spot when a body's been discovered ? You. Who else spent his time eavesdropping and ferreting round and blabbing to that bloody Inspector—— "

His vulgar and bullying manner made me suddenly lose my temper.

" I'd better tell you, Dixon," I said, " that I'm not in the habit of being spoken to like this by bastards."

It was, to say the least, an unfortunate remark. He flung off Amabel, who was trying to restrain him, and rushed at me like a bull. Luckily I stepped aside, and he went hurtling into the arms of the Inspector, who opened the door just at that moment.

The Inspector took no notice of me or Amabel, but holding Dixon by the arm led him firmly through the door. As it shut I caught the words: " I want to speak to you." The next move was made by Amabel, who threw herself on to the window-seat in a paroxysm of tears. Then Clarence woke up, or pretended to wake up, raised his head from the cushion and made a face at me. I had never felt more drawn to him. My anger left me as quickly as it had arisen, and I began to reproach myself for my tactlessness.

" I'm awfully sorry," I said when I had walked across the room. " I suppose my nerves are on edge, too. Do you think you ought to go to your sister ? "

" Oh no," he said, and lay back on his sofa. But when he saw her going towards the door, he got up and prevented her from opening it. I was longing so much to be a thousand miles away that I didn't think of trying to overhear what he said. However, he seemed to have some influence; for she retired to the window-seat and sat there quietly, with her eyes fixed on the door. Then Clarence came over to me.

" What does it matter, after all ? " he said.

" What ? " I echoed weakly.

" This whole affair. Two people, for whom we don't care. . . ."

" I liked Dr. Green," I interrupted.

He looked at me with astonishment.

" Did you ? "

" Yes. Very much."

" I'm sorry. But even so, you'd only known him for two days."

" Yes. Perhaps it isn't that."

" Then what is it ? "

This new sympathy, this intimacy of conversation after so many evasions, half-truths and sentences too deliberately framed, made me suddenly want to cry. Indeed, tears, bringing a kind of relief, did come into my eyes, and as I sat down I felt I did not care who saw them. I had gone through enough. There was no reason, any longer, to be ashamed of anything I did. This moment of utter self-abandonment was an emotional turning-point. As far as the case was concerned, the worst, for me, was over, and however much I was afterwards to be moved by pity for the calamities of others, I shed, at last, the sense of the personal wretchedness which had troubled me ever since I saw the crumpled body of Mrs. Harley on the balcony.

Meanwhile, Clarence surveyed me with sympathy.

" You see," I said, looking up, "it might have been you."

He smiled.

" Or you, for that matter. Don't worry. I'm the only one who's been in hell."

" How ? You ? "

" You see," he said with a tragic dryness, " I'm the only one of the party who has had the experience of finding that the woman he loved and who, he thought, loved him, was at the same time being unfaithful with—with . . ."

He stopped and turned away.

" But are you sure of that ? " I asked gently.

" Yes," he said without looking round. " She almost told me so. She did tell me . . ."

For a few moments we said nothing.

Then, suddenly, the door opened and Quisberg came in, followed by Harley and the Inspector. I stood up and instinctively inclined my head a little. It was like the entry of the Celebrant at High Mass, or the Commanding Officer at a review. Even Clarence seemed to pull himself together, and show a respectful, almost a solicitous, attention. Quisberg was paler even than he had been when I saw him on the terrace, but his face had somehow acquired a look of calm which made its misery less complete. He went straight to an armchair and sat down.

Harley, still the perfect secretary, drew up another and bowed the Inspector towards it. The Inspector bent down and whispered to Quisberg, who shook his head, and said: " No, no. You talk to *d*em first. You know what I want to say." The Inspector straightened himself and said, giving us a commanding glance, " Both Mr. Quisberg and I have something very important to say to you all. Will you sit down and listen to me ? It may be for rather a long time, I'm afraid." Then he sat down in his chair and toyed with some sheets of paper, while the rest of us brought up chairs and completed a semi-circle round the fire. Then, while we were all composing ourselves, crossing our legs and lighting cigarettes, the Inspector rose, went to the door, locked it, and returned to the circle, where he stood by his chair.

" You must," he said, looking at us somewhat severely in turn, " all be prepared to suffer considerable distress while you hear what I have to tell you. You may easily feel that I am wantonly revealing secrets which have no bearing on my story. This, I assure you, I shall not do. I am bound, however, to probe some very tender places, and I ask you to forgive me—if only for the sake of the chief sufferer "—here he inclined his head to Mr. Quisberg—" who has asked me to tell you his story as well as mine."

At this point he sat down. Excited and apprehensive as I was, I could not help feeling that he was rather enjoying himself. If only he had stuck to the theological college, what eloquent sermons he would have preached!

" I was called in," the Inspector continued, " to investigate the murder of Dr. Green—an apparently motiveless crime occurring in a household already mourning the sudden death of one of its Christmas guests. I say that the murder of Dr. Green was apparently motiveless, but it was not long before an examination of those cross-currents which always exist where several persons of differing temperaments are gathered together, showed me that Dr. Green, while living, was a thorn in the flesh of at least two of you here, and one member of the house-party who is no longer with us."

The parsonic pause which followed was too much for Amabel, who turned her white face on the Inspector and almost shouted:

"Where is he, Inspector? Have you arrested him? I insist on knowing."

" Mr. Dixon," he replied calmly, " has left this house, and will not return to it."

" Then," she said defiantly, " I'm going too."

" Please, Miss Thurston, you must listen to me first. Afterwards, you can make up your mind. But if you have any gratitude or consideration at all for Mr. Quisberg, you will be patient and hear me out. Perhaps I had better say now, that this public address to you all is really Mr. Quisberg's idea and not mine. Each of you, in your separate way, is deeply concerned in this tragedy, and Mr. Quisberg is desirous and, to my mind, very properly desirous, that each of you shall hear the whole truth. We could, of course, have spoken to you one by one, but apart from the labour of doing so—I might even say, from Mr. Quisberg's point of view, the ordeal of doing so—it is, I think, just as well that you should hear me in one another's presence. You will thus, each of you, be assured that there has been no concealment or misrepresentation. And it will, I hope, make your relationships with one another easier and happier."

He lit a cigarette.

" I'm going to tell you," he said after a short pause, " the whole sequence of events, as a story—not from my point of view, but the historian's. I shall keep myself out of the picture as much as I can, and shall not bother you with the clues which led me to my discoveries. For them, I have to thank my training and a good deal of luck. Try to listen to me patiently and calmly—and with sympathetic consideration for those who have been the sufferers, whether innocent or guilty.

" The story begins many years ago—before the war. Mr. Quisberg held an important position in England and was even then a very wealthy man. The organization with which he was working collapsed suddenly, and in the confusion which followed he committed an action of which he himself will give you an explanation when I have finished. It is enough for me now to say that this action involved his hurried flight from England to the Continent, where he changed not only his name, but even, through the surgical skill of Dr. Green, his physical appearance. There was at the time a very

close friendship subsisting between Mr. Quisberg
and the doctor—a degree of friendship, indeed,
which is found more often among northern than
southern nations. For a while, Mr. Quisberg lived
under the wing of his friend in complete obscurity,
but later when the passing of time had confirmed the
physical changes in his appearance, he travelled
about and engaged, with success, in various business
enterprises. During a holiday in Switzerland he met
Mrs. Quisberg—Mrs. Thurston as she was then—and
they married. I may perhaps be forgiven for saying
that it is a rare example of a thoroughly happy
marriage. And later, should Mrs. Quisberg seem to
need your sympathy, some of you will do well to
comfort her with this."

His eyes met Amabel's for a moment. Then he
continued:

" At the time of his marriage, Mr. Quisberg
decided, as I think you all know, to return to
England. He bought his wife this fine house and
lived here, respected on all sides, in happiness and
comfort—nor did anyone associate him with the
man who had left England so hurriedly over twenty
years before—until the afternoon of Christmas Eve.
By the most unhappy coincidence, there arrived on
that afternoon, as a guest of the house, Mrs. Harley,
who had before her marriage been Mr. Quisberg's
secretary. I need not say that he had completely
lost touch with her in the meanwhile, that he did
not know she was still living or married—much less
that she had a son and that this son was now his
valued helper and friend.

" Mr. Quisberg met Mrs. Harley in the hall, here, on Christmas Eve. They only spoke a word or two, but recognized each other at once. Mr. Quisberg was on his way to an important meeting in London. He had no time, even if it would have been wise, to talk privately to Mrs. Harley, or come to any kind of understanding with her. All he could do was to tell his fears to Dr. Green in a few hurried whispers on the lawn in the front of the house, and hope that Mrs. Harley would keep the secret to herself till he came back.

" And now my task is more difficult; for I have to try to explain the mind of someone who can no longer explain himself—someone, moreover, whom I have never seen. I have already told you of the close devotion which existed between Mr. Quisberg and the doctor. I gather that the doctor was a most able and brilliant man, bound by none of the scruples of conventional morality. He was able to form quick decisions, and relished them far more than prudence or deliberation. There was an element of the fantastic in his character, of that genius which is sometimes considered not far remote from madness. He was a man whose actions it would always be hard to understand, and still harder to predict—a man who in every sense was a law to himself. Some of you liked him, some of you hated him. To be indifferent to him was as impossible as it is now for us to judge him."

Again the Inspector paused and looked at us in turn. He was, I felt sure, not far from enjoying himself. Indeed, I think, he knew he was, and read my thoughts; for when his eyes met mine, his cheeks were coloured with the suspicion of a blush.

Then he continued in a deliberately quiet and unrhetorical tone:

" I can't tell you when Dr. Green formed his plan, or what form it would have taken if events had not played into his hands. You all know of Mr. Warren's accident while you were playing a game in the drawing-room on Christmas Eve. You may also know that Dr. Green, after attending very ably to Mr. Warren, gave him a sleeping draught. Mrs. Quisberg, meanwhile, had been showing Mrs. Harley to her room, but found her in a mood of such agitation that very naturally she asked the doctor if he would prepare another sleeping draught and give it to Mrs. Harley. The doctor agreed, but made, probably, a stronger mixture than he had given to Mr. Warren. Then the household went to bed, except for Mr. Quisberg and Mr. Harley, who were in London, and Miss Thurston and Mr. Dixon, who went together for a motor ride. The door of Dr. Green's bedroom faced the door of Mrs. Harley's bedroom. Soon after two o'clock—Mr. Harley, would you like to go away for a few moments ? This must be most harassing for you."

Harley, whom as usual we had all forgotten, shook his head and murmured something that I could not catch.

" Are you quite sure ? " the Inspector asked anxiously. " Very well. You know what's coming. You must try not to listen to this part. . . . Soon after two o'clock, I was saying, Dr. Green crept across the landing to Mrs. Harley's room. He took with him a bottle of some anæsthetic, ether or chloroform, we don't know which. Mrs. Harley was already sleeping very heavily under the influence of the draught. It was thus quite easy for the doctor to render her completely insensible with the anæsthetic. When he had done this, he killed her by breaking her neck. He was a very strong man, you must remember, and had an expert knowledge of anatomy. Then he opened the french window and threw out the body, expecting no doubt that it would fall right down to the terrace. Now it happened that at this very moment, Miss Thurston and Mr. Dixon came back from their motor ride and let off a firework, a kind of star-shell, which flew over the house, illuminating all the far side, and revealed, to anyone who was watching, the doctor standing by the window of Mrs. Harley's room, with her body in his arms.

" Someone was watching—the caretaker in Paragon House. It seems that the regular caretaker had fallen ill suddenly, and the agents had to engage a new man at short notice without inquiring very deeply into his character. The man they engaged was, as a matter of fact, a criminal, and had served sentences for burglary and assault and probably other offences. The fact that he was watching this house from an upper window in Paragon House is not so extraordinary as it may seem at first sight. In the first place, he had hardly anything to do, and it was partly idle curiosity which made him keep his eyes fixed on the chinks of light which appeared and disappeared in the big wall opposite. Probably he saw your game in the drawing-room through an uncurtained window and felt an improper interest in the ' goings-on.' Probably, also—though this is a guess on my part—he was spending his time planning a new ' coup.' Beresford Lodge, if I may say so, is a house worth robbing, and any clever thief tries to find out how the land lies before coming to the attack. At all events, his watch was not unrewarded; for he saw something which gave him a great opportunity—not this time for theft, but for blackmail. In a short time you will hear of him again.

" Mrs. Harley's body was found, as I think you all know, by Mr. Warren, on the balcony outside his bedroom. Most naturally, he sent at once for Dr. Green, who in turn sent for Dr. McKenzie. Dr. McKenzie saw nothing suspicious in the injuries which the body had sustained, and I think most probably that if there had been no further developments, the inquest to-morrow would have resulted in a verdict of accidental death.

" Christmas Day passed without much incident. Mr. Quisberg and Mr. Harley returned in due course from London, and it was naturally a very great shock to both of them to hear the sad tidings. Dr. Green, we may be sure, did not burden Mr. Quisberg with any confession of guilt. Mr. Quisberg was also, I may mention, much disturbed by a domestic matter about which he had asked Dr. Green to make some inquiries, and it is not surprising that the strain of his many anxieties was almost more than he could bear.

" The blow fell after dinner. By this time, the news of Mrs. Harley's supposed accident was common property in the neighbourhood. We can easily imagine it reaching the caretaker of Paragon House through the milk boy or a baker's boy, or gossip with the servants of a house in the same road. It seems that he came round to this house during the afternoon, but for some reason—perhaps because he had not fully decided what he was going to do— went away again without seeking admittance. After dinner, however, as a result it may be of further thought, or some confirmation of his suspicions, he walked round once more and demanded an inter- view with Mr. Quisberg, who saw him in the study. Mr. Quisberg was naturally so horrified by the caretaker's disclosure that he hardly grasped its threatening nature. Dr. Green, whom he quickly sent for, was better prepared. No doubt Dr. Green had not overlooked the importance of that sudden flash of light which occurred at the very moment of his crime, and was already turning his fertile mind to meet the danger. As soon as he saw the intruder, he took command of the situation and asked Mr. Quisberg to withdraw. Of what happened then between Dr. Green and the caretaker, we have only Mr. Quisberg's account of what Dr. Green after- wards told him. According to this story—which there is no reason whatever to doubt—the care- taker demanded a passage to Australia and five thousand pounds as the price of silence. Dr. Green temporized with him, and arranged to meet him on the Heath, presumably for further discussion, on the afternoon of Boxing Day. The doctor was to make his whereabouts known by playing an air on the musical instrument which was afterwards found near his body. But the same night—and I need hardly tell you that Mr. Quisberg did not know this—when he had temporarily got rid of the unwelcome visitor, he took a spade and a couple of planks from the potting shed here, made his way to a secluded spot at the far end of the West Heath, and dug a grave which he covered over with the planks, a little loose earth and leaves. I have no doubt at all that this grave was intended for the caretaker's dead body.

"Next morning, Dr. Green, despite the ordeal before him, found time to go down to London and get the information which Mr. Quisberg had asked him to get concerning what I have called 'the domestic matter.' He came back about three, and went for a walk with Mr. Dixon who, I may as well say, without beating about the bush any further, was the subject of the doctor's inquiries in London. Dixon was carrying a short but heavy stick weighted with lead. The discussion between the two men during their walk was far from amicable—we will suppose that the doctor presented Dixon with a definite and humiliating ultimatum—and ended in a violent quarrel, the outcome of which was that the doctor knocked Dixon down, took his stick and walked away, leaving him lying on the Heath some-where near the Spaniards. Dixon, after a time, continued his walk alone through the northern suburbs, and called both at a doctor's, where he obtained some attention to his injuries, and later at the house of some friends in North Finchley, where he had supper. These visits have been satisfactorily checked to-day.

" Meanwhile—long before Dixon had reached North Finchley—the doctor walked back to the West Heath and disappeared into the thicket. Had he known it, three acquaintances of his were also on or near the Heath that evening. One was Mr. Warren, who was watching the sunset from Spaniards' Row. The other two were Mr. James and Nurse Moon, who were having a disagreement while walking together in West Heath Road. The cause of the disagreement, it is only right for me to tell you, was Nurse Moon's infatuation for the doctor which, in a mood of pique or devilry, she made no attempt to hide. Indeed, when the silence was suddenly broken by the doctor playing on his little flute, she recognized the music and the player, and made as if to join him then and there. From this, however, she was fortunately dissuaded by Mr. James's protests. She knew also that she was due to be on duty here in a short time, when Dr. McKenzie was expected to pay an evening visit. Instead, therefore, of plunging across the Heath and possibly playing a part in the grim struggle that must have been occurring at the same moment, she hurried back to Beresford Lodge and changed into her uniform.. Mr. James, whom she had left behind, spent a few minutes walking up and down West

Heath Road in a mood of great bitterness. He then resolved, desperately, to meet Dr. Green face to face, and set out in the direction from which the music had come. It does not seem to me that it would have been very easy to find the doctor, with no other clue to guide one, but the fact remains—and it is a fact which I have no hesitation in accepting—that Mr. James did come across him, or rather his dead body, in quite a short time. Like Mr. Warren, a few seconds later, his eye was first caught by the metallic glint of the flute. As a policeman, I am, of course, bound to blame Mr. James severely for not immediately reporting his discovery. Humanly speaking, and knowing what I do of his state of mind at the time, I cannot be surprised that when he ran across Mr. Warren (whose innocent walk was leading him towards the same spot), he considered himself absolved from further responsibility, and sought relief from his nervous tension in a complete change of scene and the companionship of a sympathetic friend.

" Of Mr. Warren's conduct I can wholeheartedly approve. He examined the body as well as he could to make sure that death had really taken place, and after removing articles of value from the pockets, returned at once to Beresford Lodge for help.

" By the way, Mr. Quisberg, I should have handed these over to you before, as Dr. Green's sole executor. Will you take them now ? "

As he spoke, he pulled out of his pocket the note-case and cigarette-case which I had found on the body. Quisberg stretched out a hand mechanically and took them, laid the notecase on the arm of his chair, opened the cigarette-case, looked at it sadly, and shut it again.

" This," the Inspector said, " is really all my story; for we do not yet know, if we shall ever know, what exactly happened between Dr. Green and the caretaker. I am convinced, as I said before, that the doctor had lured the caretaker to that lonely place with the deliberate intention of killing him. He was quite unconventional enough to feel no kind of scruple about taking the life of a blackmailer. Evidently something went wrong. Perhaps the doctor had been thrown off his mental balance by the previous struggle with Dixon. Perhaps the caretaker is unusually agile. He must certainly have been suspicious and on his guard the whole time. At all events, there was a fight, and this time it was the doctor who lost. There is no reason, of course, to suppose that his death was anything but an accident. It is a maxim, I believe, of every detective story that blackmailers do not kill their victims. I take it that the doctor had a shot at his enemy with the stick and missed, or perhaps tripped up, and that when the caretaker had wrenched the weapon from him and gave a return blow, he struck harder than he intended. It was, of course, not a situation in which one could spend much time calculating how hard one ought to hit. One thing alone really puzzles me, and I fear will continue to puzzle me. The doctor's

plan to kill the caretaker was really beautifully con-
ceived. It had its moments of rashness, of course.
The serenade on the flute was a dangerous piece of
bravado, though not out of keeping with what I
know of the doctor's character. But, as a whole,
granted that it was a desperate measure, it had
every chance of success. It might have been two or
three days, or even more, before anyone missed the
caretaker. Even if inquiries had been made, there
would have been no reason to suppose that he had
met with any catastrophe. The agents, I think,
would merely have assumed that he was an irres-
ponsible fellow who had deserted his post. At all
events, I see no cause why any search should have
been made on Hampstead Heath, and in default of
such a search, the body, securely buried in a damp
and remote thicket, might easily have remained
undiscovered for years—or at least till the trippery
season. And by that time the doctor was sufficiently
resourceful to make away with it altogether. One
weakness alone stands out. How did the doctor
propose to kill his man? He did not know that
Dixon would set out for his walk carrying such a
convenient weapon—still less that there would be
any chance of securing it. Indeed, I am inclined to
regard this walk with Dixon as an afterthought on
the doctor's part—merely as a chance of putting in
some useful work before the time appointed for the
real task. We might, of course, suppose that he
intended to come back and fetch a weapon from
home. But if that was so, why did he take the flute
with him instead of fetching that, too? Perhaps,

you may say, he had a weapon, but the caretaker made away with it. I do not think so ; for the injury to the doctor's head was almost certainly caused by Dixon's stick, and there would have been no motive for the caretaker to conceal a weapon which he never used. One might advance as a tentative theory that the doctor intended to use the spade which was, of course, already hidden in the thicket, to give the fatal blow. To my mind this clumsy instrument would not have been at all to the doctor's liking. Think, for example, how hard it would have been to take it up and get a proper grasp of it without arousing suspicion.

" However, I am keeping you far too long over what is a purely professional line of inquiry, and must apologize for letting my interest run away with me like this. As I said before, my story is now told. I don't know, before we part, if Mr. Quisberg . . ."

He paused expectantly, and we all looked at Quisberg, who with shaking hand opened the doctor's cigarette-case again, drew out the last cigarette, lit it, and rose unsteadily to his feet. Before he spoke, he turned his tragic eyes on each one of us, till finally they came to rest on Harley.

" Dr. Green," he said at length, " was my very dear friend. He died for me. Your *modd*er, Harley, was my mistress, in *de* old days when . . . As for *de* money, which *d*ey say I stole. . . ." Here he paused pitifully and took a long pull at his cigarette. " . . . I never stole it. It was mine, owed to me by *de* company. I can't explain *d*is now, but you will see. . . ."

Then, while we all thought he was pausing again to find words, he suddenly uttered a gasping cry, put a hand to his chest, tottered and fell down, dead.

XX. SHORT CATECHISM

Reader: Was it suicide ?

Malcolm Warren: No. Don't be so heartless,
either. Can't you guess what it was ?

R.: I suppose the cigarette was poisoned ?

M.W.: Yes.

R.: By Dr. Green ?

M.W.: Yes. Quisberg's death, you see, was a
tragic answer to the problem that had been puzzling
the Inspector.

R.: You mean, the difficulty of supposing that the
doctor had set out to kill the caretaker without
providing himself with a weapon.

M.W.: Exactly. He had provided himself with a
weapon. It's quite easy to see what the doctor's plan
was. During his talk with the caretaker, he intended to
offer him the poisoned cigarette. It was all so simple.

R.: I suppose the doctor would have had to
smoke himself—as a guarantee of good faith.

M.W.: Probably he did.

R.: Then the cigarette-case must have contained
at least two cigarettes. Suppose the caretaker had
pulled out the wrong one ?

M.W.: That would have been very awkward, but
I think we could trust the doctor to see that he
didn't. A little sleight-of-hand or mental suggestion
would have been sufficient.

R.: But the plan failed.

M.W.: Yes—because, strange to say, the care-taker was a non-smoker. This came out at his trial and was fully confirmed. There was no trace, for example, of a cigarette wrapping or tobacco tin in the débris at Paragon House.

R.: What happened to the caretaker?

M.W.: All in good time! You ought to ask me first, what happened to the petrified little group surrounding the dead body in the terrace room. What did we all do? Did Amabel faint? Did Clarence whistle a bar of Beethoven? Did the Inspector swear? It's easy to be flippant about it at this distance, but it was a most shocking and awful moment.

R.: What did you do?

M.W.: As far as I can remember—nothing. The Inspector gave orders and Harley had them carried out. Clarence and Amabel went up to Mrs. Quis-berg. I stayed at the far end of the room for a while, and as no one took any notice of me, opened one of the french windows and walked down the Louis Quinze staircase into the garden. I soon realized that it was still raining, and went round to the front door, feeling damp and chilly. The front door was shut, of course. I had no latchkey and was forced to ring. Edwins admitted me, fortunately without comment, and I went up to my bedroom and changed my clothes.

R.: This is all terribly undràmatic.

M.W.: Yes, but almost more interesting than the drama, don't you think?

R.: I don't know about that.

M.W.: But surely it is. A detective story is always something of an *étude de mœurs*—a study in the behaviour of normal people in abnormal circumstances. By normal people, I mean people whose lives come fairly close to our own, people whose psychology we can follow and sympathize with. The theft of a coconut, however ingenious, in an island of savages, would, as such, hardly hold anyone's attention. Similarly, a murder occurring on a battlefield would fall rather flat. You want the revolver shot, the bloodstained knife, the mutilated corpse—but largely because they bring out the prettiness of the chintz in the drawing-room and the softness of the grass on the Vicarage lawn. You don't follow ?

R.: Yes, I do.

M.W.: If I may continue this digression for a moment, I would say that the excuse for a detective story is two-fold. First, it presents a problem to be solved and shares, in a humble way, the charm of the acrostic and the crossword puzzle. But secondly —and this, to my mind, is its real justification—it provides one with a narrow but intensive view of ordinary life, the steady flow of which is felt more keenly through the very violence of its interruption. I may be speaking too personally perhaps. I think I have told you already how much I am moved by contraries—that I never realize the full loveliness of the summer till the first autumn rain sets in. But I suppose this sense of contrast exists in most people.

R.: Be careful, or you'll become really paradoxical. Most people would say that the softness of the Vicarage lawn is only noteworthy because there's a body lying on it. You say the body is only noteworthy because it is lying on a soft lawn.

M.W.: Not quite. Though I don't know. If you press me too hard and offer me yet another whisky I might try to maintain that, from a philosophical point of view, your paradox is true. After all, soft lawns are more real and permanent than dead bodies. At least, I hope they are.

R.: I can see you're implying that my next question should be: " How was your dinner served that Sunday night ? Did you have dinner ? And, if so, was it a good one, and had you any appetite ? "

M.W.: Very good questions, too. Imagine yourself for one moment in my circumstances. Would you expect dinner to be served an hour after the head of the household had died in such a fashion ? Could you have eaten with gusto ?

R.: I don't know.

M.W.: You see, you're regarding my story as something apart from any experience you might have yourself. I'm sorry, because it's evidently a reflection on the way I've told it.

R.: Not altogether. I should love to have an answer to the questions I suggested a moment ago.

M.W.: Dinner *was* served. Amabel and Sheila did not come down. Where they had theirs, if any, I don't know. There were only three of us in the dining-room—Clarence, Harley and myself. We talked quite brightly—or, rather, Clarence did—about modern art.

R.: Let me see. Should I have talked about modern art?

M.W.: You'd have only been too delighted to find you could talk about anything. As it was, the conversation flowed fairly smoothly, and we continued it for some time in the drawing-room, till a maid came in to say that Mrs. Quisberg would like to see me. I went at once, of course. It was a very sad meeting. She was on the verge of tears most of the time, and so was I once or twice. But even then I was struck by her kindness and unselfishness. It seems that Quisberg had told her everything that afternoon and had declared himself quite ready to take whatever the consequences might be. Mrs. Quisberg's chief distress was for Harley, apart from the loss of her husband, which came to her as a terrible blow.

R.: She had already lost two before him, hadn't she?

M.W.: That is a heartless remark. You know perfectly well that really devoted wives and husbands very often do marry again, quite soon afterwards, too. Besides, I gather that Mrs. Quisberg's first marriage—with Clarence's father—was not altogether a happy one. The father, it seems, was even more difficult and wayward than the son. The Thurston marriage, I think, was happy.

R.: You haven't told us much about these two earlier marriages of hers.

M.W.: I don't know much about them. James and Thurston must have been two very different types.

R.: Did either of them leave any money ? I have gathered that Mrs. Quisberg was living on her third husband.

M.W.: I don't think James left any. This accounts for Clarence's poverty. Thurston did leave something, settled on Mrs. Quisberg for life, with reversion to the Thurston children. His money turned out to be rather important.

R.: Why ?

M.W.: Well, you see, Quisberg's death, so far from clearing up everything, led to many complications. Was his money really his, or was it owed to the Cabal liquidators ? The liquidation, of course, had been finished years before, but I understand the Crown has a claim in criminal cases——

R.: What was the outcome of it all ?

M.W.: Mrs. Quisberg was eager, at first, to hand over all Quisberg's fortune. Friends dissuaded her from being so rash, and in the end a compromise was reached, by which she handed over a quarter of a million and a certain sum by way of past interest on it. It was a quarter of a million, you remember, that Quisberg was supposed to have made away with. This left her with forty or fifty thousand pounds, Beresford Lodge, which had been bought for her in her name, and, of course, the Thurston money.

R.: Was Quisberg really a crook ?

M.W.: In the worst sense, no. There is no doubt

that he had committed a criminal offence in vanishing with the securities at the time of the Cabal crash. On the other hand, a barrister told me that a fair defence could have been put up that the money was owned by Quisberg in his own right and that the company merely held it as custodians. I don't think, either, that there was any evidence to show that Quisberg was involved in the fraudulent practices of the Chairman and Vice-Chairman—though I dare say he sailed pretty near the wind. No doubt he was less straight-laced when young than in his old age. The whole Cabal story is so involved I've never been able to follow it.

R.: Well, what became of everybody ? Let's take the caretaker first. I suppose they didn't try him for murder.

M.W.: No, they didn't. He was tried for manslaughter and acquitted. The prosecution, you see, couldn't, or didn't wish to hide the fact that Dr. Green had set out with the intention of murdering him. I think some of the jury thought the doctor was a homicidal maniac. The caretaker's attempt at blackmail was, of course, hinted at, but not pressed very strongly. The only two people who could have given first-hand evidence were both dead—the doctor and Quisberg. So the caretaker remained at large—sometimes, when I thought of him in the small hours of the night, I used to feel rather uneasy—till a few weeks ago when he was arrested for robbing a woman of her handbag and given a heavy sentence.

R.: And what of Dixon ? And Amabel ?

M.W.: Poor Amabel went through a terrible time. She had, you see, sufficient of her mother's nature in her to feel very guilty about the way she had been behaving, and she did all she could to make amends by looking after her mother during the period following Quisberg's death. When Quisberg had his last talk with his wife—an hour or so, I suppose, before the tragedy in the terrace room—he told her what Dixon's record was and said he would never consent to the marriage.

R.: How did he know about Dixon's record?

M.W.: The Inspector had read him the paper I had found in Dr. Green's notecase.

R.: Why didn't the Inspector give him the cigarette-case at the same time?

M.W.: Because one of his assistants was examining the outside of the case for finger-prints. Or so he told me.

R.: I expect he really forgot about it or hoped everybody would, so that he could keep it! What happened to the case, by the way?

M.W.: Mrs. Quisberg gave it to me—as a memento of her husband and Dr. Green. I wear it on gala occasions. (This is not one.)

R.: Thank you! So Amabel didn't go chasing after her lover?

M.W.: She wrote to him, Mrs. Quisberg told me, saying that her feelings were unchanged, but that they must not meet for six months. Dixon tried twice to see her, but she avoided him. Then, for some reason or other, he gave her up—or, perhaps, she gave him up. She's now engaged to a successful barrister a good deal older than herself.

R.: And what of Clarence James ? You made me dislike him intensely.

M.W.: I didn't like him myself, I confess, till that last meeting in the terrace room. And even after that, I never felt I really wanted to see him again. But I realize that many people would have thought him the only tolerable member of the party. Like Amabel, he also rallied round his mother for a time. Then, when the period of crisis was over, he became a Communist and got a miserably paid job on a Communist paper. This lasted for about six months, and then he quarrelled with his colleagues and flirted with Fascism. The last I heard of him was that he had been made editor, at quite a good salary, of a rich magazine dealing with the applied arts and modern " luxury articles." Since that time, I believe, his political views have changed a good deal.

R.: Perhaps he realizes that, though Communism might support a few painters and musicians, it wouldn't do much to help the production of futurist chromium vases, expensive lampshades, and silk underclothes. Did he see Nurse Moon again, do you know ?

M.W.: I'm not sure, but I gathered from Mrs. Quisberg that he didn't. Mrs. Quisberg had a letter from her—a very well-written letter, too—in which she protested that she had never meant to give Clarence any encouragement and regretted any trouble she might unwittingly have caused, etc., etc.

R.: Clarence had been very quick to fall for her, hadn't he? I suppose he first met her when Cyril began his appendicitis, and yet he was writing frightful sonnets to her a week or two later.

M.W.: With a person like Clarence I don't think such emotional speed would be impossible. But as a matter of fact, he'd met her some time before at Beresford Lodge when she came for a few days as night nurse to help Sheila through an operation for tonsils. He was attracted to her then, and, finding that they had some mutual friend in the artistic world, managed to see her at intervals till Cyril's appendicitis brought them still closer together, and love reached sonnet-pitch.

R.: How far do you think that sonnet was sincere?

M.W.: It's impossible to say. I think Clarence wrote it purely as an exercise—to distract himself. It was a type of poetry with which he'd have no sympathy at all. But I have no doubt he was very much in love at the time.

R.: You made one bad mistake, didn't you, in thinking that the nurse's companion on the Heath was Edwins?

M.W.: Yes, it was quite an *idée fixe* with me. At a distance Clarence and he did resemble one another, of course, but I oughtn't to have been so sure. My real fault was one of psychology rather than one of observation. It seemed to me just as suitable that Edwins and the nurse should be having an affair, as it would have seemed fantastic that Clarence should have taken any interest in her.

R.: Why?

M.W.: It's hard to explain. Such a difference in
mentality. . . .

R.: She had a pretty face. What does her mentality matter ?

M.W.: You don't know these precious young men.
Now had it been some short-haired sylph in Bloomsbury. . . .

R.: Perhaps you're right.

M.W.: As a matter of fact, Nurse Moon *had* what
are called intellectual pretensions. When she had
left, a book by Bertrand Russell was found in her
bedroom.

R.: Had she read it ?

M.W.: That we don't know.

R.: Well—Harley next, please.

M.W.: I was lucky enough to get Harley a job in
the City. He's doing very well. Was that twelve
o'clock striking ? I'd no idea it was so late.

R.: Don't hurry. I must ask you a few more
things before you go. The first is about the caretaker of Paragon House. When you saw him on the
Sunday morning, he was whitewashing the windows.
Why was he doing that ?

M.W.: He was questioned about that at his trial,
and his answers were evasive and unconvincing.
He admitted that he had been to see Quisberg on
Christmas Day, and said it was because Quisberg had
sent for him. When asked what Quisberg wanted to
see him about, he said that Quisberg had com-
plained of being overlooked and had asked him to
whitewash the windows. As a matter of fact, as no
doubt you know, it's quite easy to see out of a

whitewashed window—especially if you leave a
little chink somewhere—but impossible to see into
one. I think the real reason he whitewashed the
windows was to prevent any of us from seeing *him*.
You see, he was badly scared by then. It wasn't
altogether a rational act, but it's not hard to
understand.

R.: But what of the message he gave you for
Quisberg: " Tell the gentleman he won't be overlooked," and so on ?

M.W.: That, I think, was an invention on the
spur of the moment—rather a clever one, too. I
think the message was meant to call a truce and say:
" I shan't interfere with you again, so don't you
interfere with me. Let bygones be bygones." Of
course, he didn't realize Quisberg's innocence, and
thought that he and Dr. Green were in the plot
together.

R.: We can't be sure, can we, that Quisberg didn't
know that the doctor intended to kill the caretaker ?

M.W.: We can't be sure, but I think it most
unlikely. I think Dr. Green was much too fond of
Quisberg to burden him with such a secret, and I
think also that if Quisberg had known the doctor's
plan he would never have let him carry it out.

R.: Do you think Dr. Green had told Quisberg
that he had killed Mrs. Harley ?

M.W.: Not for one moment. I can imagine him
saying, after the caretaker had gone home on
Christmas night: " My dear Axel, you must be
deranged to believe such a cock-and-bull story. Let
me deal with the man in my own way, and you

won't be troubled by him again. Get this rubbish completely out of your head."

R.: And did Quisberg believe him?

M.W.: I have no doubt that he tried to.

R.: What was the object of the expedition to Paragon House, by the way, and why did the Inspector take you?

M.W.: I like to think he took me because he thought it would amuse me. Really, of course, it was so that he should have an independent witness of the experiment. I had to give evidence in Court that a body thrown out of Mrs. Harley's window at Beresford Lodge could be seen plainly from Paragon House, in the light of a "Jubilee Flash."

R.: I see. The Inspector seems to have been a pretty shrewd fellow. How did he actually find out who Quisberg was?

M.W.: That was my telephone call, I'm afraid. He had it "tapped," and quickly got a set of Cabal pictures from Scotland Yard. But, as a matter of fact—he may have told me this to ease my conscience—when he tackled Quisberg, he found him on the verge of confessing.

R.: To return to this Jubilee Flash for one moment. I can't get over the fact that it was a very unfortunate coincidence that it went off just when it did!

M.W.: I agree entirely. But it nearly always is an unfortunate coincidence that unmasks a really clever murder. If it had not been for the flash——

R.: Mightn't they have found in any case that

Mrs. Harley's injuries were not consistent with a fall ?

M.W.: That is possible. But you must remember the doctor planned to throw her right down to the terrace. If she had fallen so far her body would have been much more mutilated.

R.: He didn't reckon that your balcony stuck out so far ?

M.W.: I think the flash dazzled him, and made him aim badly.

R.: Your view is that he was really a master criminal ?

M.W.: I think he had unusual gifts.

R.: The serenade on the Heath seems to me to have been a bit risky.

M.W.: Yes, it was a fantastic notion. If the doctor had been quite himself, I dare say he'd have indicated the rendezvous in some other way. I think by that time he was a little off his balance. It must have been a great shock to him to find the caretaker trying to blackmail Quisberg. But when all's said and done, the serenade, even at such a moment, was very characteristic of him. He probably had arranged to play a few notes only—to use the instrument like an ordinary whistle—and then found himself carried away by its charms. Now——

R.: No, you mustn't go yet. Another question. What became of Harrington Cobalts ? Did you make a fortune ?

M.W.: No. When it was known that the negotiations with G—— were still inconclusive, the price dropped sharply, and I (of course) sold half my

holding in a panic. About three months later G——
made a bid of fifty-two shillings per share, which was
accepted. So I got that for the shares that I'd hung
on to. My total profit was about fifty pounds.

R.: Then Quisberg's death didn't really affect
the deal ?

M.W.: No. You must remember he was only one
of a syndicate, and his shares were all in the names of
nominees.

R.: My last question. While you were waiting for
the messenger to bring you the photographs from
Fleet Street, you wrote down a list of sixteen points
on the case. And you said, in your rhetorical way:
" Little did I realize at the time how proud I should
afterwards be of one short sentence! " Which was
that one short sentence ?

M.W.: It came in Point No. 6. This ran, you may
remember:

> " *Mr. Quisberg's visitor on Christmas night. The talk
> in the study, of which I only caught one phrase—' Why,
> in that light, I saw it as plain as I can see you!' In what
> light ? What was so plainly seen ? And where was it
> seen from ?*

R.: The gem being ? . . .

M.W.: " *Where was it seen from?* " If only I had
had the time or intelligence to answer that question!
If only I had known that Paragon House was the
viewpoint, think how " warm " (as they say in
hide-and-seek) I should have been. What was the
most likely thing to have been seen from Paragon
House ? Obviously Mrs. Harley's fall. And why

should Quisberg's visitor have made such a point of it, if the fall had been an accident ? The sentence, I think, is the key to nearly everything.

R.: As a matter of fact, I guessed the answer.

M.W.: Well, dear Reader, good-bye and thank you very much for listening to me so kindly. See you again, soon, I hope.

R: Er—yes. Good-bye.

M.W.: Good-bye.

HOGARTH CRIME

Surreptitious slaughter, and the reasons behind it, have never lost their power to enthrall. Old ladies' wills and wilful old ladies, the sleuth in evening dress, the eccentric village squire and the portly butler (who either saw, or did it) continue to exert their fascination.

Some detective stories have worn rather better than others – as a rule, those in which playfulness, assurance and ingenuity are well to the fore.

The Hogarth Crime series, in reviving novels unjustly neglected as well as those by the justly famous, offers a new generation the cream of classic detective fiction from the Golden Age.

Carter Dickson

Lord of the Sorcerers

'His usual devilish cunning' – *New Statesman*

In the sands of Egypt, an archaeologist dies from a scorpion's sting amid rumours of an ancient curse. The woman of the party, Lady Helen Loring, is dispatched by her father back to England, and to safety. But Lady Helen makes the mistake of taking a small souvenir – a priceless bronze lamp – said to have the power to blow to dust all who remove it from its desert resting place. And sure enough, on the stairs of her Gloucestershire mansion, surrounded by servants and gardeners (and even the plumber) she simply vanishes into thin air, leaving behind her a puzzle to baffle the talents of the irascible old sleuth Sir Henry Merrivale, 'the Oliver Hardy of crime'.

Cyril Hare
Untimely Death

What could be finer than to stroll across Exmoor, enjoying the larks and heather and distant sea-views? Plenty, thinks Francis Pettigrew, whose holiday turns to nightmare when he stumbles across a body on Boulter's Tussock; a rather alarming body at that, given to vanishing and reappearing in unexpected places. All the renowned detective skills of lawyer Pettigrew and his loyal friend ex-Inspector Mallet are brought into play to track the corpse's mysterious movements – and some equally startling twists of English law – before the ghost of the sleepy Devon countryside is finally laid to rest.

Gladys Mitchell
The Saltmarsh Murders

Cosy English villages can be murderously peaceful.

Noel Wells is a young curate in the sleepy village of
Saltmarsh. His life passes in helping the Reverend
Bedivere Coutts with his sermons and dancing with
Daphne to the gramophone in the vicarage study. Then
one day Mrs Coutts discovers that her unmarried house-
maid is pregnant, and the trouble begins.

Noel knows just the person to help: Mrs Beatrice Adela
Lestrange Bradley, beady-eyed guest at the Manor
House, who in her unnervingly unorthodox investigation
tackles with relish a smuggler, the village lunatic, a
missing corpse, a public pillorying, an exhumation and –
naturally – a murderer.

'The Great Gladys' – Philip Larkin

Romilly and Katherine John
Death by Request

This morning the usually hearty breakfast at Friars Cross is somewhat subdued, for the sixth member of the party is still upstairs – dead.

Who can possibly be the murderer? Colonel Lawrence is a blundering idiot; Phyllis Winter is of a frail and hysterical disposition; Mrs Fairfax and Judith Grant seem to have no motive; the Barrys all have alibis. So *did* the butler, who has unfortunately embraced socialism, do it? And can a private investigator make a correct deduction when he is in love with one of his suspects?

Death By Request comes straight from the heart of the Golden Age of detective fiction.

S.S. Van Dine
The Benson Murder Case

Wall Street reels and New York high society buzzes with shock and scandal when playboy stockbroker Alvin Benson is found in his brownstone mansion, slumped in a chair with a bullet through his head. Philo Vance, amateur detective *extraordinaire* and America's answer to Lord Peter Wimsey, is the first on the scene. Intrigued at once by the curious absence of Alvin's toupee and false teeth, Vance sets off in pursuit of an elusive murderer, confronting a host of suspects (and a number of family skeletons) in his tireless quest for the truth.

C. H. B. Kitchin
Death of His Uncle

New Introduction by H. R. F. Keating

'Kitchin's knowledge of the crevices of human nature lifts his crime fiction out of the category of puzzledom and into the realm of the detective novel. He was, in short, ahead of his day.' – *H. R. F. Keating*

A shady acquaintance begs Malcolm Warren to investigate the disappearance of his cantankerous uncle from a suburban Gothic mansion. Their search starts a hilarious trail leading them from seedy seaside hotels and gloomy Cornish coves to the Arts and Crafts Shop of South Mersley Garden City, until finally it lures the unsuspecting sleuth to a damp and sinister destination . . .